MERRY ARLAN:
BREAKING THE CURSE

Will Soulsby-McCreath

ISBN: 978-1-7399525-1-8 (eBook), 978-1-7399525-0-1 (paperback)

First Edition

WillSoulsbyMcCreath.com

For everyone fighting for their place in the world.

The world of Terya that you are about to visit is still working on its inclusivity in some aspects, but it is a world where everybody is free to be their honest selves, which includes nonbinary genders—if you're unfamiliar you may come across pronouns you haven't seen before (for example: xe, xem, xyr and ey, em, eir).

While the institutions of Terya have traditions, oversights, and biases to overcome, the world itself is one of acceptance and progress and what I hope our world will aspire toward.

In a similar vein, I have worked very hard to ensure that no content in this novel will cause harm to anyone (particularly marginalized communities), but I am aware that we all have our own areas of oversight and I, like the world I have created, am striving to be better with each day that passes.

ALSO BY WILL SOULSBY-MCCREATH

The Guardian Cadet Series
Merry Arlan: Breaking The Curse
Kitty Hughes In: An Unexpected Meeting (short story)

MERRY ARLAN:
BREAKING THE CURSE
GUARDIAN CADET SERIES

Will Soulsby-McCreath

CHAPTER ONE

"No," Commander Jonathan Whitclé said flatly.

"What do you mean no?" I snapped in response.

"You are not suitable for the position." He didn't even have the decency to look at me.

"Well, why the hell not?"

He sighed, finally looking up, leaning his elbows on the desk and steepling his fingers. "Firstly," he began, "your gender. The Brotherhood of Guardians does not accept women. Secondly, you appear to have difficulty with authority."

"That's discrimination," I spoke with venom. "What's wrong with having a female Guardian? It's not like I'm going to..." I stopped and frowned. "What is it that you think a woman would do to disrupt the Guardians?" When he didn't immediately answer, I moved on to my next point. "On the second count, I only argue when it proves necessary. Plenty of your Guardian's have the same rule – only, when they do it, you call that initiative."

"The answer is no, Miss Arlan." He looked back down at his file and picked up his pen. "You're excused."

I leaned forward, placing my hands on his desk. "What if I could prove to you that I would make an excellent Guardian?"

He glanced up just long enough to shoot me a flat look. "There is no proof you could possibly show me which would change my mind at this juncture. Good day, Miss Arlan."

-G-

"Kitty!" I hammered on the bathroom door.

Instead of a response there came a whisper and a giggle followed almost instantly by a hushed moan. I grimaced and rubbed my face, heading for the kitchen instead. Mornings had always been my least favourite time of day, something working nights had only amplified. Combine both of those with Kitty's insistence on hooking up with his new boyfriend in our shared – and only – bathroom and my irritability knew no bounds. Especially since I had lessons to get to.

Was I grumpy enough to turn on the hot tap and ruin Kitty's morning? No, probably not. It wasn't fair to turn Kitty's day bad just because mine was pre-destined to be so. I pulled some juice out of the enchanted cool cupboard. I took it and a protein bar back to my room, glancing at the bathroom door as I went. I knew too well what Kitty was doing in there. He'd known

Gergorio Valencia for four weeks and they'd been at it like bunnies ever since.

Kitty and I weren't exactly friends, so I wasn't particularly comfortable with the idea of talking to him about how difficult his boyfriend's constant presence was for me. Kitty and I hardly knew anything about each other. He had been looking for a flatmate; I had been looking for a flat. I didn't ask many questions and Kitty mostly kept to himself in his own room, or at least he had until Valencia had come along.

I sighed as I touched the charm left to me by my foster father, Arlan Tiernan. He'd died exactly three years ago. I didn't want to tell Kitty about it, even if I could have. After all, Kitty was intelligent and would definitely ask about me adopting Arlan as a surname and that was a question I didn't have an answer prepared for. I didn't tend to lie, but I wasn't prepared to give an honest answer either.

I got to campus early enough to divert to one of the bathrooms and clean up a little before my spell-singing lesson, at least wash my face and brush my teeth. It always seemed pointless to look nice for those lessons anyway. Between Professor Sorenson insisting that her students run up the stairs to her classroom and the effort we had been exerting in each session, I always finished up needing to shower afterwards.

Sorenson's classroom was at the very top of Tower Four, utilising the entire floor space as a combined office and classroom. She had nominally separated the two with a wall of crystals that acted as a ward so that, even if something went wrong in a lesson, her office would still be intact. Sometimes I wondered if she made her students run up the stairs in an aim to move to a classroom closer to the ground.

When I got home Kitty was out, his shoes missing from their usual spot by the door; taking off his shoes upon entry was definitely a habit he had picked up from living with me.

My loose shoulders tensed when I spotted a golden-brown head poring over papers at the dining table in the kitchen. I hadn't noticed him until I perched in the plush green armchair nearest to the door to unlace my boots. While the kitchen opened up into the living room, the dining table was obscured from view of the front door.

Valencia didn't look up as I squeaked something that might have been a greeting and retreated to my room. He was nice enough, I trusted that Kitty wouldn't be dating him otherwise; however the prospect of a relative-stranger's even less known boyfriend spending time unsupervised in my home was somehow not hugely reassuring.

Valencia enjoyed cooking, which was great for Kitty because he got a home cooked meal regularly without getting distracted by alchemy practice, but terrible for me since it meant I so often found Valencia in my kitchen. He probably wouldn't have minded sharing the space but I had no desire to find out whether or not that was true. Instead I showered and headed back out to campus.

Commander Whitclé took lunch in his office at midday; so I headed there immediately after my own lunch. "Good day, sir," I greeted.

The Commander was overworked if his desk was anything to go by; constantly covered in papers and files that strayed onto the floor. Presumably, the mismatched chairs dotted around the room and the brown leather sofa shoved under one window had once served another purpose, now they were resting places for yet more papers.

His lips twitched in either a smile or a grimace, I couldn't tell. "Miss Arlan," he sighed. "What can I help you with today?"

"I am petitioning to join the Brotherhood of Guardians."

"No."

"Why not?"

"We've been over this Miss Arlan."

We had. It had been a semi-constant contest between the two of us. I'd started my second year at the university almost three moons ago, and every day for the last two weeks I had sought out Commander Whitclé to petition him.

The first time I hadn't known what would happen, hadn't known that the Guardians only accepted men, hadn't known that I needed to use the word 'petition' to get anywhere. It had been a somewhat steep learning curve. Each time perfecting the petition a little further. Each time a step closer to acceptance.

"I maintain my position" I said with falsified confidence. I couldn't look directly at Commander Whitclé, so I turned my gaze to the lamp stood behind him.

I hadn't known what the Brotherhood of Guardians was until I moved to the Island of Shima five years ago but as soon as I learned about them, becoming one became my dream.

I should have known it was a bad idea to

petition the Commander when I was already unhappy, but an acceptance from Whitclé could have changed the course of my day. Not to mention I didn't want him to start thinking I was giving up.

Dejectedly returning home revealed that Kitty was still out and thankfully, Valencia had joined him. Although, his Guardian Cadet Uniform was hanging to dry in the bathroom; maybe Valencia had moved in and nobody had told me. I couldn't help but trail my fingers over the embroidered "G" in the Guardian crest on the top. I sighed and made myself a quick dinner before heading out to work.

-G-

"Kitty," I groaned from under my duvet "I told you I'm working nights, can't you and Valencia go be bunnies elsewhere? Doesn't he have a home?"

I stumbled to the door, yanking it open to find Kitty looking sheepish, hand still raised from his infernal unending knocking. His hands shifted to pull his shock of red hair into its ubiquitous messy ponytail. The cream coloured jumper he wore when he wanted to answer the door without changing out of his pyjamas swamped him, making his short frame all the smaller. The sleeves extended to cover his hands as soon as they fell back to his sides.

"Merry" he whispered, turning his face down, freckles hiding under a pink flush when he realised I was also in my pyjamas. "Are you a Sensitive?"

"What?"

"A Sensitive? I thought you were but..."

"Why?"

"Gergorio's aunt needs help." Without much more information Kitty urged me into the living room. I stared at the trio sat on the sofa, acutely and uncomfortably aware that I was still in my pyjamas.

"This is my aunt." Gergorio introduced from his position to the far right of the sofa. He gestured at the woman sat beside him.

Her ears marked her as an Elf, the tips in sharp points that aimed toward the crown of her head. Judging by her midnight blue day armour she was either a mercenary or a woman with a penchant for getting into trouble of the violent variety. I leaned toward mercenary as I noticed the dual swords strapped across her back. I looked between her and Gergorio, searching for the family resemblance. They were both Gold Elves, and had similar brown hair with gold highlights, medium brown skin, and glinting gold eyes. The sharpness of their noses matched. It was difficult to compare Gergorio's wavy hair to hers, since hers was pulled tightly back.

"Rakael Valencia" she greeted, with a nod. Definitely a mercenary then. Something about her made me uncomfortable but I couldn't put my finger on what.

I turned to look at the final visitor on the other end of the sofa to Gergorio. Another stranger.

"Kalik" he said his voice deep and clear. Tight black curls lay across his forehead. He was totally Human, musculature defined even through his Guardian Uniform — the white of his shirt contrasted with his dark skin in the same way Commander Whitclé's did, though Kalik's had a green colonel stripe under the Guardian Crest rather than Whitclé's commander red. A mercenary partnering with a Guardian was not something I had seen before. "We need a Sensitive," Kalik continued. "Are you equipped?"

"Why do you need one?" I hedged.

"There is a specific object that can only be found by a Sensitive," Rakael stated.

"What object?"

"That is strictly need to know," Kalik interrupted.

I shrugged. "I don't think I've ever investigated whether or not I'm a Sensitive. I don't even really know what it means."

"May we test?"

"What's the test?"

"You tell me what colour this crystal is." He pulled a crystal out of his pocket. The light from the light globes in the flat bounced off it, somehow not marring the colour.

"Yellowy-amber?" I offered.

"What?" Kitty blurted from over my shoulder. "It's clear quartz, isn't it?"

"Not according to the box it came in and the fact that Miss Arlan can see its inherent magic." Kalik rebutted. "What else can you tell us?" He leaned toward me.

I examined the crystal. It almost extended its glow, as if reaching out toward me. I couldn't help but lean away from it, rubbing my nose as I noticed the sensation of something brushing against it. "The longer I look at it the more it seems to want to eat me?" I shrugged.

"So, sight only?"

"No," I screwed up my nose with the need to sneeze. "Feeling too — can you put that away yet?"

Kalik closed his hand around the crystal,

shoving it back in his pocket. "Congratulations, Miss Arlan, you're officially a Sensitive."

"Great!" Sarcasm coated my voice. "And what does that mean?"

"A Sensitive," Kalik explained, "is someone who can, without effort, sense the inherent magic in an item, a person, or a situation. Where I, for example, would have to cast a spell to sense magical residue, a Sensitive would sense it in some way, sight, smell, taste, and so on."

I frowned, shifting from foot to foot as I thought about whether that sounded like me. The hum that hovered over Sorenson's classroom, the crackle of newly lifted wards when I passed closed businesses on my way home at night, the citrus smell of the Shields on the stage at Jhoto's bar and club, even my assessment of Rakael Valencia had included a feeling of wrongness that I still couldn't place.

"It also means you can find the amulet with the power we require. Our latest lead places it inside one of the Embassies on Shima," Kalik finished.

Embassies.

Everyone had an Embassy on Shima. And the Embassies were always filled to the brim with High-Born dignitaries, ambassadors with more investment in their own interests than anyone else's, and pompous jerks. But which Embassies did Kalik mean? All of them or just a few?

The most maintained and well used were the Human, Elven, and Goblin Embassies. My heartbeat snapped like a bowstring at the concept. Guardian involvement or not I didn't relish the idea of putting myself into someone else's trouble, especially not at such high risk.

"Find another Sensitive. I don't deal with

High-Borns." I sped back to my bedroom, closing the door firmly behind me and leaning on it while I focused on breathing evenly.

Don't panic. Nobody can force you into the Embassies. You turned them down very politely and didn't give enough information for them to start piecing anything together. He's not going to find you.

Rakael Valencia could find somebody else to help her. Sensitives couldn't be that few and far between.

CHAPTER TWO

A quick glance at the clock atop Tower Five told me the Guardian Gym was still open for public use. I shoved open the heavy door and pulled off my boots, leaving them in one of the wooden cubbies along the wall, before stepping onto the padded mat floors.

The large sparring floor in the centre of the room was mostly empty, with a few people doing warm ups and bodyweight exercises. I scanned the back wall for a free punching bag. Most were in use by an assortment of people both in and out of Guardian workout clothes.

The room was always humid, sweaty, and smelling vaguely of blood. But with the main door propped open, a fresh breeze flowed through the room. The clang of weights being lifted and replaced and the thwack of skin on leather soothed my prickling nerves. I took up a stance at a punching bag and started my workout, focusing on making each move as technically perfect as I could before thinking about power.

"Hey," I vaguely recognised the deep voice and that its owner was speaking to me.

Kalik looked different in workout clothes. The sleeveless black shirt displayed his muscular arms and complimented his dark skin. His hair had been loose when we first met but now most of it was pulled into a tie on the top right hand side of his head, keeping it from flopping onto his forehead.

"Hi?" I asked, pulling my hooded overtop off and wiping my sweaty face with it.

"Want to spar?" he offered.

"Sure." I followed Kalik to an open area of the sparring floor, dropping my hooded overtop at the edge of the area we claimed.

"What's your safety word?"

"My what?" I asked, stretching my warm muscles.

"Your safety word, when someone wants to stop."

I shrugged. "I don't usually bother."

"You don't usually fight Guardians."

"Actually—"

"I won't spar without one."

"Fine, okay, how about 'safety word' — it's easy to remember and it's very clear. Plus it's not something you would use day to day."

Kalik smiled. "Maybe just 'safety'? 'Safety word' is a little long if you're getting choked."

I shrugged my assent. Kalik leapt at me.

I dodged. The man was damned fast. I couldn't help the grin that spread across my face; it had been a long time since I'd had a decent fight with another person rather than a punching bag. I threw a punch, it glanced off his stomach.

"You'll have to hit harder than that," he teased throwing another punch.

I blocked and countered.

"So," he said, attempting to get me into a choke hold. "Why won't you help Rakael?"

"I told you, I don't deal with High-Borns." I tried to get around to his back.

"Why not?" he asked, dodging to keep me in front of him.

"Personal reasons." I launched a kick at his knee and leapt around him.

"Is it all High-Borns? Or just some?"

"What is that supposed to mean?"

I landed a solid blow on the back of his head and flipped him onto the mat, going for a choke hold on his prone, winded form.

"Safety" he gasped.

I helped him to his feet.

"Best of three?"

I hesitated. If I agreed to more sparring, he would continue his line of questioning. Could I fight him physically while keeping my brain moving fast enough to prevent any issues? But the glory of sparring with a skilled opponent was too appealing to resist.

We took up our fighting stances again, both a little more hesitant this time. Assessing each other.

"I asked the Commander about you," Kalik said.

"What did you ask him?"

"His opinion of you."

He almost caught me when I froze at the words.

"He's an idiot," I muttered, ducking under

Kalik's grab and rolling aside. I wanted to know what Commander Whitclé's opinion of me was but the back of my mind blared a warning that finding out could keep me from ever approaching him about anything again. Then I would never be a Guardian.

Kalik laughed. I came to my feet and tried to sock him in the jaw while he was distracted. He caught my fist and pulled me close. "What makes you say that?"

I flipped Kalik over my shoulder but probably caused myself more pain than I caused him. He was on his feet almost immediately. I backed off and rolled my shoulder. "There are many ways in which that man is brilliant and many ways in which he is a complete idiot," I said, trying to stay out of Kalik's way.

"Cryptic." Kalik threw himself at me. I tried to dodge but he caught my arm and had me pinned to the floor in an instant. "Care to explain?"

"You'd have to be an idiot to think that a thousand years old rule doesn't want updating." I bucked my body to throw him off. He went. I leapt to my feet.

Someone wolf-whistled. Kalik and I both turned to find the source of the noise.

A fluttering red sleeve caught my attention. Lior's hand blurred as xe waved at me, practically glowing in the late morning sunlight streaming into the Gym. Xyr gold-brown hair and skin sparkled in the way most Goblins' gemstone-like skin did, even if Lior's golden skin tone wasn't matched by any fully blooded Goblins. Xyr face had broken into a laugh, revealing xyr spikey tipped fangs even in their retracted state.

"Excuse me a sec?" I requested of Kalik before

jogging over to Lior. "What do you think you're doing?"

"You were supposed to meet me for lunch," xyr tone was light.

"No!" I gasped.

"Yes. I know — you're sorry. You've been covering Jen's shifts, you forgot." Xyr voice was overly patient, obviously upset but trying not to be.

"I really am sorry."

"I forgive you. Also, my mama wants to know if you can work tonight. Jen is sick — still! — and mama's completely stumped for people again."

"That's Jhoto," I sighed. Extra shifts meant less sleep whilst still balancing my course schedule but at least I got paid double for covered shifts.

Lior scruffled my hair and pushed me back to my Guardian fight. "Okay, so cancel lunch, we'll talk tonight. You go back to your fight I promise not to whistle anymore." Xe waved crossed fingers at me.

I laughed and jogged back over to Kalik.

"So, you're friends with Liorellion Folcs, child of a High-Born Goblin?" Kalik's question held almost as much weight as his punches.

"I'm friends with Lior, who is in my classes and works with me." We traded blows.

"It doesn't bother you that xe is a High-Born?"

"Lior isn't. Xyr mama is—was." Too busy defending my singular friendship I ended up flush against Kalik's strong sweaty body with his arm clamped around my throat. His other hand clamped around my torso, pinning my arms to my sides. Stuck. I wriggled. Still stuck. "Safety," I grumbled.

Kalik let me go and we stood, panting at each other.

"How about this," he offered. "Since we're at a tie. If I beat you in the next match, you have to help Miss Valencia. If you win, I stop asking."

It wasn't much of an offer. He'd only asked me once, but the implication was pretty clear. If I refused his wager he would keep seeking me out for the purpose of requesting my help. "Can you not find some other Sensitive?"

"Why find someone else when you're right here and almost willing to help?"

"Almost?" I snorted.

"Almost," he grinned.

I hesitated. Could I beat him again? There was no specific reason to assume I couldn't. Would helping Rakael Valencia really put me in that much danger? Sure I had panicked the previous day when he'd mentioned the word Embassies, but maybe it would be the Dragon Born Embassy, or the Human one. And if I beat him it wouldn't be an issue. "Okay."

We began circling each other. As Kalik turned his back to the main door a group of grey-clothed people caught my attention. Guardian Graduates. Was it that time already?

"We have an audience," I muttered.

"Does that bother you?"

I shrugged, not wanting to let Kalik know that being watched made me uncomfortable no matter what I was doing.

Weakness was always exploited, especially in a fight.

He launched himself at me. I dodged, rolling under him and to my feet on his other side. A little too slow. He grabbed me, making for the same immobilising choke hold from earlier.

I kicked his thigh, pulling away. As he regained his footing I scrambled onto his back. He didn't fall, as I had expected him to. "Strong," I found myself muttering without thought.

I kicked at the back of his knees, forcing him down. I pushed down on his shoulders and whispered, "all I have to do is slam my elbow into the back of your neck and you die."

"Really?" He asked, taking advantage of the pause to flip us over and pin me under him.

"It's mostly a question of angle and speed; anyone can do it with the right training – break the windpipe or rupture blood vessels." I fought to get out from under him, breaths coming sharply between words.

"And you've had that training?" he panted.

I managed to twist myself on top of him in an awkward and painful position. My breath hissed out between my teeth and he took his chance to pin me again.

I went to clap my hands over his ears to stun him but he grabbed my wrists, pinning them in one massive paw, his other hand holding fingers to my collarbones. My breath hitched with the beginning of panic.

"You can yield anytime," he smiled, eyes crinkling at the corners.

I huffed some breaths, fisting and unfisting my hands, testing his grip on my wrists and trying not to let my mind follow the path it wanted to go down about being trapped and at the mercy of another person.

Kalik's smile dimmed, eyebrows twitching together. "Are you okay?"

"No" I snarled. "I'm pinned to the floor by a Guardian."

"I meant—"

"Safety," I gasped, the panic flooding my systems making my already rapid heartbeat painfully fast. I'd agree to a whole lot to get him off me now.

"Think of it this way," Kalik said, helping me up. "Helping me with this is great practice for becoming a Guardian."

By the time I had finished setting up my workspace behind the bar; Lior had appeared and claimed one of the empty seats on the customer side. Xe wasn't wearing a stage costume, and xyr dark red long sleeved tunic told me xe couldn't be working as floor staff either. Jhoto demanded all working staff wear full black, although style and actual items were for us to choose.

Dark red suited Lior, disguising the fact that xe had typically Elven colouring that didn't match xyr Goblin features like xyr aquiline nose and xyr elegantly curved ears that pointed toward xyr forehead. "Okay, what's wrong?" xe asked.

"I hurt" I admitted. Lior blinked at me; usually I didn't admit things like that. Weakness will be exploited, always.

"Your Guardian fight?"

I nodded.

Xyr eyebrows jumped up. "He beat you?"

A surprised smile twitched at the corners of my mouth. "I gave as good as I got."

"I'd offer to rub it better but I don't want to embarrass you."

"I don't get embarrassed," I grumbled.

"Okay, then shall I rub it better?" Xe waggled xyr eyebrows at me.

Lior was a relentless flirt, and had been at least as long as I'd known xem. It had bothered me at first, but after a surprisingly frank conversation about my defensiveness, Lior and I had figured out my boundaries.

"There's a healing cream under the bar," xe told me. "It's mostly for when people get cut on broken glass or for the bouncers but…" xe shrugged.

"I do know where things are in here, Lior," I teased. "It's almost like I work here."

"So…? Are you going to grab it or shall I?"

"Maybe later." Healing creams always smelled so bad.

"Okay then, tell me everything I've missed in your life since last we spoke. Highlight on your Guardian fight."

Trust Lior not to care about the theory of my being at work. Between serving customers, I caught Lior up on the events of the past few days and xe returned the favour.

The spell-singing lesson had run long. Sorenson's opinion that if I just kept trying it would somehow click had left me exhausted and thinking of nothing so much as a quick lunch, a warm shower, and a pre-work nap. Kitty should still be at the library, he usually was at this time of day, which should mean I had the flat to myself. Instead I found Kalik and Rakael Valencia sat on my sofa, with Kitty in the nearest armchair chatting amicably with Rakael.

I hesitated by the door, almost not daring to step into the flat. If I left now would they notice my arrival? "Hello," I greeted.

"Good, you're here," Kalik said. "We thought we could start searching today."

"You're eager." I frowned. The dried sweat on my brow and down my back from Sorenson's lesson itched.

"Time is of the essence," Kalik stated, rising to

his feet.

"It is?"

"We didn't mention this earlier," Rakael took over for him. "Because we don't want it shared around if we can help it, but the curse has a deadline."

"Curse?" I asked.

"Miss Valencia has been put under a curse of... unknown intensity and origin," Kalik clarified. "We don't exactly know what it is or where it came from. That's why we need the artefact you'll be helping us search for."

"Oh..."

"I was given a year until..." Rakael Valencia trailed off but I could guess well enough. This curse was either going to kill her or permanently turn her into some other kind of creature, like a frog or an end table. Judging by the care she took in her appearance, if the curse was any good, it would turn her into an ugly end table at that, just to make everything that much worse.

"**D**o we really have to traipse across the whole island until one of us 'feels the thing'?" I whined as I followed Rakael and Kalik through the streets. "I do have other things to do."

The Human Embassy was enormous, taking up more than a city block of space. It made sense – Humans were the main inhabitants of Shima, the Brotherhood of Guardians had even been founded by a Human and they still made up the majority of their membership.

The grey stone building matched the other buildings in the area, with no real barrier between it and the street in front. We wandered on the far side of the road, an occasional carriage or cart blocking our view.

"Do you feel anything?" Rakael asked, ignoring my complaints.

"Nothing," I called, before muttering to myself, "except boredom."

We kept walking; Kalik fell into step with me.

After another half a block he asked, "What other things?"

"Work. Studying." Catching up on my sleep but I wasn't about to mention that. Balancing working nights and early morning lessons was always a challenge. Normally I worked the early shift for Jhoto but since Jen was still sick I had been picking up extra shifts for almost four weeks now, meaning instead of working the opening shift and half the night for Jhoto I was now working from opening to closing four nights a week, not to mention weekends.

"You'd rather be working than helping someone?" he asked.

I shrugged. "I have bills to pay."

"You're very serious."

"Is that a problem for you?" I asked.

"What do you do for fun?"

"I go to the Guardian Gym."

"Then just think of this as a workout," he grinned.

I was almost too busy glaring at Kalik to notice the woman walking toward us. Almost.

I ducked down a side alley. The smell of rubbish and bodily fluids stung my nose as I hid behind an industrial bin. I tried to tamp my magic aura down as much as possible, though I doubted she would be able to sense me even if I hadn't.

Her long dark hair had started to escape from its twist, haloing her face and neck in an unexpected way. The jewelled clasps glittered in the afternoon sunlight. Her long dress — or were those robes? — swirled around her feet as she made her way down the street.

When Halvana Magna had passed I let myself breathe again, immediately regretting doing so in the alley, and emerged into the fresh air.

"What was that?" Kalik asked, gesturing to Rakael to come back toward us.

"High-Born?" I offered.

"That was the Duchess of both Saien Houses."

"Exactly my point. Shall we continue?"

Rakael shrugged and began walking again.

Kalik and I followed.

"What?" I prompted when Kalik wouldn't stop staring at me.

"What do people call you?"

"Merry, what else would they call me?"

"Not Miss Arlan?"

"Not usually, no."

"Meredith?"

"Not ever."

"Oh?"

"I've never really liked it." That wasn't true; I had once loved my name, when it had been called with love to bring me to dinner, or used as a proud introduction; when it had been used as a comfort. But those days were so long gone I could hardly remember them at all. Just a vague feeling of pride and love and wide smiles set in a silvery face.

"I never really liked my name either" Kalik admitted after a pause

"Really? What is it?"

His face grew pinker. I didn't press, if he didn't want to tell me I wasn't going to push it. Perhaps if I left him his secrets he would leave me with mine.

We wandered a little while longer, circling almost the entire Embassy before I realised the clock was tolling six. "When was it five?" I demanded.

"An hour ago?" Kalik offered, confused.

"I'm late!" I gasped, turning back toward the Five Towers that rose above the city, silhouette cutting through the orange sunset and setting off.

"Wait," Kalik called after me but I wasn't turning around for anything less than my full evening's pay.

I pushed past a woman on the street in my hurry, throwing an apology over my shoulder. I could have sworn I heard Halvana Magna call my name.

CHAPTER THREE

When I got to work, Jhoto was, thankfully, nowhere to be found. I shoved my way behind the bar, thanking the waitstaff who had stepped in, though her name eluded me.

On the stage Lior drew all attention: dancing like each movement was for one person, singing like every note was a whisper in your ear. Xe could make everyone feel noticed as an individual. Xe was a natural born performer; with so much raw talent for spell-singing it even put masters like Sorenson to shame.

The Shields at the bottom of the stage glowed with a gentle silver light; it shimmered on Lior's hair and the silver sequins on xyr costume. Lior practically shone. Had Jhoto made the stage Shields silver on purpose? Either to remind people of coins so they would be more inclined to spend money or to disguise Lior's parentage?

When the club closed for the night and the bouncers had encouraged all patrons out of the building, Lior emerged from backstage in xyr undershirt and leggings to help me put the chairs and tables back into their proper positions.

We worked in companionable silence until Lior's jaw split in a huge yawn.

"Go to bed," I insisted.

"You're on opening to closing until Jen comes back, it's totally unfair. Like I'm going to let you set up and clean down all by yourself!"

I cleared my throat. Should I come clean with Lior about having been late?

"Oh wait..." Lior's hip jutted to one side as xe turned to face me. "You didn't set up today."

I ducked my head, peeking up at Lior's smirk. Of course xe already knew. "Did your mama notice?"

"I covered for you."

I pulled Lior into a hug. "You're the best."

Lior froze in my arms. "A hug? From you? Just for setting up the club? It's not like I wouldn't've helped if you had been here." Despite the protest Lior squeezed me tight. "I was worried." Xe sighed, burying xyr head into my shoulder. "Mama is overworking you and I got all concerned for your wellbeing."

I snickered, embarrassed by the care and affection in the statement.

Lior pulled out of the hug, taking my upper arms in xyr hands. Xe peered at me.

"I made a bet with that Guardian I was sparring with. Now I have to help him search the whole island for some stupid thing — I don't even know. But at least you know I'll be safe with a Guardian escort."

"That would be more reassuring if I didn't

know you, Merry." Xe squeezed my upper arms one last time before letting me go and turning back to grab another overturned chair.

"What is that supposed to mean?"

"You are more skilled at getting into trouble than anyone I know."

I nudged Lior with my elbow.

Xe beamed at me, breaking into a yawn again.

"Bed," I insisted, pointing to the back stairs up to the apartment. "I owe you for covering anyway."

"That's not how friendship works!" Lior sing-songed but did as I asked and headed upstairs.

A knock on the door pulled me away from my lunch. Kalik shot me a blinding smile. "Another day another try."

I sighed; at least they had left me alone for the weekend. I grabbed my boots, perching in the plush green armchair by the door to pull them on.

"You don't wear shoes in the house," he noted.

"No." I glanced up. "Old habit."

Everyone seemed to comment on it and I had no idea where I had picked it up from. Lior once told me it was common among Goblins but xyr mama had abandoned the habit upon settling on Shima.

"Where's Rakael Valencia?" I asked, noticing that she didn't appear when Kalik stepped into the entryway.

"She's following up another lead for now."

"I thought the whole reason I had to do the wandering thing was because only a Sensitive could find the thing?"

Kalik shrugged.

Ensuring the door was locked behind me; we

made our way down the stairs and headed around the Five Towers toward the North of Shima.

"It's a lead on a different way to remove curses," Kalik expanded. "You and the Amulet Of The Dragon Lord are still our best chance."

The Amulet Of The Dragon Lord, so that was what we were looking for. I'd never heard of such a thing. "I thought you were supposed to be her bodyguard."

"Only most of the time. There are other Guardians."

"Shockingly enough, I am aware of that."

Kalik laughed. "You're pretty funny Merry; I should remember that the next time we inconvenience you."

There was heat in my ears, was I blushing? No. I couldn't be. Not from one little compliment, what was wrong with me?

The Dragon Born Embassy was a lot more run down than the Human one had been. With it being rare for Dragon Born to leave the White Cliffs, and most returning quickly if they did so, there was nobody on Shima invested in maintaining the building. Kitty was the only Dragon Born I had ever come across.

The building itself had no physical barrier between its walls and the street but I could almost taste the magic filling it, metallic and spicy like a spoon dipped in chillies. One crumbling edge had been overtaken by vines that looked a little too sentient for my liking. Hopefully Kalik wouldn't want me to go near them.

Rakael Valencia stood on the corner of the street opposite the entrance: a huge black door decorated with a Dragon made out of gold. I couldn't tear my eyes away from the golden beast. It looked ready to come to life at any moment.

"Merry?" Kalik touched soft fingers to my bicep.

"Hm?" I tore my eyes away from the Dragon. It couldn't be real anyway, Dragons hadn't been seen in centuries.

"Do you sense anything?" He tilted his head, as if he had already asked me that question.

My eyes drifted back to the golden door Dragon. "There's a lot of magic coming from that building."

"What kind of magic?"

"The kind that makes me not want to go near it."

"Anything else?"

"Is now a good time to reiterate that I don't know what I'm looking for?"

"You'll be able to sense it," Rakael declared. "We should walk around the Embassy just to be sure. Check all sides." She strode off with purpose, the Guardian who had been stood with her trailing after like a puppy.

I allowed myself a big sigh before rolling my shoulders back and following the pair.

"She's the kind of person who has to be doing something or she panics," Kalik explained.

"That's not exactly my problem."

"So what is it?"

"I don't like to fail."

"Okay...?"

"If I don't know what it is I'm trying to find then we could easily just walk past the thing and we'd never know. I'm not trying to say I'm incredibly invested in Rakael's plight, it'd be great for her to not be cursed but that doesn't mean I'm the only one who could help her and I'm hoping you're still trying to find another Sensitive. I won't lie and try to convince you I desperately want to help Rakael, but I have accepted a part in this task and I don't like to fail. And the sooner we succeed the better for everyone involved. I can go back to my old life, you can get back to proper Guardian duties, she can be not-cursed."

He nodded. "If you're doing a job you want to do it properly."

"Exactly."

Silence settled over us then Kalik shrugged. "You'll know it when you sense it."

"Very helpful," I tried imitating Lior's tone of ridiculousness but it didn't stick. "You've solved all my problems."

Kalik's eyes sparkled as he smiled. He lowered his voice to a whisper. "I have no idea what you're supposed to be sensing either."

I laughed and fell into step with Kalik as we wandered around the perimeter of the Dragon Born Embassy. Every time we wandered a little closer a pressure descended on my torso, the sensation of being pushed away.

My feet ached by the time we finished up and I headed home. At least Jhoto's was closed on an Unday night so I could head straight to bed.

The sun streamed through my open curtains, pulling me to awareness. Kitty wasn't up yet, which gave me free reign of the entire flat to get ready and head out to my spell-singing lesson.

"I know you can do this better, Merry," Professor Sorenson said, waving her hands to dispel the residual magic loitering in the classroom.

"Better how?" I panted, exertion pulling on my limbs.

The rose-coloured light from the crystal ward surrounding the room died down as the magic faded.

"Your defence is weak, meaning you're overusing your offence. You're haemorrhaging energy just trying not to get hit. You need to invest some in a Shielding spell."

"I don't know any Shielding spells."

"Even a basic one would be better than nothing."

I bit my lip. "I don't know any."

Sorenson pushed her long, salt and pepper hair away from her flushed face. "I haven't taught you any?"

"No."

"Next lesson."

The bell in the clock tower rang out, announcing the end of the hour and the end of our lesson.

"I expect better next time, Merry," Sorenson called after me as I pulled open the door to the stairs. If I hurried I might be able to catch Commander Whitclé during Petitioning Hour.

"I do not have time to deal with you today, Miss Arlan," Commander Whitclé snapped when I opened the door.

"I wish to petition to become a Guardian."

"I said I don't have time for this today," he said through gritted teeth. The pile of paper on his desk appeared to have multiplied.

"Did I miss Petition Hour?"

"Technically, yes."

I sighed. "Then I'm sorry to have bothered you while you're busy." I turned back to exit, muttering under my breath, "With me helping your paramour, I'd have thought you'd be more inclined to hear me out."

Kalik passed me on the stairs, shooting me an exasperated smile as he entered the office. "What is going on?" he demanded, pushing the door closed behind him.

Commander Whitclé's response was too muffled for me to make out as I traipsed down the stairs, lingering soreness in my feet calling for my attention as over-exertion pulled at the rest of my body.

"We're doing everything we can," Kalik's voice carried clearly down the stairs, obviously raised with emotion. "You need to put your personal life aside. This is completely inappropriate."

Jhoto's bar was already bustling when I arrived. I'd briefly stopped at my flat only to find Valencia, once again, at my kitchen table. He hadn't even looked up when I came in, his books spread out over the table's surface like autumn leaves on a pond. I'd enquired as to Kitty's location only to find out he wasn't there. Somehow I managed to refrain from letting the tired-grumpy part of me ask if Valencia ever intended to leave.

I'd worked at Jhoto's so long that the clinking of glasses and bustle of chatter had shifted from overwhelming to home-like. I dodged the people filling the entryway — they never did fully migrate to the bar area or the seats by the stage.

When I finally emerged from the crowd it was to find Jhoto standing behind the bar. She smiled, shoulders falling in relief as I pulled on the uniform apron and settled into my usual spot. Barely a second to breathe before orders started flowing. I filled glasses from casks under the bar and bottles lined against the mirrored back wall, shoving used and dirty glasses into the sink at the back every chance I got.

"Merry," Jhoto called from the end of the bar. "I need you to perform."

I almost dropped the glass I held. "Perform?"

"On stage." She gestured to the empty and unlit platform.

"No." I shuffled over, wiping my hands on my apron. "Jhoto, I don't do that. I'm a bartender."

"Well, Liorellion isn't here and I need a performer. People are getting restless. You study spell-singing."

"Not that kind of spell-singing." Battle spells were hardly appropriate in a crowded bar, unless someone started a fight and even then a Battle Song was probably overkill.

"You can make it work."

"No, Jhoto, it's not just that I—"

She grabbed my upper arm; tugging me out from behind the bar and into the backstage area. We passed the store room, the door to upstairs, Jhoto's office and stopped outside the dressing rooms, wrapped in the black curtains of backstage.

"There has to be somebody else," I protested as Jhoto pulled the apron off me. "Anybody?"

"Nobody else on staff has any singing training. I would ask Baz to juggle but the advert says it's a spell-singing night and people are already getting antsy at having to wait." She shoved a tight band on top of my head, like a circlet for a royal but far less expensive.

"But Jhoto I—"

"No more protests." She shoved me on to the stage.

I stared out at the crowded bar from my new

vantage point. The circular tables were almost full, some chairs turned to face the stage rather than their respective table. It looked different from up here, the bar small and tucked out of the way. Hidden.

The lights at the base of the stage started to glow, Shields raising and coating everything in a hazy sheen.

Jhoto's was the perfect representation of Shima. Goblins, Elves, and Humans milled about, sitting in groups and talking or drinking or both. Some groups were mixed and some were exclusively Humans or Elves or Goblins with no outsiders. There weren't any Dragon Born to be seen, usually easy to spot with their tell-tale shocking red hair; even Red Elves had brown hair with red undertones rather than the bright red hair of a Dragon Born.

The table closest to the stage held a band of beautiful women who turned their faces up at me; expectant. The silver haze of the Shields lent themselves to the ladies' blue undertones. Blue Elves. I swallowed thickly.

Did I know any spell-songs that weren't Battle ones? A lullaby? A work song? A silly warm up? Anything? What did I have in my repertoire that would appease these people?

These people wanted Lior. Confident, self-assured, sultry Lior. Lior, who could weave exactly the right magic to make people have fun, drop more coin on drinks and tips, and go home with only good things to say.

I was no Lior.

Somewhere in the back of my mind a memory pinged. A tune. I started to hum the melody, letting the trained magic in my voice amplify the tune. A lullaby? A folk tale. The words came slowly.

When I was a child I used my voice to make little light tricks. Now I let that childish magic play out on the stage, rising and falling with the melody. If I concentrated just right I could almost make figures out of light who mimicked the story.

As the song came to a close I glanced at the side of the stage. I didn't have anything else to offer.

In full sparkling costume, Lior stood, like a hero from an epic tale. Xyr hand blurred in a frantic wave, eyebrows drawn together and up.

I retreated from the stage as the lightshow faded, magic lingering on the Shields longer than I held it.

"Where were you?" I hissed.

Lior's face pulled into a grimace. "Sorenson wouldn't let me go. I'm so sorry Merry. I—" Xe glanced at the empty stage. "I'll explain tomorrow?"

I nodded, wiping at my face. What were legs anyway because I certainly couldn't feel mine. I leaned against the wall and took a few deep breaths.

Stay calm. Just because a few Blue Elves happened to be in Jhoto's when you were on the stage doesn't mean they figured out who you... I gripped the charm on the chain around my neck.

I pulled the headdress off and tossed it back into the costume box before heading back to the bar.

Jhoto was still behind the bar when I went back. I gestured for her to follow me into the stock room.

"What in the name of Shima was that?" I demanded, clinging to my charm to buck up my confidence.

"What?"

"I'm a bartender not a performer."

"You're a spell-singer. What else is spell-singing for?"

"Either way that isn't my job."

"Merry, I am sorry but I didn't have any other options. People were getting restless and I needed someone to keep them entertained. You knew this job had a level of flexibility around it."

"Jhoto?" A voice called from the doorway. I turned to find Rakael Valencia, still in that midnight blue armour — did she own any other clothes? — stood with one shoulder resting on the frame. "Can we borrow your bartender?"

"You still dating Whitclé?"

"Yes."

"Then, no."

Rakael stepped into the room. "Jhoto, I..."

The pair moved close together. It looked intimate, the way Jhoto's face softened, the way her shoulders loosened. The way Rakael Valencia stood.

I ducked out of the storage room and back behind the bar.

"Miss Arlan," Kalik greeted, leaning an elbow on the bar top.

"You really can call me Merry."

He nodded toward the stage, upon which Lior was doing one of xyr quintessential sensual song-dance combos. "Saw you up there."

I ducked my head, ears heating.

"You were good."

"Thanks," I muttered, but he wouldn't be able to hear me over Lior's amplified voice let alone the chatter of the patrons.

"I've never seen anyone weaving Illusion

Magic with their voice before."

"I don't think it's Illusions, not strictly speaking."

"Well, whatever it was it was fascinating."

"Why are you both here?" I asked.

"We have a new lead on the amulet and were hoping Jhoto will be happy to let us borrow you for the night."

"Couldn't have waited until tomorrow?"

"We're on a deadline."

"So my life doesn't matter," the bitterness in my voice was so strong it almost had a taste. I rubbed my face. "Sorry, that was rude."

"What's up?"

"That," I gestured toward the stage, "was very much not my job."

Kalik let a hissed breath out between his teeth. "That's... not great."

"And now you're asking — are you asking? Can I say no? Or if Jhoto agrees am I just expected to do it? — you're demanding that I leave my wage-earning job to help out a pushy Elf and her pushier sometimes-bodyguard."

Kalik looked at me, eyes intense. "You can say no."

I yanked some empty glasses from the waitstaff station at the end of the bar and tossed them into the sink. "Can I? I lost a bet with you to do this in the first place. Is it really an option for me to refuse at this point? Even if that weren't an issue, the fact that between you, you have decided to ask my boss first and me second means that, if Jhoto agrees, I don't get much of a choice. I'm forced into this, whatever way you look at it, if you actually bothered to look."

Kalik was quiet long enough that I turned to start washing the glasses.

"You're right," he admitted.

"What?" I turned, dripping suds onto the floor.

"You're right. We've been so focused on getting this amulet to fix Miss Valencia's problem that we haven't really taken into account that you're a person with a life and school and a job. You're right. We trapped you and we didn't bother to look and I'm sorry."

I shrugged. It wouldn't change anything. Apologies never did.

Rakael and Jhoto emerged from the store room, Rakael grinning at Kalik. "She said we can borrow Merry."

I didn't argue; if Jhoto had made up her mind I wasn't going to be able to change it. I wiped my hands dry on the towel by the sink and headed out to the cool night air.

"So what's the lead?" I asked when we stood outside the club. I rubbed my arms. If I'd known this evening would have included standing on cold street corners talking with a Guardian and a mercenary, I might have brought something warmer to wear. The weather was only just starting to change and the distance from Jhoto's toasty-warm bar to my own toasty-warm flat usually didn't necessitate warmer clothing yet.

"The amulet's last recorded location," Kalik answered, leading me away from Jhoto's and the Five Towers and toward the east of the island.

"How did you stumble upon that?"

"It's in an old Guardian report."

"Great. Where was it last?"

"There was an ownership dispute that was taken to the Council of Colonels — that's the six Colonels who function as command for things the Commander can't or won't deal with, or if something happens to him."

"I know."

"Right, you've petitioned before, you have to know that."

I did not know that part, but I wasn't about to share that with Kalik.

"The ruling was that the amulet would be returned to the Elf who had reported it stolen — or to their descendants at least."

I stopped still. "What?" my voice came out quieter than I intended.

"Reportedly," Kalik continued, either not having heard me or having misunderstood. "It never left Shima and has just been sat in the Elven Embassy for the last hundred years."

"No." Still too quiet.

"I couldn't believe it either!"

"No." I pushed the words out. "I'm not going to the Elven Embassy."

Finally Kalik stopped, turning to see that I was almost two buildings behind him. "What?"

"I'm not going to the Elven Embassy." It came out steadier this time.

Kalik and Rakael shared a glance.

"But we can't go through proper channels," Rakael said. "Apparently the Lord who officially owns it — what was his name? Never mind, it doesn't matter — apparently he's a miserly type and would be unlikely to allow us use of the amulet. If we made the request and he said no it would be impossible to steal it afterwards."

I backed away, glancing down a side street. Would that get me back home or would it lead to a dead end?

"You went to the Goblin Embassy," Rakael continued. "And the Human Embassy, and the Dragon Born Embassy."

"It doesn't matter what I did or didn't do

before. I'm not— I'm not going anywhere near the Elven Embassy." The latent magic in my voice prickled at my stress. I tried to dispel it with a few deep breaths.

"Merry, please. We don't have time to search out another Sensitive," she begged. "This is the only way. It took moons to track you down. We don't have time."

"You have to— I can't— I—"

"I'll talk to the Commander about your petition," Kalik blurted.

"How do you know about that?"

"I overheard some of your conversations with him."

"If you're such an adept spy, you break into the Elven Embassy."

"We need a Sensitive. Only a Sensitive can find the amulet." Kalik was sympathetic but an air of the same desperation that coated Rakael carried under his words.

"You don't understand," I whispered, taking another step back.

Kalik stepped up to me and guided me into the opening of the backstreet I had considered running away down. "Merry, your refusal is finite. We won't force you to do anything."

"There's a but coming, isn't there?"

He smiled sadly. "This is a big thing for you isn't it? This was the whole reason you refused to help in the first place. Something that outweighs your desire to be a Guardian?"

I shifted on my feet.

He nodded, attention shifting to Rakael Valencia. Her hair shone with gold even in the blue of the street lights.

"She's turning to gold," Kalik muttered.

"What?"

"She had a year from the activation of the curse before it happened. It took us almost a moon cycle to find out about the Amulet Of The Dragon Lord. Then half a year to find you."

"What... how?" The words came out soft and unintended.

"Miss Valencia, as you have so aptly assessed, is a mercenary. She is also skilled in Finding Magic — you know about that from school?"

I gave a half shrug. It was a self-explanatory title. Magic used to find things.

"She was hired to find and return a wedding ring. Her employer, as it turned out, was less reputable than she had expected. She found the ring and returned it but the client wasn't satisfied."

"Wasn't satisfied?"

"The employer started asking questions about where she had found the ring."

My shoulders slumped and I rubbed my face again. "The wearer. Her employer asks where she found the ring and follows the person running away."

"When she wouldn't answer..." he shrugged. "Apparently it doesn't take a long time to set a curse on someone."

I looked away from Kalik and from Rakael Valencia, desperate to keep my thoughts from turning to my own attempts to outrun my past. If Rakael Valencia had been hired to find me, would she have decided I was worth the risk of an unfinished job?

I forced myself to look at her. The people I was running from wouldn't have been so nice as to only curse her. "Sensitives are really that rare?"

"Rare as Dragons."

"If I do break in, it's not like going in through the front door; the whole point is not to run into anyone, right?"

Kalik's gaze snapped to my face. "You'll help us?"

"Against my better judgement."

CHAPTER FOUR

Tall white stone walls surrounded the Embassy grounds, obscuring the building itself from view. The very top peered down at me, like an overbearing invigilator during a test. Something about it reminded me of the Goblin Embassy. Outwardly they had nothing in common: wrought metal fences to white stone walls, the darkness of the squat Goblin building compared to the polished marble tower of the Elven Embassy.

My knuckles brushed against the wards. Sparks crackled against my fingers. I flinched away. Ah. The wards.

"So, what's the plan?" I whispered. It didn't matter that we were around the corner from the main entrance and well out of sight of its guard station; some small part of my mind was convinced someone would hear us and come running.

"You go in, find the amulet, and bring it out to us," Kalik replied.

I stared at him. "That's the plan?"

"I like to keep it simple."

"That's beyond simple! That's barely even a plan!" I took a deep breath, trying to calm my racing heart. "How am I supposed to get past the huge wall?"

"There's a gate a short way down from here, a servant's entrance," Rakael supplied.

"Lackey," I corrected without thought.

"What?"

"Never mind. What about gate wards?"

The embassy building sparkled in the light of the half full moon. More white stone, peppered with large, stained glass windows. It reached for the stars.

Shadows stretched in odd and monstrous shapes from the hundreds of statues of Elves — presumably historical figures — placed on the ground, the balconies, and jutting from the building itself as if they had been trying to escape and been turned to stone.

Gaudy pretending to be refined.

The balconies dotting the upper floors had no discernible pattern beyond being stationed outside huge windows. I clambered up a statue below one such balcony, with no regard for the fact that I was putting my dirty feet all over the face of some important historical Elf. I pulled myself over the balcony and slid through the window to find myself in an office.

It was dark and empty of Elves — or anyone else for that matter. I spared a quick glance over the desk as I moved past it and the high backed chair in front of the window. Neat piles of paper but nothing of relevance.

A set of shelves sat against one wall, filled with books and the assorted junk people tended to accumulate in offices. The likelihood that the amulet would be in this random office was so low it seemed absurd to waste time searching it. Nevertheless I let my hand drift across the various items on display, testing and checking for inherent magic.

If I were an amulet of power where would I be? If I were a High-Born Elf where would I keep it? The archives? The Elven Embassy must have archives. Where would they be?

Well, here goes nothing. Ignoring the way my heart jittered in my chest, I pulled open the door to the office.

"Miss?" a patrolling guard — if the uniform was anything to go by; who still had people wear tabards in this day and age? — asked in Elvish.

I grabbed at something on the shelf nearest me without looking. "I'm new," I said, the Elvish coming out a little rusty but clear enough. "The Lord asked me to put this in the archives but I don't know where it is." I held up the thing I had grabbed. A child's bracelet, delicate blue and clear crystals encased in silver wire.

I blinked down at it. The clasp held none of the typical signs of wear – no tarnish, no shift in the mechanism; a brand new clasp on a well-used bracelet. It would have suited a young Blue Elf, or even a Half Elf with a level of blue undertoning. Why keep a broken-and-recently-fixed child's bracelet in an embassy office?

The guard gave me directions to the archives, which were, of course, in the basement just beyond the dungeons. Elves and their love of irony.

Walking through the Embassy, I tried to look like I belonged despite the tension pulling my shoulder blades together. I kept my eyes forward, not looking at anybody I passed. Why couldn't there have been a servant's staircase to use? Why did I have to pass through the huge entrance hall with its mosaic tiled floors and echoing grandiosity?

Just beyond the door to the dungeon, the gaudiness stopped. A utilitarian space, though still done out in white stone and light woods. The doors to each cell were solid, pale wood, banded with metal and with a covered window around head height through which prisoners could be viewed, talked to — hopefully fed. I tried not to think about it.

The doors I passed were all open. Empty cells with wooden benches — presumably some semblance of a bed — and a translucent screen that probably hid some kind of bathroom, though I was hardly inclined to investigate.

Surely, aristocratic Elven Lords wouldn't want to wander through the prisons to get to the archive. Surely they would consider it distasteful to have to pass prisoners. Then again, they could always send their Lackeys to retrieve their artefacts.

The archive itself was packed full of cases and shelves that contained every manner of object considered important to Elves in some way. The power styles and levels were overwhelming like too many smells in a soap shop.

I tried to shake off the feeling, tried to ignore the plethora of sensory information. Who came up with the idea that only a Sensitive could be sent into a room filled with things that will trigger their senses in the hopes of finding one specific item?

Was the itching at the back of my neck something in the room or my own paranoia?

I rubbed at the back of my neck, realising I still held the child's bracelet. Should I leave it here? Would that be too obvious? Did I take it with me? How was any of this questioning relevant to the task at hand?

Without any idea of what the Amulet Of The Dragon Lord looked like, speed was out of the question. I ran my hands over each shelf and cabinet. Did anything call more than the others? This was definitely not the best way of doing this but it was the only way I had.

Finally my free hand grew warm as I held it over one display case. I shifted it away to find the cool, stagnant air of the dungeons and archive once again.

Somehow I had expected it to be bigger, maybe because its importance had been stressed so strongly, maybe because of the power signature it gave off. It was no wonder they needed a Sensitive to find this thing. This little piece, not even as long as my thumb at its longest point, would be easy to ignore if you couldn't sense the magic sitting inside it.

When Kalik had said 'amulet' I had expected a piece of metal shaped like something, maybe a Dragon, or maybe forged by Dragon Born, but no, this was obviously stolen from a real Dragon. Whoever The Dragon Lord was, whoever had forged this amulet would have had to subjugate or kill the Dragon in order to extract one of its front teeth.

The root was shattered and had been cleaned

up. It shifted from white, through shades of grey, to charcoal black at its tip. Probably from a fire Dragon with that level of carbonisation.

A silver cage surrounded the tooth, a small hoop at the top to thread it through a necklace chain. Who would ever have been bold enough to wear a Dragon tooth around their neck on a chain? Any Dragon would have murdered them on the spot — not that a Dragon had been sighted in centuries. Not to mention, any Dragon Born who spotted it would begin a tirade of recrimination that would probably make anyone wish for a Dragon to appear out of thin air and murder them just so they wouldn't have to listen anymore.

I grabbed the amulet. Searing pain shot through me, sending me clattering to my knees, display case tumbling with me. I clutched at my hand, teeth clamped around my lip to keep from crying out. It burned. It tore. My hand was being sundered from my arm.

When the pain finally faded I rose on shaky legs, leaning heavily against one sturdy cabinet.

I froze.

Someone else was here.

CHAPTER FIVE

His magic was familiar and foreign all at once. The feeling of fresh snow, stepping one foot into a frozen puddle, ice cracking and collapsing with a splash far deeper than your expectations, as the frigid water seeps all the way into your boot. I turned to face him slowly.

"Meredith?" He seemed shocked, head rearing back. He must not have recognised me until I had turned. His eyes flicked over me from head to toe to head again. The twitch of his eyebrows radiated disapproval, probably over my choice of clothing. Baggy grey and black weren't exactly his aesthetic. "What are you doing here?" His usually even tone was absent, as if he had to search for each word before he could speak.

I didn't answer. I had no answer. Even if my breath hadn't still been rasping up my throat from the pain, I couldn't tell him the truth; that I had come at the behest of a random Layman Elf to steal an item from him. How could I have thought he wouldn't provide me with any item I could have asked for?

"No matter," he continued. "You're home now and that is all that matters. Come."

I didn't follow as he stepped toward the door.

"Meredith."

"I..." Finally I found my voice. "I can't."

"Can't? Do your legs not function?"

"They function." I ducked my head, staring at my own worn black boots. Boots he absolutely wouldn't approve of.

"Meredith, we've talked about this. You need to look up; you're a proud member of the Smeeten family, you can't look so ashamed all the time." His cold fingers pressed against my chin as he lifted my face up. His fingers were always cold.

A voice called from the doorway, "Lord Smeeten?"

We both turned to look.

Nathaniel Larrings was just a weaselly as I remembered.

He should have looked like Smeeten: they were both Blue Elves with the pale skin and blue undertoning expected of that description, but it almost didn't matter. Larrings' blue eyes were darkened with hatred where Smeeten's were icy cold. Larrings' hair was always sullied by grease where Smeeten's seemed as if the delicate platinum strands were enchanted to be perpetually freshly washed.

Their base looks weren't the only variables. Smeeten chose clean cut and elegant clothing, icy coloured robes typical of his station as a Lord. Larrings tended toward shirt and trouser combinations, neither of which ever seemed to fit: trousers always too tight and shirt always too wide in the shoulder and too short in the sleeve — how could it be too wide in the shoulder and short in the sleeve at the same time? Larrings' arms weren't an abnormal length, it made no sense! The ill-fitting nature should have mattered to Smeeten, since Larrings was his personal Lackey, meaning he wore the Smeeten colours: delicate icy blue silk and the silver Smeeten stripe down the sides of his trouser legs.

Larrings stepped into the glow of Smeeten's personal light globe, revealing something new. A scar slashed across his face; starting at his forehead and moving in a sweep down his nose and across his cheek.

"What?" Smeeten demanded of him.

"I was concerned for your welfare, my Lord." Larrings dipped into a respectful bow. "You responded to the Archival Alert and then I heard nothing more."

I could have kicked myself. With all the power streaming from the archives I hadn't even thought to look for wards. Smeeten must have set one up, or perhaps it was tuned to alert all the Court Elves in the Embassy. It made sense. The archives were right next to the dungeons, they held the most important Elven artefacts, of course there were wards.

"A fair point, Larrings. Meredith, what are you doing here?"

Again I didn't answer. This time it wasn't ignored.

"I asked you a question."

Cold sparkled in the air. Frozen pinpricks of ice that would look like the prettiest snow from outside its range.

"Are you deliberately ignoring the question or are you just too stupid to answer," Smeeten snapped.

I bit my lower lip and ducked my head again.

The sound of the slap assaulted my ears as much as Smeeten's ice cold hand had assaulted my face. Warm blood trickled down my cheek where his Courtier's ring had cut my skin.

"Larrings," Smeeten snapped, pinching the bridge of his nose. "Take my niece away; I can't look at her right now."

I stepped back, stumbling on the artefacts strewn over the floor. There was nowhere to run; the only door was blocked by the Elves I had most wanted to avoid. Larrings stepped forward and grabbed me by the wrists. Hand clamping like metal, he dragged me from the room.

CHAPTER SIX

The activated light globes cast an ominous blue glow over the small rectangular room. The door was bolted from the outside and the viewing window was similarly locked. When I approached it the sizzle of wards buzzed over my skin.

In my childhood I had read that all Elven prisons kept lights on throughout the day and night in order to deprive prisoners of sleep so that they would be more likely to talk. I had never expected to be in a position to find out for myself.

Why had Smeeten decided to lock me in the cell in the first place? I wasn't exactly a person he wanted to show off at the best of times but the cells seemed a little extreme.

Pacing the length of the cell took me exactly five steps, not enough to build any momentum or any ideas. What was I going to do? I should have known this was going to happen. I shouldn't have come here. I shouldn't have listened to Kalik. I should have trusted my gut.

I toyed with the charm on my necklace as the restlessness toyed with me. Eventually I lay down on the pallet to sleep.

The deactivation of the wards tugged my attention away from putting my hair into tiny plaits. There was no time to undo the half-heads worth of plaits before the door swung open on well-oiled hinges.

Smeeten placed a tray of food on the pallet as the wards rose behind him, door swinging closed with a quiet thunk. He peered at the absurdity of my half-finished hair, eyebrows drawing together.

He watched me eat the full meal before he spoke. "I'm sure you're sorry for everything."

I stared at the tea, ceramic mug releasing steam in elegant swirls. Tea. My least favourite drink, especially when laced with milk and honey the way Smeeten served it.

"Drink your tea, Meredith."

I did as he told me, trying not to grimace at the taste.

"I want you to know you really hurt me by running away. I thought we were a happy family, but then you did that to me. Was I not providing enough for you?"

I looked down at the empty tea cup in my hands. The warmth should have been comforting. I put it on the tray.

"Meredith, how many times do I have to tell you to look at me when I am talking to you?"

My head jerked up to meet his icy gaze.

"I gave you food, books, shelter. I took you in after the death of your parents, even with you being... well... even with my brother having married... even with you not being a fully — even with your existence polluting the Smeeten line. Even so, I took you in, cared for you. I gave you everything you could possibly have needed! And you chose to run off and leave me devastated. Why?"

I didn't know how to answer. I couldn't answer. Smeeten had given me everything I needed to survive but he'd kept me on a short leash, like a show dog, except that I wasn't shown to anyone. "I needed to be free," I said finally.

Smeeten's robes made a soft "swooshing" noise as he sat next to me on the wooden pallet. He took one of my hands between both of his. "I was concerned for your safety, Meredith. You disappeared without any of my guards. Nobody could tell me where you went. There was blood all over your bedroom, and poor Larrings had that huge slash on his face. I thought you had been kidnapped. I sent out search parties but nobody had any word of you. I was so certain something horrible had happened."

"It didn't," I tried to reassure him, squeezing the hand under my own.

"This is why I didn't want you to go outside Meredith. People do all sorts of horrible things. You could have been taken, forced to do vile things."

"But I wasn't. Nothing happened. I'm fine, see?"

It was easy to tell when Smeeten was angry. The air got still like a frosty morning before anyone has emerged to break the silence. "Maybe nothing happened to you this time,

Meredith, but you are still too young and naive to be left out there alone."

He swooshed from the room.

I flinched at the slap of the wards slamming closed behind him.

When my heart stopped racing I finished plaiting the rest of my hair. Once complete I started undoing the plaits, leaving it loose around my head. Usually I wore my hair in bunches or plaits on each side of my head — always designed to hide the tips of my ears. Smeeten would be pleased if I left it down; maybe it would appease him a little. The cloud of it obscured my view at the edges, weirdly lightweight compared to normal.

The wards played out against my nerve endings, like a gentle sunburn, pressing on my every move. It was hard to rest or think with the pressure of it.

Their sudden disappearance almost bowled me over. I glanced up, expecting to see Smeeten once again. Instead, Larrings stood in the doorway. He stared at me long enough that my heart started punching against my sternum.

"My little mongrel," he said finally, voice as greasy as his hair. He stepped toward me, wards and door closing behind him.

"Nathaniel."

He sneered. Larrings had always hated it when I called him by his first name, something about not affording him the proper respect of a title.

"What were you trying to steal, little mongrel?"

"I don't know what you're talking about."

Smeeten was predictable, Smeeten was worth attempting to please, if you did as he wanted his rage usually didn't present itself. Larrings, on the other hand, was like a beaten dog; he would bark and growl but he wouldn't do anything without his master's say so. He wasn't a real threat, not if I kept Smeeten on my side.

"Why else would you have been in the archives?"

"Admiring the artefacts."

"I'm going to find out what you wanted little mongrel, you might as well tell me now. Maybe I'll even put a good word in with Lord Smeeten if you do."

I rubbed my hand where it still hurt from grabbing the Amulet Of The Dragon Lord. If Kalik was right, Larrings wouldn't even notice the amulet, and even if he did, then what? Even if he told Smeeten, then what?

"You can't keep secrets from me, and you know it."

CHAPTER SEVEN

As it turned out, Elven prisons did keep their cell lights on all the time. Between the lack of light cycles and the lack of things to do, it was getting harder and harder to tell how much time had passed. I could understand why Elves thought their prisons worked: prisoners would say anything to break the monotony, for the chance to get out.

Not that there was any such escape for me. I'd bet money Smeeten hadn't even recorded my presence here with the rest of the Court. It wouldn't matter to Smeeten that I was an adult by all definitions, that I was legally free to make my own choices. To him I was property. To him I was the family shame and to be hidden away.

It didn't matter whether I told Larrings or Smeeten or both what my purpose had been in the archives, this cell would be mine until

Smeeten had gathered a way to transport me back to his house.

Smeeten's robes were more silver than blue this visit so it must be a different day. The next morning? Or had a whole extra day passed in between?

Smeeten held a tray of food once again, as he had done the last time, and, once again, he waited for me to finish it before he spoke. "I am willing to forgive you."

"Forgive me?"

"For running away and for your insolence yesterday. Your time away has corroded your manners, but that is repairable, and I am willing to forgive you. I am willing to let you come home."

Home. The word was weighted. Home. My flat with Kitty, my job at Jhoto's, my life with Arlan Tiernan.

Smeeten took my hand in his again. His cold hand smoothed over my own. "Don't you want to come home?"

The brush of air surprised me enough that I looked up to see where it came from.

Curtains fluttered in a midsummer breeze, its partnered sunlight tinting the clean white rug filling most of the floor slightly gold. I could have sworn it was late autumn, and the last time I had been in this room was mid-winter.

The bed was softer than I expected it to be. I looked down at it. I sat on my old bed, pale wood and soft mattress with clean white sheets. The posts at each corner were wrapped in ice blue and dawn pink fabric, the same fabric the curtains were made from. I couldn't quite place the feeling of wrongness it instilled in me: this had always been my bedroom. What had I been expecting?

I looked down into my lap with a frown and jumped to see my knees were bare. The clean white dress finished just above the knee. My head jerked to look at the door; I knew I should see a pale wooden door left ajar. It was closed, banded with iron, and prickling with wards.

No.

I wasn't in Smeeten's home. I was in a dungeon in the Elven Embassy on Shima.

The first thing to change back was my clothing. Back to my baggy black trousers. I let out a slow breath and the remainder of the Illusion shattered with a crack, the sound of a foot breaking through ice.

Smeeten wrenched his hands from mine. "Have it your own way, Meredith," he snapped. The door and wards slammed closed behind him.

I curled my knees up to my chest, hiding my face in them.

My hand hurt.

It couldn't have been long after that that Larrings appeared. His presence announced by the sound of the bolt sliding back.

His greasy smile made me grimace. After the toll of Smeeten's conversation with me, breaking out of his Illusion Magic, and the pressure building within me from being trapped in the cell, Larrings was the last person I wanted to see. Then again, was Larrings ever not the last person I wanted to see?

"Are you ready to tell me why you came back yet?"

I didn't have an answer he wanted to hear, so I kept my mouth shut.

"Lord Smeeten isn't exactly happy with you, Meredith."

I frowned as Larrings sat next to me on the pallet bed. He never called me Meredith.

"He wants to know why you were in the archives. He wants you to come home. He wants—"

"I don't care what he wants." My voice was quiet even as the snap exploded from me, unbidden. I turned my face away from Larrings, staring at the screen that hid the sink and toilet from view.

"Shall I tell him you said that?"

I took a deep breath and kept quiet again.

"Shall I tell him about all your insolence?"

Larrings waited for me to respond. I decided he would have to wait forever. I told myself I didn't care what he did.

Larrings snorted a breath like a horse that was impatient to move. "I would be more inclined to answer if I were you. You may not have experienced Lord Smeeten's wrath before, but he is displeased enough with you that your position of privilege is liable to change."

"You can try your schemes all you like, Nathaniel. I have no answer to your questions, at least not one you want to hear."

Larrings huffed again and stormed from the room.

I stared after him, taking another deep breath. He would have his little tantrum and then he would be back, asking the same questions and receiving the same answers.

It would be in his best interest to suggest Smeeten perform his own interrogation but that probably wouldn't get him anywhere. Lackeys were Lackeys. Regardless of the Lord they worked for, or claimed to work for, they were never taken as seriously or treated with as much respect as a Lord. In many ways, Lackeys had the worst of it, less than a Lord for not having Lord status but looked down on by Laymen for swearing fealty.

The next time the buzz of the wards flickered away I expected it to be Smeeten. Larrings should have cried to him, begged him to make me behave, as he had when I was younger. Instead of an icy robed Smeeten, it was once again Larrings in the doorway. His face was frozen, reddened slightly on one side. Smeeten must have slapped him.

What could have caused Smeeten to have slapped Larrings?

Larrings stomped across the room toward me, his hands fisted at his sides, and I abandoned the thought process.

The pain had dulled by the time Smeeten next turned up. He didn't bring food. Was it a different day? Had he forgotten? Was this some passive aggressive action? Did the reason even matter?

He stood at the door, watching me as I debated with myself whether it was worth the pain of sitting up or whether I should let him see what Larrings had done on his order.

"You really hurt Larrings' feelings," he prompted.

I bit my tongue against the sarcastic remark that wanted to be spit out. I pushed into a sitting position. Hurt his feelings, did I? I tried to ignore the pain in my ribs. Broken or just bruised?

Smeeten sighed, delicately placing a hand against his forehead. "Meredith," he said, moving toward me finally to sit on the pallet. "I know he's only a Lackey, but you must treat your staff well or they will try to leave you."

Because slapping Larrings definitely constituted treating his staff well.

"Then again, you'd know all about leaving, wouldn't you?"

The urge to pour out all my confessions bubbled in my stomach. To tell him about all the things Larrings had done to me. To explain that my rudeness wasn't without reason. I clenched my jaw against it. What would it accomplish?

"You could do better than him," I said finally.

"Always searching for better, Meredith. That is what led your father down such a dangerous path."

I froze at the mention of my father. Smeeten rarely referenced him. A bigger shame than me, at least I hadn't chosen to be what I am. "You taught me to expect the best."

"Larrings has his purpose."

"Your attack dog?"

"Lackeys sully their hands so Lords will not have to. You should know that."

"And Laymen? Where do they fit in?"

Smeeten smiled. "Laymen are to be ruled and protected."

"Have you ever even spoken to a Layman? Asked them what they wanted?"

"Have you?"

"Yes, actually."

Smeeten blinked at me, as if reassessing everything he knew about me. "And what did that Layman want from you?"

"Nothing."

"I highly doubt that, Meredith."

"Have your doubt."

"Did this Layman know who you were?"

"You told me never to reveal my lineage."

"That would explain it then."

"It's not that simple. We're friends — of a sort."

Smeeten laughed. "Friends with a Layman? You'll tell me you are friends with a Goblin next!"

"Well..."

"It's my own fault, I suppose," he interrupted. "I should have cultivated your social group beyond that of my own employees, given you proper friends for your social standing."

"You would grant me friends?" I whispered.

Something twitched at the edges of Smeeten's lips, a tightness in his eyes.

"I made friends on my own just fine," I said.

"The wrong friends."

"Who says they're the wrong friends? My best friend is the child of a Goblin Duchess." Technically Jhoto had given up her duchy but Smeeten wouldn't appreciate that fact and, really, he didn't need to know.

"Goblins, Meredith?"

"I think Elves need to be less xenophobic. Actually, I think Elven Lords and Lackeys need to be less xenophobic, most Laymen don't care."

"Xenophobic?" Smeeten choked.

"It means unfriendly to or wary of strangers."

"I know what it means, Meredith."

"You seemed confused."

"We are insular for our own protection."

"The wars are long in the past. Shima has been independent for a thousand years, which means the wars have been over for—"

"War is always a possibility. It is the role of

Elven Nobility to preserve Elven Culture."

"You're acting like there's harm in learning about other cultures."

"Next thing you know you'll be professing the benefit of the Brotherhood of Guardians, as if it isn't a human scheme to destroy all other cultures."

I stared at Smeeten. He shook his head and left the room without another word.

The next time Larrings came to visit me, he held the broken bracelet. His stance was cocky and confident.

"I found this," he declared, surging toward me.

"I have no idea what that is."

"Your mouth says one thing but your eyes say another, little mongrel." He stood too close; he always did when he was confident Smeeten wouldn't interrupt us.

"Why would that thing have any relation to me?"

"Because this used to be in Lord Smeeten's office, which means you were there too, which means you wanted something that belongs to him, which means all I had to do was search the archive storage unit that was strewn all over the floor — or rather the record for that unit — for Smeeten artefacts and correlate the missing piece. So where is it?"

"Where is what?"

"The Amulet Of The Dragon Lord."

"What do you mean?"

"What do you mean," he repeated back to me. "Not what is that? So I'm right. That is what you wanted."

"Not 'what do you mean' rather than 'what is that,' 'what do you mean' as in what are you babbling about?"

"Okay, we can do this your way. Why do you want the Amulet Of The Dragon Lord?"

"I don't want it." Somebody else did.

"Why did you come to retrieve it?"

That gave me pause.

Larrings shook me by the shoulders, rattling the pain in my ribs. "Where is it?"

"I don't know!" I had dropped it, hadn't I? But, no... I had grabbed it and then there had been all that pain and then... then Smeeten had been there.

Larrings stepped away, almost stumbling. "You don't... you don't know? How do you not know?"

I held up my hands, giving up, begging Larrings not to hurt me again. I couldn't take it.

His fingers clamped around my left wrist, yanking my hand closer to his face. "What the fuck?"

CHAPTER EIGHT

"Merry. Merry." The hand shaking my shoulder stopped my breath. How had I not woken up to the change in the ward pattern? Was it Larrings? Smeeten? "Merry, come on, wake up."

It couldn't be Larrings or Smeeten. Neither of them would call me Merry. My whole body ached like a combination of a bad sparring session and a rough shift on Etta's ship.

Kalik's smile was soft in the harsh light of the cell's light globes.

"Are you real?" I asked.

"As far as I know."

"Wait. No." I shoved myself up into a sitting position, biting my lip hard against the cry of pain that tried to escape. Someone was stabbing me, my ribs, my head, my hand. What had happened? It hadn't been this bad before. "You can't be here," I whispered desperately to Kalik.

"They'll— you'll— your job."

"Just have to make sure we're not caught. Can you stand?"

Kalik helped me push to my feet, catching me when I stumbled at the sight of the open cell door, wards disrupted, nothing between me and freedom but the rest of the Embassy grounds.

"I can only keep this up for so long," a voice called quietly from the other side of the doorway. I glanced at Kalik. That had almost sounded like... but that was impossible. There was no way Whitclé would have broken into the Elven Embassy for any purpose let alone to rescue me.

"Shut up, Jonathan," Kalik called back, voice barely carrying through the stone room.

I shifted my stiff and aching muscles. How long had I been here? How long had I been asleep?

More importantly how was Kalik here? How had he broken in? How had he found me?

I pushed the questions aside; there would be time to ponder them on the outside of these marble walls. I headed through the cell door.

Against all logic, Commander Jonathan Whitclé stood in the hall, hands plastered to the door frame, blocking the ward from activating.

When Kalik and I emerged from the cell, he let it go. The sizzle of the released ward shot through me like a lightning bolt, adding to the pain filtering around me.

I touched a hand to my head. What had happened? The last thing I remembered was Larrings attempting to interrogate me about the Amulet Of The Dragon Lord.

"Coast is clear," Rakael Valencia called from the end of the hallway.

"What happened to the theory of a smaller group and being less likely to get caught?" I muttered.

"That was for item retrieval, not a rescue mission." Kalik's jovial tone didn't fit in with the situation but somehow it put me more at ease. I couldn't imagine anyone being so jovial in a situation like this, so it must be real.

We crept to the stairs up to the ground level of the Embassy. Before we could start up them I pulled Kalik to a stop. "Wait, what's the plan here?"

"We escape the Embassy without getting caught."

What was I expecting? A real plan from Colonel 'I like to keep it simple' Kalik?

With more pain than I should have had, I managed the stairs and trailed after Rakael Valencia into the Embassy kitchens, thankfully empty. Each wall had a counter sticking out from it, broken by cooking equipment like a stove and a sink. Each surface was laid out with gadgets and other cooking paraphernalia that I couldn't put names to. In the centre of the room a huge wooden island stood, surface warped from use. I peered through the windows, desperate to see the night sky after so long without. The full moon peeked out from behind clouds.

My hands landed on the wooden block in the centre of the room as the air left my lungs.

"Merry?" Kalik asked, hand hovering close enough that I could feel it on my back but not so close as to touch me.

"Full moon," I managed.

"Yeah, we've been missing you."

Tears prickled my eyes.

"Now, let's get you out of here."

Rakael Valencia and Commander Whitclé hovered by the door, one watching the outside, one watching me and Kalik.

I wiped my eyes and followed my rescue team out of the door and into the rear courtyard of the Elven Embassy. The cobbles seemed to rear up to trip me. Kalik's hands flashed out, ready to steady me. I touched one hand to his forearm.

Rakael Valencia dashed forward to open the gate, the wrought iron gate laced with flowers through which I had entered so long ago.

I tried to increase my pace as Commander Whitclé reached the gate but the stabbing in my lungs stopped me. Kalik put his hand over mine on his arm as I gasped for painful breath.

"Merry?" he asked, voice carrying further than I wanted in the silent night.

"I can—" I wheezed.

Alarms blared and wards slammed up over the outer walls and the gates of the Embassy. The magic was like a slap to the face. I stumbled back, colliding with Kalik. His arms closed around me, so soft it would be easy to break the hold but sturdy enough that I wouldn't fall.

Whitclé and Rakael stared, ashen faced, through the translucent wards. The gate was still open in Rakael Valencia's hand.

CHAPTER NINE

The Elven Embassy Guards dragged us to stand in front of the recently awakened Elven Court. From what I knew, most Elven Courts were made up of an odd number of people so as to never have an equally split vote, and they never contained less than eleven Lords. The Court Kalik and I stood in front of contained only six Elves of varying colourings, genders, and states of dress.

I ducked my head, counting shoes of Court members on top of the mosaicked floor of the main hall of the Embassy. Nine standing shoes, a well-built pair of crutches on either side of the single foot, and one pair raised from the floor on wheelchair rests.

The blue silk shoes of Tellyn Smeeten had my head jerking up, as if he was snapping at me to show the Smeeten pride. I flicked my gaze over the tops of the court members heads; every one of them had their ears on display. Some of them wore their hair scraped back like Larrings — although none of them had hair as greasy as his — where others had cropped hair like Smeeten.

I didn't dare meet the eye of any member of the Court, or even glance in Smeeten's direction. He would be disappointed — no, he would be angry. A rare response. It was easy to frustrate or disappoint Smeeten, but he was too cold and logical for anger. Anger made you sloppy. Anger made you forget the important things. Anger made you oblivious to the subtle signs.

"You are charged with breaking and entering, trespassing on Elven Land."

The speaker was a Red Elf, impeccably put together; her clothes might as well have been donned and hair coiffed only seconds before she emerged to rule over the council session. Perhaps she had been working late, or maybe she always looked this perfect. Maybe she was the image Smeeten had been trying to hold me to all these years.

"What have you to say in your defence?"

"I was concerned for the welfare of a friend who was being held against her will," Kalik's voice came steady and even.

I turned my head to look at him. He stood at ease, arms behind his back, apparently relaxed. It was hard to believe.

"Do you have a reason for not following protocol? For not requesting official permission to access the Embassy?"

"I did not believe my friend was being held in an official capacity, rather, I believed she was being held without an official Elven Embassy ruling."

"What?" The Lead Courtier's red eyes shot wide in surprise.

"She is not a subject of the Elven Crown and therefore should not have been held here beyond one night. Not only that, but if you were to look at my friend you will see how poorly she has been treated while here. I presume the way she has been treated is not standard of prisoners of the Elven Crown?"

The Lead Courtier captured my gaze with her own, weaving magic between the two of us. She stared deep into my soul. Hours could have passed without my knowledge. "A Sensitive," she breathed.

"Indeed," Kalik affirmed, his words distant like hearing through water. "As I'm sure you know, there is a long history of the mistreatment of Sensitives amongst all societies due to their rare and useful natures. You can, therefore, see why I held reservations about whether she was an official prisoner, and why I believed the Court would not be able to help me."

"Do any on this Court recognise this Sensitive?"

Finally her magic released me. I could have drowned in that power. I sucked in a breath deeper than my damaged ribs would allow, air immediately escaping as I doubled over in pain. The rasp of my agonised breaths echoed in the otherwise silent chamber.

I pulled myself back to standing, trying not to grimace, trying not to look at Smeeten. If he didn't want to claim me I wouldn't force him.

"She is Meredith Smeeten," Smeeten's voice came clear, even, and steady. Cold. "My niece and my heir."

Kalik's face jerked toward me, eyes searching

out every signifier of familial connection between me and Lord Tellyn Smeeten. Same ice blue eyes, same platinum hair that shifted blue in the right lighting, same pale skin. He would find the undercurrent of blue that wasn't there, since I wasn't flushed pink to dispute it.

"If this Sensitive is your niece, she is a subject of the Elven Crown," The Lead Courtier said.

I managed to find my voice, "I am studying at the Five Towers University."

"And claim the neutrality that goes with it," Smeeten finished between clenched teeth.

"Smeeten," the Lead Courtier snapped, "are you telling me that your niece and heir has been held here against her will at your knowledge?"

"Must we discuss this in such an open setting, My Lord?"

The Lead Courtier turned her attention to me once again. I focused my eyes on her full lips so as to avoid her holding gaze and the magic within it. After more time than I could count she shifted her attention to Kalik. "Due to the nature of the situation, I think we can all agree that you are both hereby banished from the Elven Embassy until further notice but no other action will be taken against you. Miss Smeeten, you will be permitted use of the Embassy once your studies are completed. Does any of this Court disagree?" She didn't pause to let them. "Guards, please escort these two from the premises. Court, we shall retire to the Courtier's Chambers to discuss this further."

-G-

"Merry," Kitty hammered on my door, yanking me out of the depths of sleep.

With a quiet groan, I dragged myself out of bed and over to the door. Finding Kitty fully dressed in his usual green leggings and fitted cream jumper I asked, "What time is it?"

"Commander Whitclé is here to see you."

"Here in the flat?"

"Yes. Here in the flat and asking for you. He's got that Colonel — Kalik — with him, and Gergorio's aunt."

I looked down at myself, still in the clothes I'd worn to my last shift at Jhoto's, minus the shoes. "Two minutes," I said, closing the door a little harder than I intended. I winced at the noise even as I pulled off my shirt, a muted squeak of pain escaping as I did so.

Commander Whitclé sat in the centre of the sofa pressed up against the living room wall, Rakael Valencia on one side. Kalik had claimed the armchair on his other side, the one I usually pulled up next to the door to pull my boots on and off.

Whitclé didn't fit in the room, all strong shoulders and formal attire surrounded by Kitty's choice of plush cushions and pale greens.

I let my tired body sink into the armchair opposite Kalik, my back to the kitchen. I would rather have stood, but the exhaustion pulled at my limbs and my ribs ached so I sat.

When Kitty had suggested armchairs for the living room I had shrugged and told him to do as he pleased, I hardly spent any time in there anyway. Turned out, Kitty had comfortable — if overly green — tastes in furniture.

"Miss Arlan," Commander Whitclé started his voice serious. "I need you to report on both yesterday's activity and the need for it."

I sighed, glad I had sat down. "You were there, why do you need my report?" It slipped out before I had chance to debate it with myself.

"Had you not run away last night before debriefing—"

"Run away?" I interrupted, incredulous.

After being escorted out of the main gates of the Elven Embassy — a pair of enormous shining silver things woven to display patterns and Elven legends — Kalik and I had found Commander Whitclé and Rakael Valencia in the shadows of a shop doorway almost opposite the front entrance. Commander Whitclé and Kalik shared a few short words before we started back toward the Five Towers. My feet had been heavy in my boots. I could think of little else but curling up in my own bed. When we finally reached the turn off for my flat, I had been trailing so far behind the others that I hadn't bothered to call out to them.

"Jonathan," Kalik's voice was cautionary.

"Guardians are expected to turn up to debriefing sessions after a mission," Whitclé snapped.

"Perhaps if I was a Guardian I would have known that," I muttered under my breath.

"Excuse me?"

"I said perhaps if I was a Guardian I would have known that. As it stands I don't see how you can have expected me to have this secret knowledge at your disposal. Did you really think I had run away? That I was purposefully being rude or inconvenient? And, while we're on the subject, do you expect your injured — physically or psychologically — Guardians to turn up to a debriefing immediately after their release? What welfare efforts have you included in such a practice?"

The way Whitclé pressed his lips together reminded me of Larrings when he was angry. A small part of me wanted to push him, to find Commander Whitclé's breaking point, to see what would happen if I pushed him past that. I was already hurt, what more could he do?

"What Jonathan is trying to ask," Kalik's tone was pointed but his hot gaze remained fixed on Whitclé not me, "is for you to recount the events leading up to last night."

"And the amulet," Rakael Valencia blurted. "Did you find it?"

I took the time to collect my thoughts, to form them into something I could begin to explain to the Commander of the Brotherhood of Guardians, to the woman who had so desperately asked for my help, to the man who had promised me a stepping stone toward Guardianship. "Kalik and Rakael came to me at work," I started. "Asking me to break into the Elven Embassy for the amulet — I'm guessing you know about that?"

"You asked her to break in?" Commander Whitclé snapped at Kalik.

"I managed to find the amulet," I continued before Kalik could answer. "But I must have tripped an alarm because..."

Rakael Valencia shifted in her seat, leaning toward me, impatient to hear about the amulet's whereabouts.

"And something went wrong with the amulet anyway." I rubbed my face. "I don't... I don't really know what it was. I tried to pick it up, to bring it out, but I think I dropped it."

"You dropped it?" Rakael cried.

"There was this overwhelming pain and I... next thing I know there are artefacts all over the floor and Smeeten is there."

"Lord Smeeten?" Kalik asked.

I didn't dignify that with a response, what other Smeeten would it have been?

Kalik shifted to face Commander Whitclé, "Lord Smeeten is the last recorded owner of the Amulet Of The Dragon Lord."

"What?" I whined, but it was lost underneath Kalik's explanation of how Smeeten had come into possession of it. Why couldn't they have said Smeeten that first night? If they'd shared the miserly Elven Lord's name, if I'd know it was Smeeten I would never have agreed – no matter how little time Rakael had, no matter how far up the Guardianship ladder Kalik could have got me.

"Please continue, Miss Arlan," Whitclé said to me.

What to tell them, how to tell them, and, more importantly, what to keep to myself. I forced my shoulders into a shrug. "I guess Elves don't take too well to finding someone creating chaos in their archives. I got arrested. Next relevant thing is Kalik shaking me awake and I presume the Colonel's report covered that."

"It did." Whitclé watched me, silence growing in the room until it was almost suffocating before Rakael Valencia couldn't contain herself any longer.

"What happened to the Amulet Of The Dragon Lord?"

I shifted in the armchair, uncomfortable in the seat, uncomfortable with the attention. "I don't know."

"You don't know? How do you not know?"

The same words Larrings had snapped at me landed like a physical blow. Tears prickled in my eyes but I blinked them back. "I'm sorry, I don't remember. But Larrings couldn't find it."

"Larrings?"

"He's my un— he's Smeeten's, Lord Smeeten's Lackey. He was investigating my purpose in the Embassy. He re-catalogued the artefacts and the Amulet Of The Dragon Lord was missing."

As Commander Whitclé and Rakael Valencia turned to each other, engaging in a hissed argument, Kalik shifted over to crouch by me. "I haven't mentioned your familial connection," he whispered. "But with you being publicly claimed, we will have to follow some procedures and file some paperwork. Come to my office at some point this week and I'll get it sorted without needing a public announcement about the whole thing."

"Why?"

"I'm under the impression that you wanted to remain Merry Arlan: individual. Am I mistaken?"

"No."

"You're telling me," Whitclé bellowed, "that you convinced Kalik, a Colonel of the Guardian's, to ask a random civilian to break into the Elven Embassy, steal an artefact, and return it to you? Not just any civilian, but one with no formal training or thieving experience and who isn't even an Elf?"

I decided not to mention my short stint working on a pirate ship. It wasn't like I had been involved in the piracy aspect of things, just the ship duties. And my heritage, as Kalik had alluded, was something best kept to myself, even if I could have pushed past the training by Smeeten to never tell.

Rakael Valencia stared up at the now standing Whitclé and slowly folded her arms, as if daring him to continue the argument. He spun to face Kalik and snapped, "Kalik, what possessed you to go along with this?"

"My Commander ordered that I do everything in my power to remove Miss Valencia's curse." Kalik's voice was soft as he remained crouched beside me. "I took a calculated risk."

"A calculated risk!"

"Only a Sensitive can locate the Amulet Of The Dragon Lord. There are currently no Sensitives registered within the Guardian ranks. My calculated risk backfired, but it seemed the only real option."

"And you?" Whitclé turned to snap at me.

I flinched away.

Kalik rose to his feet. "Jonathan." A warning.

"No! I want to know what could possibly have convinced her to take up your hair brained scheme."

"I offered to sponsor her Guardianship Petition."

Whitclé fell silent, staring at Kalik; mouth ajar from where he had been cut off.

"I had intended to follow the proper channels to do so but you leave me little choice. I hereby sponsor Meredith Arlan in petitioning to become a Guardian Cadet. As Primary Colonel on the Council I can go over your head with this. I would rather not."

Whitclé's lips thinned as he huffed out a breath through his nose. "You and I will talk about this later," he growled at Kalik before turning to me with forced neutrality. "Meredith Arlan, you are invited to audition for the Brotherhood of Guardians. You will have a combat assessment after the next Cadet Training session — for which your sponsor will collect and accompany you. Your tutors within the Five Towers University will be asked for a recommendation. Your report will be presented to the Council of Colonels. Your sponsor will return with our verdicts within one week of your physical and combat assessment."

And with that he left my flat.

CHAPTER TEN

The Guardian Personal Trainer was built like a wall. Sturdy, solid, and surprisingly short. A scar cut across his lower lip and onto his chin, making it all too easy to read his face as disapproving with no real reasoning behind the thought. I stood on the sparring mats of the Guardian Gym facing him, letting my weight rest on the balls of my feet. I waited for him to move. He didn't.

Kalik had come to collect me from my flat and escort me to this audition. We had arrived at the Guardian Gym as the Cadet Training Session finished up. Kalik had led me over to a pair of non-Guardians, dressed to fight, loitering at the edge of the room.

They had all chatted amiably with a Guardian Captain who was giving them tips on the best ways to defeat PT. "PT is at least as strong as he looks," the Captain had said, "if not stronger."

Dismissing the Guardian Cadets in a wave, PT had stepped toward us, bald head shining in the sunlight streaming in through the windows. He hadn't looked up from his clipboard as he took up his position on the sparring floor and called me forward.

Once I'd stepped forward, bare feet sticking to the stain-resistant material, PT dropped the clipboard and took up a fighting stance.

We had stood, assessing each other, each waiting for the other to move.

Paranoia grabbed me. In most sparring sessions I started out waiting for my opponent to move, a residual habit from learning to fight like a bouncer. But what if that wasn't what the Guardians were looking for. Reactionary fighting was all well and good but maybe in an assessment you were supposed to hit first.

I took a cautious step, trying to step out of the anxiety making me look inward and instead focus on my opponent.

PT was legendary, even to non-Guardians. He never lost a fight. Nobody knew his real name. Nobody knew how long he had been a Guardian. It was said that he trained this Commander, and the last, and probably the one before that. I wasn't sure how much I believed exactly, but looking at his gently lined face now, I could see the base for such rumours.

I feinted toward his face. He didn't flinch; instead he grabbed my other wrist, the one that had been aiming for his ribs. He yanked me off balance, attempting to pull me into his chest — the same immobilising hold I had fallen prey to with Kalik in our sparring match bet.

I countered. Grabbing his shirt for balance, I kicked his leg behind the knee and shoved him toward the ground.

Pain radiated through my torso as I scrambled to get an arm around his neck.

With a single arm sweep, PT shoved me to one side.

I hit the ground in an agonising roll, gasp of pain escaping and hand flying to my ribs as I squinted up at PT. He stood over me, staring down. Fuck. I'd messed up. He was disappointed. I was a failure.

"Kalik," he bellowed.

And now I'd ruined Kalik's reputation along with my own. I was a manipulative jerk and I should have taken no for an answer and found a new profession. It wouldn't be that bad to work as a mercenary — potential curses aside.

"You brought me an injured Petitioner."

I peered up at Kalik to see his wide eyes fixed on PT.

"Fix your mistake."

I got painstakingly to my feet and walked from the room. Kalik would either follow or he wouldn't. I turned to exit the Five Towers campus, aiming to slink home but Kalik stopped me with a hand on my shoulder.

"What?"

"Healers," Kalik answered.

"I don't need to see a Healer."

Kalik moved as if to poke my ribs.

I dodged and hissed as pain ricocheted around my torso.

"Healer," he demanded.

This was going to be a disaster. How could I wriggle my way out of this? Healers wanted to know things about you, like your origins, history, and how you had got hurt in the first place. The last time I had gone to a Healer, Captain Etta had accompanied me and her hands on her twin daggers had quieted any uncomfortable questions.

"Who did this?" Kalik asked, pulling my attention away from the looming Healers tower. It was identical to the other four towers, sand-coloured stone with regular windows, reaching toward the sun. Yet, somehow, Tower Three had always made me nervous in a way the others didn't manage. "Was it your uncle?"

"Smeeten has never been big on violence. I mean the occasional—" or more common "—slap is one thing but he's much more fond of moulding people, manipulating them into the shapes and roles he wants them in."

"He does this a lot?"

I shrugged, wincing at the pain in my ribs — had it been that bad this morning? "I've seen a few iterations but it was mostly just me and Larrings — not that he was moulding us to be similar, of course."

"Oh?"

"Yeah, I was supposed to form into the pretty perfect poised Elven Lord. Larrings is his weapon of choice."

"His weapon of choice?"

"Smeeten is lousy with magic; he's the strongest mage I have ever met. His power level is... it's impossible." I hadn't ever noticed it when I was younger, but meeting him again at the Elven Embassy, the sense of his magic had been so strong I could smell it, taste it, feel it. It had pressed against me like heat in a smithy. "But he dislikes physical violence. He wouldn't sully his hands with such things. It's not proper for an Elven Lord to use their own hands for physical violence. That's what Lackeys are for."

Larrings had been changed in the time he had worked for Smeeten. He'd started out bright eyed and quietly watching, but as time passed he had become the twisted vindictive man I knew best. Smeeten had moulded him how he wanted him. The degradation had been so strong it showed: Larrings' eyes darkening, hair becoming slimy with grease. Smeeten hand crafted him in the same manner he had crafted me.

Entering Tower Three we were greeted by a very pretty young woman with tightly coiled black hair and equally dark skin. She offered a bright smile and greeted Kalik by name. "Colonel Kalik, what can we do for you today?"

"My associate here needs Healing."

The Healer picked up a clipboard from the long desk behind her. "Full name?"

"Merry— uh— Meredith Arlan," I answered.

"Origins?"

"Origins?" I frowned at her.

"Are you a Human? Goblin? Something else?"

The words stuck in my throat. "Half-Elf."

"And?"

"And?"

"And half what else?"

I swallowed around the lump in my throat. "Does it matter?"

"Of course. Typically Goblins are allergic to lavender, so that's important."

"I don't— I'm not— I think," I forced the words past the paralysing fear. "Goblin."

The Healer nodded, eyes skittering over my face and shoulders. "You do have mostly Elven features," she murmured.

I could have contradicted her. I could have told her about my fangs that extended like a Goblin's did. I could have showed her my picture perfect Goblin ears. I could have mentioned how everyone in my life besides Kalik, who seemed to be present for every revelation of my long held secrets, thought I was Human.

She invited me into an examination room. Clean white walls stopped me in the doorway. Clean white sheets on a plain bed pushed up under a small window had my heart pounding in my chest, each thump sending waves of pain through my ribs.

"Merry?" Kalik asked.

I focused on breathing, despite the pain. In and out. Nice and even.

"Can I stay with her?" Kalik asked the Healer.

"If she wants you to."

"Merry?" Kalik's deep brown eyes invaded my vision, replacing the stark white room. "Do you want me to stay?"

I nodded.

When I finally made it into the room, though I refused to sit on the bed when invited, the Healer asked me a few more questions, scanning over me with her magic to assess my injuries. It pressed against me like a heavy blanket.

"I'm going to start Healing you now," she said. "It may be a little uncomfortable."

The pressure of her magic changed from heavy blanket to a thousand needles. Without warning my fangs descended, sickly sweet venom filling my mouth. That hadn't happened in a while. I curled away from the Healer's hands.

Kalik hands lifted mine, giving me something else to focus on as he pressed gentle fingers into my knuckles one by one, finger by finger. "You're okay," he murmured.

A strangled yowl escaped me.

"I like your fangs."

I tried to glare at his soft smile. My fangs were my business and nobody had seen them beyond Larrings and Smeeten, at least not in my memory. But Kalik and his innate ability to see through every wall and barrier I had built, of course he saw them too. Wait, he liked them?

"What inherent magic do you have?" the Healer asked her own magic disappearing. "Something is trying to block my Healing."

I panted, ribs tugging and scraping with each breath. I poured my focus into retracting my fangs. Kalik had seen them; Kalik said he liked them, what did that mean? – Never mind that, I didn't want the Healer to see them too. I'd like to keep some semblance of my privacy intact.

"Merry's a Sensitive," Kalik offered.

"That would have been useful to know," the Healer said. "But it shouldn't be making this much difference."

Kalik squeezed my hands. "Is there any — wait, what is...?" he trailed off as he flipped my left hand over.

We all stared down at it. It looked like a well healed but slightly raised scar. No bigger than a coin, shaped like a fang that had been broken at the root.

"Is that...?" again he trailed off but I knew what the end of his question would have been. Is that the Amulet Of The Dragon Lord?

"Yes," I squeaked. "At least, I think so."

With soft fingers Kalik moved my hand to and fro, examining the amulet as the light shifted over it.

"What is it?" the Healer asked.

"An ancient magical amulet," Kalik answered quickly. "Confidential."

"Okay." The Healer chewed her lip. "This

might be a little less easy than I was expecting."

This time her needle-like magic only stabbed at one area of my body. My breath hissed out between my teeth.

"I never meant to become a Guardian," Kalik said.

I squinted at him. What was he talking about?

"My brother wanted to join and I had nowhere else to go. Our parents weren't exactly wealthy, and I was only sixteen when they died. I was working when it happened so I only have Jon's story, he could have told me anything. We both signed up for the Guardian's straight away."

"Where is he now?" I gritted out. Why was Kalik telling me this part of his history?

"He's doing his own thing."

"Is he still a Guardian?"

"Yeah. We entered under different surnames — I took mama's name, Kalik, I always liked it better. People can usually pronounce it on the first try too."

"That's part of why I picked Arlan," I muttered without thinking.

"So you get it."

"Okay," the Healer interrupted. "You are as Healed as I can manage in one session. Your options are to come back in two days for my next shift or let the residual magic work for the next week and avoid combat and heavy lifting."

She looked tired but Kalik led me from the room without mentioning it. Healers would have recuperation techniques, right? There's no way professional Healers wouldn't be prepared for this kind of thing. I couldn't help the last glance over my shoulder at the Healer leaning against the white wall, alone.

No sparring meant no time in the Guardian Gym, which meant no word from Kalik or anyone else about my audition. I didn't know whether it would be rearranged and I had no way to find out. When I tried visiting Commander Whitclé's office, ribs protesting at the magnitude of the stairs, I found a note on the door stating that he was out of office for the next week and to take all requests to the Council of Colonels.

Sorenson signed me off lessons for recovery, since spell-singing with mostly healed ribs was a bad idea.

When I turned up early for my shift at Jhoto's, Jhoto met me behind the bar with a glare. "What do you think you're doing here?"

"My shift."

"Now you turn up for a shift?"

I frowned, heart thumping hard against my sternum. "What do you mean?"

"Where have you been?"

I opened my mouth, closed it, took a deep breath and said, "You remember that night Rakael Valencia asked you to let me leave with her and the Guardian Colonel?"

"Of course I do, that was the last time you turned up for work." Jhoto huffed out a breath, grabbing a cloth from under the bar and wiping down the surface. "I should have known better than to let Raka do what she wanted. I should have known she'd get you into trouble." She flung the cloth down on the bar top. "I'm gonna get Lior to help you set up. We'll sweep this aside for now."

I watched Jhoto disappear into the back. Minutes later Lior appeared with a pout.

"Lior?"

"Where have you been?" xe hissed.

I flinched from the animosity; xyr fangs were practically extended with it and busied myself setting up glasses. "Indisposed."

"Come on, Merry. If you were that mad at me for being late you could have just said something, you didn't need to avoid me for two weeks."

"Two weeks?" The glass in my hands fell to the floor, shattering where it landed. I stared down at the broken pieces of glass, glittering prettily in the light. I could see myself in the shards, just as broken, just as shattered.

Two weeks. Half-moon, full moon. How had I not put it together myself? I tried to forgive the oversight. Being kept in a windowless room with no day to night cycles would mess with anyone's timeline. Between that and the injuries, and the stress... But still, guilt tugged at me.

Lior grabbed the broom and started sweeping up the mess. "You didn't know?"

"No... I..." I tugged the broom out of Lior's hands and propped it against the bar then held my arms out for a hug. Lior dove into the embrace. Xyr arms tightened around me, squeezing on my recently Healed ribs. "Ooft, careful."

"You're hurt? Again?" Xe held me at arm's length.

"Again. Sorry."

"Sorry for being hurt?"

"For everything. Lior I..." I wiped a hand over my face before tears had a chance to gather. "It's been a really rough two weeks."

Lior tugged me into the stock room, pressing the door tightly closed behind us. "Talk to me."

"I broke into the Elven Embassy."

"You did what? Merry!"

"Shh! Yeah. I've been working with this Guardian to find some snazzy amulet or whatever." I focused on not flexing my hand, which currently contained said amulet. "And he found out it was in the Elven Embassy and asked me to break in."

"That's absurd."

"Do you want me to tell you or not?" I teased, slipping back into the easy comfort of friendship with Lior. For just a moment I could almost believe there wasn't an amulet embedded in my hand and I hadn't been named heir to the Smeeten Lordship.

"Obviously I was caught because I am not, in fact, a burglar," I continued. "And this is where it gets bad."

Lior's eyes widened with disbelief. "This is where it gets bad? It's already bad!"

"My uncle found me." I released a slow breath, both relieved and tense at the idea that I was telling someone else about my heritage. Sure, Kalik now knew, but he'd found out somewhat organically, it wasn't like I had *told* him. "He's who I've been running from, hiding from."

"How is your uncle involved in the Elven Embassy? You're not even an Elf! Arlan is a Human name."

"Technically, it's a fake name."

"Whoa."

"Merry is my real name — original name. Meredith I mean."

Lior's hand landed on my upper arm, comforting in a way I didn't deserve.

"I'm sorry I've been lying to you."

"It's okay, like I'm not super jazzed about it or anything but I get it. Tell me about your uncle."

"He's... he hasn't changed. He's immensely powerful. He wants me to be the quintessential Elven Lord, and is supremely hurt and disappointed that I failed at that and ran away. He has this one particular Lackey—"

"Sorry, my knowledge of Elven hierarchical structure could use a little topping up. What's a Lackey?"

"Okay. My uncle is a Lord, the highest — he's in the Queen's Court and everything — it's the equivalent of a Goblin duke, duchess, or duchen. The people who work for Lords, they're called Lackeys — it's a role you're born into though, whether you actually work for a Lord or not is up to you. Beyond that are Laymen, like, um, the stage Shield technician, she's a Layman."

"Okay, carry on."

"So Smeeten — my uncle — has this one Lackey, he never liked me or he wants to exert power over me or whatever. I don't know. But he's..." I trailed off. Maybe I shouldn't unload this on Lior. It wasn't fair even if I could get it out. And what if this got out, not that Lior was a gossip, but it would impact Smeeten. And what if he traced it back to me?

"He's what?"

I rubbed my face. "I got hurt."

"Are you okay?"

"I'll be fine. Nothing a week off physical activity won't cure." I curled my hand around its new addition, the amulet warm under my skin. "Just a couple of broken ribs, and a wrist, and a couple of bruises. Normal stuff."

Lior tilted xyr head to one side then rolled xyr shoulders back and grinned impishly. "So what perks do you get for being an almost Lord?"

"None. Only downsides."

"Well that sucks and you should opt out."

A laugh escaped me.

"I didn't even know you were an Elf."

"That was on purpose."

Lior studied me. "You're just filled with secrets, aren't you?"

"You can ask."

Xe smiled. "Thank you, but I don't need to know. Anyway," Lior linked my arm and brought us back out of the stock room. "I found out that your roommate's boyfriend's aunt is my mama's ex! Recent ex."

"No way!" I gasped.

Lior chatted at me through the rest of set up and well into the night, even so far as to gain xyr mama's irritation.

Almost a week after I had been to the Healers, I once again found Kalik at my door.

"You were out?" he asked as I approached from the stairway.

"Quite the detective, aren't you?" I said, sarcasm resting heavy on the words.

"Well, I am a Guardian, don't you know," Kalik joked.

"I was doing a restock at Jhoto's. Normally it happens on the weekend but the whiskey delivery was late this week," I said as I unlocked the door.

"What's in the bag?"

"Lior and I had lunch after we were done. Xe sent me home with leftovers for dinner."

I left the door open for Kalik to enter through as I headed to the enchanted cool cupboard to put away the food. I shifted back into the living room to take off my boots just as Kalik set a box onto the coffee table.

"I'm here about your assessment," Kalik said when my boots had taken up their regular space by the door. "Do you want me to take off my shoes too?"

"It's fine." I gestured for him to sit, which he did, in the armchair by the door. It was starting to seem like his regular seat.

I settled across from him in the opposite armchair and waited for him to tell me I had failed, that I would have to find a different future because Guardianship wasn't in mine. After all, PT hadn't even reassessed me.

"Meredith Arlan, welcome to the Brotherhood of Guardians."

"What?" I gaped.

"You are officially a Guardian Cadet."

"But I didn't fight PT."

"Technically you did."

"But—"

A soft smile broke out across his face. "Why are you arguing this?"

"I just... I don't really believe it. It doesn't seem real."

"Believe it. In this box," he gestured, "are your Guardian Cadet Uniforms and your training schedule."

I lifted the lid off the box to look inside. The Guardian Crest greeted me, staring up at me from a neatly folded grey top. I traced my fingers over the embroidered G, the pentagonal shield surrounding it that must be the Five Towers from above, and the soft fabric of the rest of the garment.

I pulled the shirt from the box.

"They're all styled to fit human men, but judging by your current clothing choices I don't think that'll be too much of a problem," Kalik continued.

The shirt was softer than I expected. Lightweight and silky. "What is it made out of?"

"A specific Guardian only weave that makes it resistant to crossbow bolts and arrows. They're also fire resistant."

"Impressive," I muttered.

"They're also ergonomically designed to keep your body temperature consistent," Kalik gushed before settling into the chair and clearing his throat. "You'll be expected at Cadet Training sessions this week, do you already know the times?"

"Yeah, you can't use the Gym when they're in session."

Kalik nodded, a smile creeping over his face again. "I'll let you explore the box." He let himself out of my flat.

I carried the box into my bedroom and unpacked it carefully. Guardian Cadet Uniforms.

I lay each piece on my bed. Five light grey coloured shirts, and two matching hooded overtops with the Guardian Crest embroidered over the heart. Two pairs of dark grey, almost black trousers with the Guardian Crest over the right hand pocket.

My very own Guardian Cadet Uniform.

CHAPTER ELEVEN

"Cadets, we have a new initiate." PT's voice echoed through the Guardian Gym.

I stood behind him, squirming at the attention of the line of Guardian Cadets in front of me. The only uniformity among them was their Uniforms – and the fact that they were all men. I had always assumed Humans made up the majority of the Guardian ranks, but looking at the line now I realised that wasn't true. Relatively equal numbers of Elves, Goblins, and Humans stood along the sparring mats.

I'd also imagined they would all look like Valencia, all lithe and tall, with glistening golden skin, hair, and eyes. Instead the Cadet line ran like a mountaintop in height, peaks and valleys between the Cadets. Their skin tones ranged from the palest of Blue Elves and opal-skinned

Goblins, all the way through a multitude of shades of brown, to the deepest tones similar to those of Kalik and Commander Whitclé.

"Please welcome Cadet Arlan. Before anyone starts questioning anything," he shot a meaningful look at the line of Cadets. "Commander Whitclé and I are well aware that Cadet Arlan is a woman. This is not a point of contention. This will not be debated. You will treat Cadet Arlan the same way you would treat any new Cadet. Am I understood?"

"Yes Sir," the Cadets barked in unison.

PT jerked his chin toward the line and I scurried into place, ducking my head in the hopes that the attention would shift away from me soon.

PT began pacing up and down the line as he continued to speak, hands clasped behind his back. "Today you will be continuing what you have been learning this past week. Jenkins?"

A young looking human, slight of build and wearing an overly baggy overtop dashed forward to meet PT. The pair walked over to me as the other Cadets started to partner up. "You can catch Arlan up."

"Yes Sir." Jenkins nodded. "Hi," he waved at me. "You can call me Al, everyone does."

"Merry."

"So, shall I just walk you through it?"

"I guess?"

"Right, sorry, I'll give you a little background. I take riding lessons as part of my Cadet Training and I fell off the horse and broke my arm... and my leg... and a little bit my skull..."

"Wow."

Al laughed, rubbing the top of his arm. He glanced at PT. "Yeah, not my finest moment. I'm all healed up but PT is a stickler for following the Healers guidelines so I'm not allowed to spar for a while, or do anything to risk further head injury, so catching you up is a better use of my time."

"Makes sense."

Al walked me through the movement required. His teaching style was so similar to the first mate on Etta's ship that I re-examined his soft jawline, autumn-leaf brown hair, and pale skin in an attempt to find other similarities. Al was a little more nervous than the pirate, but just as patient.

Before long, we were blocking out the movement with one another slowly.

PT called the end of the session. "Don't worry," Al muttered. "We'll move on to something else next week and then you'll be just like the rest of us – still no clue what's going on."

I laughed with Al as we exited the Guardian Gym, stopping when I spotted an unhappy Lior loitering in the hedges near the grass pentagon in the centre courtyard. I waved goodbye to Al as I headed over to Lior.

"I knew it," xe hissed. "I knew you would abandon me if you got onto the Guardian Cadet Programme!"

"Lior, I'm not abandoning you."

"Yes you are! You don't show up for our lunches, I never see you at the club anymore, you're dumping me for a whole new set of friends."

"I'm not dumping anyone!"

"I just saw you laughing with that Cadet! And you've been missing our lunches for weeks!"

"I was—"

"I know, you've always got a perfect excuse. If

you don't want to be my friend anymore, or spend time with me anymore, that's just fine!"

It didn't sound fine but Lior wasn't done.

"Just don't do it like this! At least have the decency to tell me."

"I'm not— I don't— I want—" I rubbed my face. The sudden switch from working nights at Jhoto's, the two weeks of no day-to-night cycles, and then the Healing fatigue had scrambled my brain. Not to mention the nightmares. "It's not like I turned up at your mama's club every night just to hang out."

"So you don't want to spend time with me!"

"That's not what I was—"

"Fine! I guess I'll leave Little Miss Guardian to her Guardian Business."

"Lior," I called but xe had already made it half way across the green. I stared after xem until xe disappeared into a group of students.

Guilt tried to eat at me. Had I been neglecting the friendship? Since officially quitting Jhoto's — a shockingly painful conversation — I hadn't wanted to go anywhere near the club.

Had I really put any effort into my friendship with Lior since my disappearance? More importantly, had I missed another lunch with xem without even realising? I rubbed my face. I had some serious apologising to do. Best to leave it a few days to let Lior calm down first.

"You haven't been practising," Professor Sorenson said, skirts swishing as she crossed through the crystal ward to her desk.

The way the afternoon sun lit the space was weird, I had previously had dawn-ish, early morning lessons. The shift in lighting illuminated the office side of the circular room, and the shelves bolted to the wall, with gaps for the windows that had used to be the main source of light for my lessons. The shelves were stuffed full of standing files each labelled in Sorenson's elegant script.

"I..."

"You're normally so dedicated, what happened?"

"It's nothing," I lied, absently rubbing my left hand over the amulet where pins and needles seemed to have onset.

"I'm aware you've been accepted into the Guardian Cadet Programme," she said, flicking open a file on her desk.

"Yes."

"Is that the issue?"

I paused. "No."

"Lots of people struggle to adjust to the rigours of the Guardian Cadet Programme. Especially students who were previously part time." She raised an eyebrow at me. "Particularly ones who used to work nights in a bar, come straight to lessons with me, and then sleep in the afternoon."

I winced. I didn't think Sorenson had known about that.

"But if you're not having any issues with the sudden and huge change in your life then there's no excuse for your slip in practice. Take the rest of the week off and I expect you to have learnt these spell-songs by next week and if you're not up to the task, don't bother showing up." She tossed a pile of papers at me. "Off you go. Lesson over."

Numb, I exited her classroom and headed back down the stairs.

I flicked through the papers: three new spell-songs. Between having to learn their melodies by sight instead of Sorenson singing them out for me, figuring out the words and their meaning, and putting the right kind of power behind them... that was a lot of work. Usually we talked over the pieces one at a time, never more than one a week; and she usually insisted that each piece be perfected before moving on.

Professor Sorenson had always stressed the importance of practise. Two hours daily, except for rest days. She said voices and magic were muscles and the only way to get stronger and improve was through training. I'd held to her expectations without fail since I started at the Five Towers the previous year.

Lior had always been good at sight singing, but if xe was still mad at me for taking xem for granted xe might not be willing to help.

Plus I'd have to find xem somewhere that wasn't Jhoto's club. The idea of returning to the site of my old job after having to go through the gut-wrenching ordeal of telling Jhoto I quit was daunting to say the least.

CHAPTER TWELVE

I tried to hold in a yawn as PT explained our task for the morning. It boiled down to basic sparring with the added challenge of working around an enchantment that prevented the use of magic. The enchantment stone in the centre of the Gym left me needing to sneeze, as if my nose was blocked or I'd accidentally inhaled sea water. I scrunched my nose, trying not to sniff.

PT pared us up. My partner was a Cadet I didn't yet recognise. He didn't bother to introduce himself so I didn't either. I positioned us on the outer edges of the sparring floor, managing clean breaths every five or so.

The sparring followed the pattern I was beginning to expect from Guardian Cadets. That was, of course, until my guard slipped as I tried to hold in another yawn and the Cadet punched me straight in the face.

I put a hand to my bleeding nose and blinked

the water from my eyes. I hadn't even seen the fist coming. I poked at my nose, trying to ascertain whether it was broken or not.

"Arlan." PT strode over, dodging sparring cadets. "Let me see."

I dropped my hands.

"Healers," he ordered. "Cadet Valencia, you've done well this session, you can escort Cadet Arlan to a Healer. You two," he pointed at our respective sparring partners, "s'partner up."

S'partner — sparring partner. Ugh.

Valencia and I headed out of the Guardian Gym and toward the Healers tower.

"I really don't need a Healer," I said, wiping my nose again as I slowed my steps in the face of the tower. "See," I turned to Valencia, "it's not even bleeding anymore."

Valencia smiled easily. "This is part of the reason PT assigned an escort. The other part is to ensure the injured Cadet can still walk."

"Do they baby the Graduates like that too?" I snarked. "Send you to a Healer for bruised knuckles and scraped knees."

Valencia laughed. "You have no idea. I have read the Guardian rule book back to front and some of the stuff in there is just absurd." He continued babbling about Guardian rules all the way into the Healers tower. Before I knew it I stood in an examination room, playing with the hem of my shirt in an attempt to distract myself from the nerves of being in the clean white space.

Valencia waited outside, sitting in one of the uncomfortable looking chairs and chatting with anyone who hesitated near him.

The same Healer who had seen me the last time entered the room with a placid smile on her face. She passed me a healing patch and told me to put it on for an hour when I got home.

After reassuring Valencia that I was perfectly fine and allowed to leave I headed straight off campus and into the entertainment district. Jhoto's was closed, so I knocked on the door to the supply entrance.

It took a while before Jhoto opened the door. She stared at me; brown eyes filled with a cold aloofness which was far too reminiscent of my uncle's familiar expressions.

"What?" she asked, voice filled with the same coldness as her eyes.

"I'm here to see Lior."

She huffed but stepped away from the door and disappeared into the club — probably heading to her office. I took what little invitation was there and headed upstairs to Lior's bedroom.

"Merry?" xe asked when xe opened xyr bedroom door.

"Can I come in?"

"I guess." Xe stepped back.

Lior's room was, as always, neat and tidy, with everything in its proper place. The blinds shifted in the mid-morning breeze from the open window over the tidy desk. The open ledger and discarded pen told me that Lior had been working when I knocked.

To the right of the desk sat Lior's perfectly made bed. Thoughts of my own bed with green duvet — Kitty's provision — scrunched up at the end where I had kicked it that morning filled my head. Opposite the bed on the left-hand wall of the room were Lior's bookshelves, every millimetre filled with neatly arranged papers, books, knickknacks, awards, and ornaments.

I hovered near the door, not wanting to step

dirty boots on the clean yellow rug.

"What happened to your nose?" Lior asked, leaning on xyr desk.

"Guardian Cadet Training," I answered, touching what I estimated would be an intense bruise. "I have this from a Healer to put on when I get home," I waved the healing patch at Lior before stuffing it back in my pocket.

"You really should put that on as soon as possible."

"She said to wait until I got home."

"I think she meant for you to go home and put it on, not come here and... why are you here?"

"I'm sorry."

"What?"

"I'm sorry. I abandoned you, you were right. I didn't mean to but I did and I'm sorry." I started to pace. "I've only been in Cadet training for like three days, so it's not that. I've been taking you for granted; you've been putting all the effort in." I sank down on the edge of Lior's bed, regretting my destruction of xyr organisation as I messed up the covers. Merry Arlan: creator of chaos and mess wherever she goes.

"Merry. I don't mind being the instigator most of the time, I just... I'm scared I'm going to lose you. You're my best friend."

"You're my best friend too." I sniffed and winced.

"Give me your healing patch." I handed it to Lior who pressed it to my nose. "I'm sorry too."

"For what?"

"I got all paranoid about you making other friends. You're a really nice — if slightly damaged — person. You'd be the perfect candidate for friendship."

"Damaged?"

Lior scoffed, "After what you told me the other day?"

I tried to scowl at xem but the movement tugged on the healing patch. Lior sat back in xyr desk chair.

"I'm not the perfect candidate for friendship," I protested. "Why on Shima would you think that?"

"The only person standing between you and a hundred thousand friends is you and the little voice inside your head that doesn't want you to take the risk — and a little bit me but I'm going to try and stop doing that."

"I don't know the rules of making friends."

"The rules?" Lior laughed.

"Shut up, I'm serious."

Lior examined me. "You really are, aren't you?"

I focused my attention on examining the rug in detail.

"Just be you, Merry. The way you were talking with that Cadet."

"What about it?"

"Give it a little time and that could turn from friendly to friendship."

"Even if it does — which I don't believe — I don't want to replace you Lior. You're important to me and you should know that losing you is not something I would choose to do."

"I know." Then Lior grinned impishly, "Would you come rescue me if I got kidnapped?"

I laughed. "Would you fight for me, Lior? 'Til the rays of the sun turned blue from the strain?"

Lior rose to xyr feet dramatically and picked up the song. "'Til the black of night turned opal white and the stars faded from view. I'd go to the ends of the world for you."

We both broke into laughter.

"How long are you supposed to wear that thing?" Lior asked.

"An hour."

"Best you stay here then."

"What were you doing before I came in?"

Lior groaned and poked at the ledger on the desk. "Homework. From Sorenson."

I groaned. "She kicked me out of my last lesson with three new songs to learn on my own."

"Kicked you out?"

"For not practising enough."

"Because it's not like you've been recovering from Healing, or started a new training regime, or had to readjust your body clock, or just had a traumatic experience or anything."

A smile tugged at the corner of my mouth. "Any chance you want to help me out?"

"Sure. Beats this snore-fest. Hey, Cadet Training is in the morning, right? When's your new Sorenson lessons?"

I told xem.

"No way, your Sixday one is right after mine! I'll hang around and we can do homework together."

"Right," I said, sarcasm filling the room.

"You're such a goody two shoes and you're trying to tell me you don't do homework as soon as it's assigned?"

"Unlike you, who puts it off until five minutes before it's due!"

"What of it?"

"I'm saying that we are never going to actually do homework after that lesson. Not to mention we'd need a place to do it."

"Library?"

"You're not supposed to talk in the library."

"Your place?"

"Kitty and boyfriend."

"So kick them out for a change." Lior laughed. "No. I know. Um... Here?"

"I'm not your mama's favourite person right now."

"Because you quit?"

I shrugged.

"Did she go all Ice Queen?"

"That's a normal thing she does?"

"Absolutely. I face it at least once a fortnight."

"How do you handle that?"

Lior shrugged. "I'm just used to it, I guess. I'll think of a place, now let me at your spell-songs, I'm dying for something new to do."

My knee bounced of its own accord as I examined the other people sat in the mismatched chairs that lined the hallway outside Commander Whitclé's office: one Human with pink-tinged skin and wheat coloured hair in formal looking attire, and a Goblin with amber skin and eyes, hair hidden under a headscarf.

Why did Whitclé call for me to come see him? Why had he asked PT to be the one to tell me? I smoothed my hands over the top of my hair, settling down the exercise frizz that had escaped the pair of plaits over my ears. Hopefully PT calling me back after training wouldn't colour the other Cadets' views of me too badly.

"Cadet Arlan," Commander Whitclé called from inside his office.

When I entered, he was sat behind the mess of a desk in his mammoth chair. I stood between the pair of mismatched chairs opposite him. "Sir."

He looked up from the mass of papers, gesturing to the chairs to invite me to sit. I chose the comfier looking one.

"Cadet Arlan," he closed the topmost folder on his desk, shifting his intent gold eyed attention to me. "I wouldn't normally ask a Cadet to perform extra duties on top of their training, especially so new a Cadet as you. Between training and your classes, I'm sure you have more than enough to keep you occupied. However, I find myself in a unique position with you."

I tried not to wince. How many times had Commander Whitclé used that exact reasoning to refuse my petitions? That he would have to treat me differently than the other Cadets. I had assured him it wouldn't be true. I had been wrong.

"With you being attached to the Amulet Of The Dragon Lord, and our only lead on Miss Valencia's case, I have to request that you go above and beyond your duties as a Cadet and aid on the Rakael Valencia case."

"Wait, what?"

"You will be aiding Colonel Kalik in the Rakael Valencia case on top of your Guardian Cadet Training."

"Yes Sir." I was dazed. He was only picking me out because of unfortunate circumstances. He was barely picking on me at all.

"Dismissed," he said, head already back down and folder open.

Kalik pushed the book away with a frustrated grunt before looking up to find me poised in the open doorway, hand raised to knock. "Merry," he greeted with a smile.

"Something wrong?" I asked, gesturing at the

abandoned book, the only thing on the top of Kalik's shockingly tidy desk. Somehow I had expected all Guardian offices to be as disorganised as Commander Whitclé's, but Kalik's could not be more dissimilar.

The rectangular room had a west facing window that looked out on the city streets rather than into the Five Towers campus. Below it he had a Solar-Glow crystal that would light up when it sensed low sunlight. A sturdy desk, not dissimilar to Whitclé's, filled most of the space, a pair of comfortable looking plush chairs set in front of it and another matching chair behind it where Kalik sat. Behind him stood a series of filing cabinets, pressed up against the wall.

Everything seemed to have a place, if the pencil pot on his desk was anything to go by: a tidy clay thing with indented designs typical to Human pottery techniques.

"Nothing," he said. "What can I help you with?"

"Commander Whitclé said something about me helping with the amulet research."

"Oh, well, I'm not sure there's much you can do at this point. I've been researching as much as I can about the amulet — how it was used, when it was made, why it's stuck to you, how to get rid of it. But every piece of scholarship I've found is in one ancient dialect or another, so it's taking more effort than I had thought."

"Thus the frustration," I supplied.

Kalik glared at the still open book.

With one final heartbeat of hesitation, I stepped into the room to peer over his desk at it. "Is that *Magical Artefacts and Their Effects* by Llaven Beenen?"

"You know it?"

"I've read it before."

"You read Ancient Elvish?"

"Almost exclusively." It wasn't meant to sound pretentious, but I didn't want to admit to Kalik that I had never officially learnt other scripts. Tellyn Smeeten had stressed the importance of learning Elvish history from Elvish sources. The abundance of Human writings on Shima still tripped me up.

"Then, actually, I could use your help deciphering this." Kalik pushed the book toward me.

"I didn't think the Amulet Of The Dragon Lord was in there." Not that I had been looking for it the last time I had read it.

"I was also reading up a little on Sensitives — for the possibility that it might impact this whole situation. I don't have much base knowledge about Sensitives beyond the test I gave you."

I perched in the plush chair on the other side of Kalik's desk. Kalik shifted around the table to sit in the chair next to me, notebook open on his lap.

"Basically," I started, reading through the text. "It says that Sensitives can interact with some magical artefacts differently than other people. It talks about Calypsiate — I don't know what that translates as, maybe an artefact name? — but, um, it says that a non-sensitive can use items as described in chapter five. However, a Sensitive would be overwhelmed by the Calypsiate — maybe the souls? Or the power? I don't know — contained within."

I kept reading and attempting to translate until the end of the chapter. When I finished, Kalik looked down at his notes, poking at words with his pen.

"So," he said, "even if we found a user manual

for the amulet, there's no guarantee it would work that way for you." He sighed, tapping his pen against the page thoughtlessly. "Maybe you being a Sensitive is part of why it attached itself to you? Although, for all we know, it does this to anyone, or there's some other reason it likes you so much. The real questions are," he shifted the pen to start scribbling each question as he said it. "Can we use it? Can we separate it from you? And is it going to harm you in any way?"

I examined the amulet in my hand. It wasn't noticeable — as proven by how long it took to notice it in the first place. At a glance it would be easy to mistake it for an old burn scar. Only upon closer examination did the shape begin to reveal itself. Only in the right light did the colours become noticeable. The silver cage was almost invisible in my pale skin except where it crossed the darkest part of the fang.

"When I was looking at it before..." I started slowly. "It looked like it was supposed to be on a chain."

"So it probably doesn't attach to everyone," Kalik sighed, writing that down too.

I let out a long breath and fisted my hand around the amulet. Maybe I should buy some gloves to hide it. It was getting to the right time of year to wear them anyway.

Kalik tapped his pen against his notes again, some ink splattering on the unintelligible scrawl. It was like a pen had been enchanted to life and made some effort to imitate the kinds of movements it had been used for before, but with no real knowledge of how words or letters worked. How could such a tidy person have such messy writing?

"We'll keep looking," Kalik assured me.

"How did you fare with those songs?" Sorenson asked.

"The Holding Song gave me some challenge," I admitted, flicking through the pages to find it. Lior's elegant pencilled notes covered the page.

"That's not your writing," she said once I'd placed the sheets on the music stand.

"Lior helped me out."

Her eyebrows rose. "You asked for help."

"Is that against your rules now?"

She laughed. "No. I'm glad you worked with another student. Liorellion Folcs is an expert spell-singer, even if xe has no interest in Battle Magic. That may have been where your issue with the Holding Song arose though."

"Maybe," I hummed.

"So, you're settling into your new schedule better now?"

My hand flicked to the charm on my necklace. "Somewhat," I hedged, pins and needles settling into my hand around the amulet.

CHAPTER THIRTEEN

"Last week of the moon cycle, you all know what that means," PT's voice rang out in the quiet room.

I glanced blankly at the Cadets around me.

"Put this moon cycle's techniques into action," PT continued. "Arlan, you're new so I suggest you partner up with a more experienced Cadet who can help you catch up."

"I'm happy to do it, Sir," Valencia piped up from next to me.

"Good. Carry on."

Valencia's stance was lazy and unsteady with plenty of weak points to exploit. I let my weight rise to the balls of my feet.

It took me exactly three moves to get Valencia pinned. Turned out he could take a hit as well as he could maintain his stance: not well at all.

"Wow Merry, how did you do that?" he asked,

rubbing his jaw where one hit had landed a little harder than I had intended.

"Three different sets of training."

"From who?"

I wracked my brain for a way to explain away or even evade the question before realising that all my careful words, actions, and attempts to hide my past had been destroyed. I was officially claimed as the niece and heir of Lord Tellyn Smeeten, that wouldn't stay private to the Elven Courtiers we'd faced for very long. "Pirates, a mercenary, and then bouncers."

"Never mind me teaching you, do you have any tips?"

I blinked. "You want me to give you tips?"

"Yeah! You took me down so fast! I watched you land a hit on PT, and your sparring sessions with Colonel Kalik are legendary."

I winced. "Legendary?"

"Colonel Kalik and PT train together every once in a while. Colonel Kalik sometimes comes to teach us Cadets too. The Colonel is about the only person anyone has ever seen give PT a real run for his money."

"Oh..." I looked over at the other sparring Cadets, PT shifting between them to give pointers and praise. "I guess I could tell you what I know, if you really want."

"Great!" He waited expectantly.

"You mean right now?"

He nodded, grin splitting his face.

"Your stance could use some work."

For the rest of the session Valencia and I worked on improving his stance. I pointed out his weakest points, and we tried short sparring stints so he could try maintaining it as he used the techniques PT had been teaching, talking me through them as he did so. Captain Etta had always stressed the importance of working within the stance and trying out moves.

"Arlan."

I stopped manoeuvring Valencia's arm so that it guarded his face without blocking his vision.

"What are you doing?" PT's voice was harsh.

"We're working on stances, Sir," Valencia answered.

"Is your name Arlan?"

"No Sir." He hung his head.

"Arlan?"

"If he held his hands like that he couldn't see," I said.

"You were supposed to be sparring."

"We were sir, but it seemed pointless."

"Pointless?"

I gulped, looking straight into PT's red face, trying to balance my argument before I spoke but not leave PT waiting. "With Valencia's stance as it was he had too many weak points."

"I asked her for some tips," Valencia cut in.

"Did you two spar?" PT asked.

"Yes."

"How many rounds?"

"Five."

"Five?" his head reared back.

"After the first one we started going until one of us landed a hit that wasn't successfully blocked or dodged."

"Why?"

"Otherwise I'd be beaten to a pulp, sir," Valencia said.

"Excuse me?"

"You haven't really seen Cadet Arlan fight, have you sir?" Valencia's easy tone belied the way PT's red face and booming voice made me contemplate hiking to a nice solitary cave and living the rest of my life as a hermit. Maybe I could grow to like mushrooms.

PT folded his arms. "I did assess her, Valencia."

Valencia snorted a laugh. "While she was injured."

"What's your point, Cadet?"

"Merry is a skilled fighter, and I still have a lot to learn."

"The purpose of these sessions is to put what we have learnt into practice." PT's booming voice had quietened to a more conversational tone.

"Yes Sir." Valencia turned to me with a half shrug and took up his newly improved fighting stance.

I shifted into my bouncer taught de-escalation stance.

PT remained where he was, observing our interaction.

I let Valencia throw the first punch, easily reacting to push it away.

"If you want to teach him stance improvements, should you not be exemplifying them?" PT asked as Valencia and I traded slow blows.

"I thought it would be better to fix — um, improve his current stance rather than teach him a whole—" I shifted out of Valencia's range "— new stance."

"You don't use it though?"

"Not usually." When I had fought PT at my audition I had mirrored his stance rather than falling back into my favoured one.

Valencia's next punch flew too close to my face. I caught his hand and yanked him past me, using his momentum to throw him off balance.

"You're letting him off easily."

I didn't know how to respond. It was true. I swept Valencia's feet out from under him. He crashed to the mats.

"Do you allow all your opponents off so easily? Are you without follow-through?"

Smeeten's voice crept into my head. "Anyone with Smeeten blood should excel in all she tries."

My body moved of its own accord. Next thing I knew, Valencia was double tapping the mat in surrender.

"You don't even think about it," Valencia whined as I helped him to his feet.

I shrugged a half apology. "Muscle memory."

"How long have you been fighting?" PT asked.

"Since I was fifteen."

PT sighed. "Valencia, if you want extra sessions with Arlan, you need to schedule them outside Cadet Training hours." He walked away from us, calling to the room that the session was over and we were dismissed.

"Would you?" Valencia asked as I headed over to the cubby I'd left my boots in.

"Would I what?"

"Schedule some extra sessions with me? You're a really good teacher."

"I..." I already had so much to do, between Guardian Training; lessons with Sorenson; any amulet research Kalik wanted my help with... But Valencia's wobbly guard would either keep him for graduating or, worse, get him killed. Whatever I felt about him, Kitty was important to me and Kitty would be devastated to hear that something bad had happened to Valencia. "When?"

I hadn't spent much time in the Five Towers library in my year and a bit of study. I always expected it to be noisy, filled with the cacophonous ticking of the clock, since it was under the clock tower, but it never was. The silence was unnerving. But if I wanted to find research on the Amulet Of The Dragon Lord the Five Towers library was the place to look.

It would be easier to work independently, that way I wouldn't have to explain to Kalik that when I said I read Ancient Elvish "almost exclusively" I hadn't meant by preference.

A flash of shocking red caught my attention. Kitty's bright hair fell in his face as he beamed at me, sending me a small wave and almost capsizing the massive stack of books in his arms. Was he waving at me? Why? Did he want me to come over? I lifted my hand in an almost wave back as Kitty grabbed at his toppling books.

"I haven't seen you here before." Kitty pitched his voice low so it wouldn't carry through the silent space.

"No," I agreed half-heartedly.

"Need any help? I spend way too much time here."

My eyebrows drew together as I tried to decipher Kitty's motives. "I... was looking for artefact books."

Kitty gave easy directions to the sections I might find useful. "And, of course, you have to pass the poetry section." He laid one hand over his chest, face turning smooth and emulating bliss. "Swoon. Did you ever read any of that Ancient Elven romance poetry? I studied it as an extra course last year."

Before I could begin to think of a reply one of the librarians strolled past and shushed us. Kitty clapped a hand over his mouth, waved again, steadied his books and moved away.

Even with Kitty's directions, searching through the shelves was more effort than I had expected. Smeeten had a large library in his home, but it was nothing compared to this. Even if it had been, he had never allowed me to spend much time in there. Smeeten said books were for learning not for fun. Though, occasionally when he was away, Larrings would bring me a book filled with stories of romance or poetry. I'd ended up with quite the stack hidden under my bed, always fearing Smeeten would find them.

Larrings had told him about my hiding spot on one birthday. Smeeten hadn't been angry, he'd said, just disappointed. He took my stack of books and locked the door to the library. Even Larrings hadn't been given a key.

The memory of those strange beautiful works had me lingering as I passed through the poetry section of the Five Towers library. I ran my fingers along the spines of the books whose titles I couldn't read and those I could. I tried to tell myself to leave, that these weren't the books I was here for, but I couldn't help picking up a dusty old volume. The book was thick, covered in old brown leather. The title had almost faded off, the pages yellowed with age, and something in me clung to it.

The poetry book and I made our way to the section on magical objects, looking for anything printed in Elvish.

I carted the pile of books I had gathered home, arms beginning to ache as I trudged up the stairs. I had barely dumped the books on the rarely used desk shoved into the corner of my bedroom when there was a knock on the front door.

I spared one last glance for the messy pile of books as I dashed to answer the insistent knocking.

"Lior?" I blinked. "You're here? At my flat?"

"Surprise!" xe greeted.

"In the nicest way, why are you here?"

"You asked for help with your spell-songs."

I led xem into the living room. "I do not believe you're here to do homework."

"Homework and a Congratulations Basket!"

"What is a Congratulations Basket?" I turned to find Lior holding out a basket filled with a plethora of items.

"Its things for your Guardian-ness."

I sank down on the sofa, staring at the basket. Lior put it on the small table in the centre of the room and sank down on the green rug next to it to rifle through. Really, Kitty needed to get a handle on his obsession with green: it had spread so far over the flat that it even invaded my bedroom. And when had he put that rug in anyway?

"Okay, so it's got things like soap — because you're going to get stinky, protein bars — because I know you're a terrible cook, and a calendar — so you can remember when you're supposed to meet me, and other stuff like that."

"You really didn't have to do this," I said but I couldn't keep the smile off my face.

"No, I did." Lior sighed; folding xyr hands in xyr lap. Compacting in on xemself. "Here I've been all worried about what it would mean for me if you were in the Guardian Cadet Programme but I didn't think of what it would be like for you."

"What are you...?"

"I mean, along with getting busy and stinky and hungry, you're following your dream! That's amazing! Dragons know I don't have a dream to follow."

"Come one, Lior, I'm sure that's not true"

"No it is." Xe got up and starting moving about in the kitchen. I stayed where I sat on the sofa, watching Lior through the archway that nominally separated the kitchen and the living room. "I've never had a dream. I'm just stumbling along and making the best of things but I don't know what I want out of life. If my mama didn't own the club, I probably wouldn't have even started spell-singing. I'm that aimless." Xe came back with two steaming cups, holding one out to me. I took it with a sigh, everybody so loved tea it was inescapable. "It's chamomile," Lior clarified, plonking down next to me on the sofa.

I winced as the guilt heated my ears. Of course Lior knew better than to try and give me tea. "So what if you don't know what you want to do, is that really so bad? You have plenty of time."

"I know that. I just... I see people like you who have real ambition and it reminds me that I don't have any. I got insecure and I didn't celebrate your thing. So, even though it's been two weeks and we've been chatting about it and everything, I am here to celebrate your thing. You, Merry Arlan, best friend, are in the Guardian Cadet Programme!" Xe dug around in the basket, pulling out an enchanted light popper.

A loud pop and sparkles of multi-coloured lights descended around the room.

"Are those safe in such small spaces?" I asked.

"Probably not! Let's do another one!"

I laughed.

"To making history!" Lior crowed, setting off another popper.

"Cuffs are a vital component of a Guardian's kit," PT stated, holding up a set of manacles he pulled from a box at the edge of the sparring floor almost overflowing with the tarnished silver chains. They clattered against each other, a bright tinkle that didn't match their dark appearance. "You will use them to contain criminals and some suspects. Guardian cuffs are enchanted so as to prevent the wearer from using magic."

That explained the creeping feeling sliding up my spine.

"This week, you will be learning how to put someone into cuffs and let them out. You will be practising this skill when the person is compliant and when they are resistant. You will also be learning the best way to combat your cuffs if they are turned against you."

Maybe it was the dampening effect of the manacle enchantment, maybe it was the prospect of allowing myself to be at someone else's mercy, but tension crept into my shoulders. I glanced at Valencia, whose eyebrows had pinched together.

"Every other person in the line come and grab a pair, then find a partner."

I ended up paired with a Goblin Cadet. His hair was buzzed in a similar style to Commander Whitclé but where Whitclé had tightly coiled hair, this Goblin Cadet's hair was flat and straight, causing it to obscure his forehead. His smile was wide as he swung the manacles in one hand so they caught the light.

"Manth," he said. When he spoke, his fangs peeked out at me.

What reason could he have to extend his fangs? While some of the bouncers at Jhoto's kept their fangs extended for their entire shifts as intimidation, it didn't make sense that Manth was trying to intimidate everyone at Cadet Training.

Lior had told me about the Goblin 'Reaver Hormone', an apparent reaction to one's own venom. People with Reaver Hormone Response had an adrenaline-like reaction to the venom excreted by extended fangs. Their strength and speed increased at the expense of logic and often magic. Lior still didn't know about my fangs, nobody on Shima besides Kalik did. Maybe Manth had Reaver Hormone and used Cadet Training to learn to balance it.

"Arlan," I replied.

"Arlan?"

"Merry Arlan." I gave him the benefit of the doubt, assuming he was confused by my Human first name for a surname.

"Oh, right. Aionda Manth."

I nodded, glancing at the manacles as they caught the light again.

"I've done this session before," Manth said, clicking the cuffs open. "So I know what I'm doing. I'll demonstrate on you and then you can try on me, yeah?"

"You've done it before?"

"I've been in Cadet training for a while, no previous combat training so I keep getting looked over for Graduation." An edge crept into his tone and that bright smile returned, wider this time, showing his second set of fangs. "There's no need to be nervous, I'll let you out fast. You don't have to worry about me."

I tried to hide the hiss of pain that came over me. The amulet in my hand stung. I curled my hand into a fist, keeping my eyes glued to Manth. He was still speaking, each word making sparks fly up my arm and into my head. I tried to focus on his words, blinking rapidly to clear my head. What was happening to me?

When his hand clamped around my wrist, my lungs stopped working. The grip morphed from Manth's calloused brown skin to pale blue-undertoned skin belonging to someone else.

I couldn't breathe. Couldn't hear anything past my heart pounding in my ears.

The cuff that followed the hand was cold. Like ice. Ice Magic used to control, to freeze in place, to contain.

No. It's just a cuff. It's a Guardian cuff, for training. This is a safe place.

With no breath I couldn't spell-sing and, as the cuff clicked shut, my connection to my magic rendered.

My arm was numb. It might as well have been detached from my body. The ice feeling spread, like frost on a window in winter.

When a warm hand grabbed at my left wrist it burned. I wrenched away from the force, frozen no longer.

I still couldn't breathe. Each attempt ripped up my throat. If I stayed where I was something bad would happen.

Muscle memory kicked in.

CHAPTER FOURTEEN

The blood wouldn't come off my knuckles before my lesson with Sorenson but she didn't mention it. When I headed to the door to leave she called me to wait and told me PT had asked her to send me his way after my lesson was over.

PT's office was a barren space, containing only that which it needed to function. A table working as a desk with a mismatched set of drawers shoved underneath. On each side of the desk sat a single chair. None of the items matched in colour or style. Had PT put his office together from other people's discarded furniture, or had he bought each of these items individually with no care as to what image they presented?

It hadn't been easy to find, even with Sorenson's directions. How much of that challenge had been due to the tucked away nature of the office and how much of it was the balloon inflating in my chest was hard to tell.

He was definitely calling me to his office to kick me out. Who wanted a Guardian who couldn't cope with cuffs?

"Are you still working with Valencia outside Cadet Sessions?" PT asked, leaning back in his uncomfortable looking chair.

"Yes. Troiday and Septday after Cadet Training."

"Good. The rest of the week we'll be working on cuffs. You have a leave of absence from regular sessions so long as you train with Valencia according to your current schedule."

"Sir?"

"A leave of absence for the rest of the week. I know a panic attack when I see one, Arlan."

"A panic attack?"

"I'm guessing this has something to do with those broken ribs and your unorthodox entry to the Guardian Cadet Programme."

"Unorthodox entry?" I squeaked.

"In case you hadn't noticed, Arlan, the Brotherhood of Guardians doesn't accept women yet."

I gulped.

"Anyway, the Healers can help you with the panic, they'll give you strategies to cope or provide you someone to talk to."

I couldn't help but grimace at the thought of sharing my weaknesses with someone else.

"It's not an official recommendation, but as a Senior Guardian to a Cadet, this is something well worth considering. As it stands, your immediate reaction, while a little extreme, can be worked on in training. I'll warn you now, Arlan, if you haven't improved on this by the time the cuffs course rolls around next year, it could become a real concern." He leaned forward and tapped two fingers on the desk, making a hollow thunk. "Look into the mental Healing stuff."

I nodded.

"I'll see you next week, Arlan."

Walking into the Guardian Gym as the lingering Cadets left training the next day felt like it was against the rules. The confused or narrow-eyed looks from the Cadets had me ducking my head so as not to meet anyone's gaze as I yanked the boots off my feet. At least the barrels with the cuffs in had already been put away.

Valencia loitered in the centre of the sparring floor, chatting with Al, who let out a boisterous laugh at something Valencia said before clapping him on the shoulder and jogging off to grab his own boots.

"Merry!" Valencia grinned, waving far too enthusiastically for a man who had just endured two hours of training.

Ducking my head once again I dashed over to him.

"You're going to be super impressed!"

I couldn't help but smile at his enthusiasm. "Am I?"

"Yup. I actually used my guard today. Albeit, it got me cuffed, but I used it and PT said I did really well with it too." He took up the stance, weight shifting more easily to the balls of his feet, guard up in a way that protected his face without obscuring his vision.

"Any issues?" I asked.

"Yeah, one." He lowered his guard. "I'm having some issues going back to it after I've done something. Say I block a blow or something, I've been having a tough time getting my arms back in the right position without taking my eyes off my opponent."

I nodded. I remembered that issue. "When I was struggling with that, my teacher used to just yell 'guard' at me when I was doing other things and if I didn't get it up in time she'd swipe at me with her scarf."

Valencia laughed. "That's so unexpected."

"It's not exactly appropriate to punch someone every time, but she firmly believed in reinforcement."

"Please don't start throwing scarves at me."

"Do I look like the kind of person who wears scarves?"

He laughed again.

"Maybe if we do other exercises, like bodyweight stuff, and go back to guard regularly? Or I'll just yell at you to do it, if that's what you'd prefer? That way you can get used to it outside a fighting environment."

"That sounds great. Burpees!"

I squinted at him. "How are you excited about burpees?"

I walked into the Guardian Gym although the memory of the trip from my flat seemed absent from my head. It didn't matter. Today was going to be a good day. I had made up with Lior, I'd even utilised one of Lior's gifts — enchanted notes that stuck to the wall, I'd written up a schedule with everything from lessons to home practice and stuck it where it was easy to see. For once I'd even got a good night's sleep. I was going to make today a good day.

"Cadets, we have a new recruit," PT boomed.

Had he just appeared out of thin air? I could have sworn he wasn't there before. "Welcome Cadet Larrings."

My head whipped around to see him. Nathaniel Larrings, looking as weaselly as ever in a Guardian Cadet Uniform.

"Excuse me, miss," one of the Cadets said, pulling my attention away from Larrings. "The Guardian Gym is closed to civilians during Cadet Training. You'll have to come back later."

"But I am a Cadet," I said, looking down to find, not my Uniform but the white dress Smeeten always used in his Illusions.

"I'm sorry about this, she gets confused sometimes. Come home now, Meredith." Tellyn Smeeten put cold hands on my shoulders, leading me from the room.

"No, wait. I am a Cadet."

As Smeeten escorted me from campus I spotted Kalik hovering by the green in the centre of campus.

Why wouldn't my legs do what I wanted? "Kalik," I called. "Kalik, tell him. Tell him I'm a Cadet"

"Miss?" Kalik asked.

It was still dark when I awoke but I got up anyway. There was no way I was going back to sleep after that.

I yanked open my wardrobe to find my Guardian Uniforms in perfect order. Overtops hanging from the rail, shirts on one shelf, trousers on another, and the remainder of my clothes stuffed haphazardly on the bottom shelves. Everything was where it should be.

I took a deep breath and let myself out of the bedroom, relieved to be able to open the door without issue. I left the door ajar as I wandered into the kitchen, noting Valencia's boots propped up by the door next to mine and Kitty's. When had he picked up that habit?

I opened the enchanted cool cupboard and pulled some juice from it. I poured it into a glass and sipped. Maybe PT had been right. Maybe I needed to find a solution to this. But the idea of telling my innermost secrets to someone whose job was to pretend to care rankled at best and tightened my chest at worst.

I needed to do something. Something to rid me of the excess energy flittering around in my limbs.

As the dawn light peeked in through the kitchen windows I headed back to my room to get dressed. If nothing else I could see whether Kalik had got any further with his investigation.

When I arrived at Kalik's office the door was still locked. Before I could decide whether to come back later or wait around for him to arrive, Kalik appeared from around the corner, looking refreshed in the way people did when they actually slept at night.

"Merry." A smile broke out across his face. "What a pleasant surprise."

I shifted from foot to foot. "I wondered if you needed any help with the amulet research today?"

"Don't you have Cadet Training in an hour or so?"

"Uh... no. I'm on a leave of absence."

Kalik pulled a key from his pocket to unlock his office. "Well then, I'd welcome any help you can offer."

Once again Kalik sat next to me in the plush

and comfortable visitor's chairs instead of across the desk. He set a pile of books in front of me. "These are all things I've kept back about Sensitives if you have any interest in that." He set another pile in front of him. "And these are the books I haven't looked through yet," he sighed.

We worked in companionable silence as I read through the passages Kalik had marked, toying with Arlan Tiernan's charm on the necklace, sliding it back and forth on the chain.

"What is that?" Kalik asked, leaning back in his chair and stretching his arms over his head.

"Hm?" I looked up. "It's just a necklace."

"It looks like a ring."

"It belonged to my foster father," I said without thinking. Well, that opened up a line of questions. I held the charm out for Kalik to see.

"I think I've seen that before." He pulled a book out of one of the piles, toppling the stack. He flipped through the pages, quickly discarding it into a new stack and flicking through another. "Yes. Here!" He turned the book to show me.

Ring of Concealment
The ring is sized to fit the finger of an average Dragon Born, or that of a small Human, Elven woman, a small Goblin man, or a child. It is silver in colour, although the material from which it is made it hotly debated among scholars. Unsurprisingly, the ring is difficult to find for research purposes.

The patterning on it appears to be some kind of leaf style, but it is incredibly faded, so much so that it is almost impossible to discern that it is patterned at all at first glance.

The properties of the ring are far more fascinating than its appearance, however. The

Ring of Concealment, as the name might suggest, conceals the wearer from magical seeking through whatever means: Finding Magic, scrying, and Searching Rituals.

The Ring also conceals the wearer from notice of those who would intend them harm, making the wearer less visible to those who seek to harm them and, in extreme cases, even disconnects the wearer from their name when it is spoken to the one who seeks them.

This is, however, not its only interesting quality...

I stopped reading and took the ring off the chain to examine it. I had thought it was a trinket, a pretty thing that Arlan Tiernan had given me to encourage me to trust him, because he'd seen my eye drawn to it on his little finger.

"He must have had small hands" I muttered, slipping the ring onto my ring finger and pulling it back off.

"Did you get it after he died?"

"No." I closed my hand around the ring, as if I thought Kalik would try to take it. "He gave it to me a few weeks after I moved in. Called it my moving in present and told me it was without strings; that I didn't need to pay him back, that he really wanted me to have it."

"There's something about gifting it in here too." Kalik picked up the book I had abandoned, scanning until: "if given as a gift, the charm gains extra properties, largely dependent on the parties involved. — well that's helpful and descriptive." Kalik sighed, letting the book fall onto the desk.

"It's not what we're looking for anyway," I said, feeding the ring back onto its chain.

"No, but at least it felt like we were getting somewhere."

"Maybe we should take a break?"

"Do my ears deceive me or did Merry Arlan just call for us to take a break!"

"I don't understand why you think I'm such a—"

"Focused and committed person?"

"It doesn't sound so bad why you put it like that," I muttered a little bitterly.

"I never meant for it to sound bad, Merry."

"I do believe in taking breaks."

"As you should."

"Plus, reading for too long gives me a headache." And a little rage but I didn't want to mention that. That was something I was working on alone.

"We should get lunch," Kalik declared.

"What?"

"Lunch. The midday meal. Come on." He flipped the book closed, tidying the piles before shooing me out of his office.

Kalik led me to a small café inside the Five Towers campus. The ambient noise of the people filling just over half the space reminded me so much of Jhoto's on quiet nights that I half expected to find a stage propped in one corner. Opposite the entrance sat a large glass bar-like structure filled with sweet pastries and savoury snacks, leading to a wooden counter top with the till. Behind the glass case a series of machines sat, with one staff member dashing between different steaming spouts in a frenzied fashion.

To the left of the counter the area opened up in square wooden tables with sets of two or four chairs surrounding each one. People littered the space in a casual, haphazard fashion, each with mugs and plates and some with papers and notebooks.

"Kalik," the person behind the counter greeted. "Your usual? Oh! Are you on a date?"

My ears heated at the implication.

"Work break," he smiled. "This is Cadet Arlan."

The person behind the counter pouted a little but smiled at me. "What can I get you?"

CHAPTER FIFTEEN

The sound of the door pulled me from the dry archaic description of a fang-shaped artefact that might have been similar to the Amulet Of The Dragon Lord; if it would only describe the thing as more than just "fang shaped" and "magical." Instead the author had taken great pains to describe the many absurd and long-winded details of the horrors of the Goblins who had stolen so many Elven artefacts. Such was the issue in these old texts, especially ones written during the war eras, when Shima had been the battleground at the centre of the Elf and Goblin territory and cultural disputes.

I flipped the book closed, half-way to hiding it under the seascape patterned tablecloth before I realised what I was doing. Even so, my heart pounded in my chest at the prospect of being caught with a book.

I rose from the chair as Kitty let himself in and toed off his shoes. "Hi," he greeted, hair falling out of its ponytail and into his face. "You don't have to leave just because I'm here."

"I..." was about to do exactly that, wasn't I? I sank back into the chair, fingers playing over the edge of the book's cover.

"What are you up to?" he asked at he wandered into the kitchen and opened the enchanted cool cupboard to pull out a ball of beige something. I grimaced. "It's not cooked yet, judgey-butt," Kitty muttered.

"Sorry. I'm just doing some Guardian research."

Kitty groaned. "Don't tell me *you're* going to start reading, re-reading, and reciting the Guardian rules like Gergorio does!"

"Uh... no."

"Thank Hisloeper for that."

"Hisloeper?"

Kitty waved one hand, dumping the beige thing out of its bowl and onto the surface. "Ancient Dragon, turned into a regular saying. What are you researching?"

"Nothing much," I lied, rubbing the pins and needles away. "Do you know about Valencia's aunt?"

"The curse?" Kitty asked, shoving his hands into the beige stuff, stretching and compressing it like badly washed laundry. "Yeah, I know."

"Basically that, or ways to fix that."

"How come they've got you doing it? Gergorio barely gets to do anything but training."

I played with the edge of the book again; glad Kitty wasn't facing me as I didn't answer his question.

"Is it because you're a Sensitive?"

"Kinda."

"That's gotta be hard. You holding up okay?"

I shrugged. "Sure, I guess."

Kitty hummed once and seemed to focus in on his beige blob. I tucked the book against my stomach and retreated to my bedroom.

When I emerged from my bedroom, dressed in Cadet Training Uniform and semi-ready to return to training, I found Valencia loitering in my kitchen, one hand resting on the back of the dining chair he seemed to have claimed as his own. I frowned at him. Mornings were the worst and, foolishly, I had expected to be left alone during them.

Valencia handed me a plate of fluffy looking white bread buns. "Kitty made them and insisted I feed you before we go to training."

I rolled my eyes but bit into a bun, the inside was filled with some kind of savoury deliciousness. My grumpiness at not being alone faded, replaced by discomfort at the prospect of someone offering this kind of care. It always came with strings, or betrayal.

Valencia and I walked to the Five Towers in companionable silence, squinting against the rising sun and the cool morning mist.

We had shifted onto the sparring mats to find partners when Al rushed through the doors. He looked a little sick, paler than normal and with bags under his eyes. PT shot him a look but didn't say anything, letting Al partner up with Valencia while I matched with the sullenly silent Cadet who'd sent me to the Healers on my first week.

When the session was over PT pulled Al to one side as the rest of us headed over to put on our shoes. Lior waited by mine, leaning against the cubbies and grinning at me.

"What are you doing here?" I asked, breath still shortened from exertion.

"I have the night off tonight so I don't need my mid-morning nap and thought I might come visit with my favourite friend." Xe stood up to pat me on the upper arm but stopped before xyr hand made contact. "On the other hand, you might want to hit the showers first."

"Showers are for male Cadets." I rolled my eyes and swiped a self-conscious arm over my forehead.

"Merry?" Kalik called from the entryway. He spotted the two of us and jogged over. "Glad I caught you."

"Is it about the amulet? Because I might be pre-booked."

"It's not that. We've opened up a disused barracks for you."

"Just for our Merry?" Lior teased, voice dripping with assumptions and innuendo.

Kalik looked at Lior, taking in xyr small stature that indicated xyr Goblin heritage even if xyr ears had been covered, which they never were. With light brown hair, golden eyes, and skin that glinted like sunrise on a lake, Lior's heritage as Half-Elf was clean as air too.

Kalik smiled blandly and offered his hand. "Colonel Kalik."

"Liorellion Folcs." Lior shook Kalik's hand. "Merry's best friend."

"Kalik, what are you talking about? What barracks?" I interrupted before they could move on to the awfulness that was small talk.

"We needed a little time to clear out the floor and update some aspects. There's a big debate on the Council of Colonels as to whether to call it the women's barracks but," he shook his head. "Now you have a place on campus."

I hesitated. "Do I have to move in?"

"No, there's no requirement that Guardian Cadets, or any Guardians really, move into barracks. Most choose to but it's not a requirement. It's a holdover from the encouragement for Guardians to become family men but it works for a lot of other reasons too."

"That explains Valencia," I muttered, throwing a quick look over my shoulder to make sure he didn't hear my hushed complaint. It had been needless and rude and I did like Valencia, I just liked my privacy too.

"Rakael?" Kalik asked.

"No, Gergorio. He never leaves my flat."

Lior's eyebrows waggled. I had the urge to shove xem playfully but put it aside. I was too hyped up from training to do it safely and hurting Lior wasn't on the cards.

"Cadet Valencia is always at your flat?" Kalik asked carefully.

"Yeah. My roommate is his boyfriend."

"That makes sense. Shall I show you the barracks?"

I glanced at Lior.

"Yes. Go. Shower. Please. Although I do actually have a question for you, Colonel." Lior fell into step with Kalik, xyr hand on his arm.

"Yes?" Kalik asked, looking down at the connection. He didn't say anything about it, leading us out of the Guardian Gym and into the long stretch of building connecting Tower One and Tower Four.

"If this is to be a women's barracks, where do the nonbinary people go?"

"The aim is to revamp the whole block of barracks and relocate the Guardians to it, making it a gender neutral block. As yet, there aren't any nonbinary petitioners, unless you're changing that?"

"No." Lior seemed horrified at the very idea but xe didn't unlink from Kalik as we all traipsed up a set of stairs onto the second floor.

"Where did these barracks appear from anyway?" I butted in.

"They used to be the emergency war barracks from when the Five Towers were first built. The Council of Colonels and the Commander couldn't see a reason to keep them in reserve. We don't conscript anymore, I mean we never should have, but it's against the Guardian Code now since it endangers civilians. The only possible use for these barracks is as refugee shelters, and they're really not a high enough standard for that in their current state, so either way they needed an overhaul."

He pushed open a door to reveal a long corridor with regularly spaced refurbished wooden doors, all of which were ajar and letting in the late morning sunlight, as much as there was straining through the clouds. Light globes came to life as we stepped into the corridor, illuminating the sanded wooden floor all the clearer. Behind each door was a well sized room, only a little smaller than my bedroom in the flat. They were equipped with a comfortable-looking bed against one wall with a chest of drawers pushed up against the foot-board, and a desk pressed up under the window.

Kalik led us to the end of the corridor and pushed open another door to reveal a series of shower cubicles, all open for now, frosted glass with strategic opacity to cover most of a person's midsection and barring the possibility of peering over the tops or under a gap in the base. Opposite the showers stood a row of sinks with mirrors above them reflecting the room back to itself.

"What was wrong with it before?" Lior asked.

"No running water," Kalik said, twisting a tap to show that fact had changed and flipping it back off almost immediately after. "The beds — or, more importantly the mattresses were centuries old." He sighed. "It wasn't good. I mean, the current barracks aren't great either, huge rooms filled with beds because who needs privacy, right?"

Lior chucked.

"Anyway, yeah, this place was my pet project but I couldn't get the go ahead without good reason since it's a high cost, low reward situation — at least according to the rejection forms I kept getting. Now we're just stuck on whether to make it a mixed gender barracks or not."

"Which they won't decide until Merry has graduated or failed?" Lior suggested.

Kalik shrugged but the movement was tense. "Anyway, Merry, you're welcome to use these as you need. I made sure there were extra linens like bedding and towels in the supply cupboard, along with some Guardian Uniforms."

"Please try them now, stink-bug," Lior added.

I shot a falsified glare at xem and grabbed at the bottom of my shirt.

Lior clamped a hand over xyr own eyes and xyr other one over Kalik's. Kalik's skin flushed underneath Lior's grip. "We'll leave you to it." Xe backed out of the bathroom.

Lunch with Lior was great. I headed home with more energy than I had started the day with. Not only had Lior splurged and bought us both an extra slice of cake, but chatting with xem had settled the residual anxiety of working with a Cadet I couldn't get a read on. Was his sullenness to do with me or just his personality type? Lior had waved a hand nonchalantly and asked me whether it mattered. "Either accept him how he is or ask him why he's like that; the hypothesising is going to kill you."

I pushed open the door to my flat.

At this time of day, Kitty would be in his room, most likely with Valencia, which meant I could tidy up the communal spaces in private. The sight that greeted me when I opened the door was so far from what I expected that I dropped my keys to clatter on the ground.

Kitty was pinning Valencia to the sofa, head tucked into his neck, ponytail bobbing as he moved. Valencia grasped tightly to the edges of the sofa, and I was pretty sure someone was purring.

I jerked my head away from the sight.

"Merry!" Kitty's voice, higher than usual. "I'm so sorry!"

I risked a glance back at them as I bent to scoop up my keys. Kitty, now stood, was pushing loose tendrils of hair out of his face. Valencia's shirt was missing. I looked away again. "In the living room? Really?" I squeaked.

"We got carried away. We didn't mean to," Kitty insisted.

The amulet in my hand buzzed and warmed.

"We— we won't do it again."

The buzzing intensified. I absently rubbed at it. "Okay..." I offered, retreating to my bedroom without even taking off my boots.

The walk to the Guardian Gym the next morning had Valencia quieter than I had ever experienced before. The silence sat awkwardly, the first time since I'd known Valencia that he had walked anywhere without devolving into mindless chatter. Whenever he'd met my eye his face had flushed gold and he'd quickly looked away. I almost missed his babbling, especially since every time he blushed it cast my mind back to his shirtless self on the sofa the previous day. What would it be like to be so enamoured with a person that you forgot there was another person living with you?

A whole host of Guardians loitered around the edges of the sparring floor. The coloured rank stripes on their Uniforms painted them as everywhere from Private to a single Colonel. A Colonel I recognised.

We lined up along the same edge of the sparring floor we always stood on, awaiting PT's orders. My eyes roved over the Guardian's in front of us. Kalik's green colonel stripe drew attention amongst the men facing me, especially since he stood with a Private — stripe-less dark Uniform shirt contrasting with Kalik's white button-down and green stripe — chatting in the friendly manner I had come to associate with Kalik.

"Patrols," PT began, bringing the accumulated ranked Guardian chatter to an end, "are a vital part of a Guardian's day to day life and work. Paperwork is a vital part of a Guardian's day to day life and work. Working with civilians is a vital — the most vital part of a Guardian's day to day life and work. These are not things that can be learnt on a sparring floor in a Gym. These are not things that can be taught in a classroom. These are things you can only learn through action."

He paced up and down the line of us Cadets. Kalik leaned over to whisper something to the Private, who covered his mouth with his hand to hide his quiet laughter.

"To this end," PT continued. "You will be partnered up with an experienced Guardian. You will shadow said Guardian for the next nine weeks, working with them on patrols, paperwork, and learning everything you can from them. And before anyone starts, yes, that does in fact cover the Midwinter break offered by the Five Towers. While your training currently affords you the traditional Free Days, a Guardian's role is to protect the civilians on Shima, crime doesn't take a holiday so neither can the Guardian institution. Come chat with me if you have an issue to raise."

PT waved the swarm of Guardians forward. I tried to maintain my position but the crowd was overwhelming as Guardians and Cadets met one another, asking for name after name. At least when it had been busy like this at Jhoto's, I'd had the bar to separate me from the crowd.

"Sorry." A voice I recognised. In the chaos that surrounded us he was difficult to locate. "I was helping the Private. He's never done partnering up before."

"Okay," I hedged.

"I'm your patrols partner," Kalik clarified. "And I already knew where to find you."

"I thought Colonels didn't do patrols."

"Typically we don't."

I waited for Kalik to elaborate but instead he told me what time to meet him and where before dashing off; calling over his shoulder that he needed to get back to work. I was left stranded, surrounded by Cadets and their respective Guardians as they got to know one another.

CHAPTER SIXTEEN

It was always easier to get up to Lior's room when the bar was just opening, especially on quiet nights like Deuday. Between the front of house being open, being recognisable to the rest of the staff, and there not being enough visitors that staff got protective over the back room, I could walk right through and up the stairs.

"Finally!" Lior greeted, pushing away from xyr desk. "I've been dying for a distraction." Xe spun to face me. "Why the serious face?"

"We've been put on Guardian patrols."

"Oh?"

"Paired up with a fully-fledged Guardian on their patrol route."

"That sounds... good?" Lior offered. "Sorry. I don't know anything about this whole Guardian thing and the words sound like a positive but your face says otherwise."

"Yeah...it's hard to explain." I perched myself on the edge of Lior's bed. "Can I explain or would you rather I didn't? I know you're not exactly hyped about the whole Guardian thing."

"I appreciate your care," Lior said, choosing xyr words with xyr own care. "But I can handle this."

"You sound weird, what's happening."

"My mama put me in therapy," xe grumbled.

"For what?"

"Anxiety." Xe huffed out a sigh. "I mentioned being worried about losing you to the Guardians and she got all concerned."

I frowned. "Your job is performing in front of a bar full of people."

"Being on stage is one thing, being face to face with people is a whole separate thing. Anyway, you tell me about this patrols thing and I'll tell you all about therapy."

I laughed. "Okay. I'm partnered with Kalik."

"He does patrols?"

"Not normally..."

"That's the issue?"

"It's just another example of me being treated differently."

"Maybe Kalik is just invested in your success."

"But why would he be so invested?"

Lior waggled xyr eyebrows, moving to sit with me on the bed.

"What are you insinuating?"

"Kalik's invested in your success," xe sing-songed. "He's coming out on patrols for you, advocating for your Guardianship, rescuing you from the Elven Embassy, and the way he looks at you..." xe nudged me.

"He's probably just on patrols with me because Commander Whitclé doesn't trust me and wants someone high ranking to step in. He promised to sponsor my Guardianship if I helped Rakael Valencia. He rescued me from the Elven Embassy because he was the reason I was there in the first place. And what do you mean by the way he looks at me?"

"Come on, Merry, you can't be that oblivious."

"Oblivious to what? He's doing his job."

"You just said patrols aren't his regular job."

"Being a mentor then."

"I bet he could mentor you in the art of romance," Lior muttered.

"Don't be so ridiculous."

"You ever heard the Tale of the Moon Prince? It's an old Goblin legend."

"Yeah. Goblin is captured by Elves, prays to the moon for rescue, the Moon Prince comes to Terya to rescue him."

Lior blinked at me. "It loses a little of its romance and poetry when you phrase it like that. How do you know it anyway?"

"I used to be a Goblin."

"You used to be a Goblin?" Lior enunciated each word clearly.

"No. I mean I used to live with the Goblin side of my family."

"The Goblin side of your family?"

"Yeah..." I hesitated, wondering how much to tell Lior. "I used to live with my great-aunt when I was really young. But my uncle—"

"That Smeeten guy?"

"Yeah, he made a claim for me and, being my father's brother, he had a closer claim so..." I shrugged. "But my great-aunt used to tell me the old legends."

"Can I ask the inappropriate question?"

Again I hesitated. "Okay."

"Why didn't you go back to your aunt when you ran away? I mean, obviously I'm glad you came here but..."

"I didn't know where she was, or how to get to her, or whether she even wanted me. Plus he would have found me there — can we not talk about this."

"Sure, sorry. How goes making friends with the other Cadets?"

I scrunched my nose. "I have a few tentative friend-ish things..."

The soft chime of the clock tower bells had both of us turning to the window. Lior pushed to xyr feet. "I should get ready, I'm on stage tonight."

"Need any help?"

"Nah."

I headed to the door and hesitated when I got there. "Wait, what happened to telling me about therapy?"

"Next time," Lior promised, neatening out the tiny imperfection in xyr bedding from where we had sat.

"Okay Cadets." PT paced up and down the line. "It's time to shift the Battle Magic you've been practising earlier this week into sparring matches. Your focus is on subduing your partner; you should aim to use your magic to supplement your hand to hand training. I expect you to do better than just throwing magic at one another."

He picked out our partners for the session, pairing me and Al once again.

I had never been to the top of a mountain, but the way Al's magic kept me short of breath matched Etta's first mate's description of the effects of such height. It was as if Al had turned all the air around me to syrup, a challenge to breathe in, even more difficult to move in.

With my movement slowed, Al had more time to dodge. He bounced around like a humming bird, never staying in one spot for more than a few seconds.

Frustration bubbled in my chest at being so slow and unable to catch him, making my fangs itch to descend. I couldn't even take a deep breath to try and settle the emotion.

Boom.

The blast made everyone stumble. Even PT looked unsteady on his feet. Al's magic snapped from existence, leaving me light-headed and stumbling to find my feet.

Where had that come from? Who had used that much power?

The thunk of a body hitting something solid grabbed me like a pair of hands spinning my shoulders toward the source of the noise.

Valencia lay half off the sparring floor, head on the solid entryway of the Gym. I was moving before I could think.

It didn't matter that PT would know what to do and I didn't. It didn't matter that I didn't have Healing Magic. My legs pounded across the room and sank down next to Valencia's head, hard floor pressing against my knees.

"Gergorio?" Who had done this to him?

"Tch, bet she's his girlfriend." I didn't care who had said it but looking up, it was obvious that Manth had been the one speaking.

"I would bite my tongue if I were you." It was something Smeeten would say and the fact that I had sounded like him sent shockwaves of disgust rocketing through me, mixing unpleasantly with the fear and useless anger.

"What if I want you to bite it for me?" Manth sneered.

My gums stung as my fangs extended. I spun back to Gergorio, hiding my lack of control in his dazed face.

"Cadet Manth," PT barked. "Is that how you address your fellow Guardians?"

"No Sir," Manth said.

"You're all spikey," Valencia mumbled at me, words slurring a little.

"You need to see a Healer," I insisted.

"Not for scraped knees or bruised knuckles."

"Arlan, can you get Valencia to the Healers or do you need assistance?" PT asked.

Kitty poked his head around the kitchen archway when I opened the door to the flat. "Oh, hi Merry, is Gergorio with you?"

"Um..."

"He was supposed to come up after training, but he's been getting distracted lately — says me I know but..." He canted his head to one side. "Why are you looking at me like that?"

"Don't panic." A bad start for anyone, but especially a Dragon Born – known collectively for their protectiveness. "He's in the Healers overnight." At least, but I wanted to hold that one off for a little while.

"What!" Kitty roared. "Why?"

"There was an accident in training. He's fine. It's just a concussion, but they're keeping hold of him."

Kitty took three deep, even breaths before refocusing on me. "What's put you out? You're all spikey."

"Why do people keep calling me spikey?"

"I think it's the fangs, Merry."

"What?" I clapped a hand over my mouth. Sure enough, my fangs hadn't retracted yet. Which meant the entire time I'd been at the Healers I had been... spikey. "Don't you want to go visit Gergorio before visiting hours are over?" I asked, muffled around my hand as I tried to make my fangs go away.

"Yes, but I get the distinct impression that if I don't get the answer out of you right now, you'll have had a chance to come up with carefully crafted half-truths and avoidances. As your friend, I want you to know I'm here for you, brutal and scary truth included. Plus I made lunch for Gergorio and it's wasteful to leave it."

My eyebrows drew together.

"I need a chance to calm down and focus on something else, Merry. Please?"

I perched on the edge of a dining chair, Kitty sitting next to me, leaving Valencia's favoured chair empty. It loomed over the room.

He would be fine, the Healers were skilled and they'd worked with things like this nine-hundred times before. Still, the dazed mumble wouldn't leave me, "not for scraped knees and bruised knuckles."

CHAPTER SEVENTEEN

I rubbed my face as I started up the steps to Sorenson's classroom. Time to face the consequences of missing her class yesterday. I hadn't even thought about it. Taking Valencia to the Healer and providing them the information they needed hadn't been a quick endeavour. Then I'd wanted to tell Kitty immediately, even if the way I'd done it had been a little unexpected. I'd completely forgotten that Sixday Cadet Training led straight into a Sorenson class.

As if that wasn't bad enough, nightmares about fangs and Manth being Larrings in disguise and me being thrown out of the Guardians had plagued my sleep.

When Cadet Training had ended I had headed to the Healers tower to check on Gergorio, finding Kitty sat next to his bed with a stack of books that could have rivalled a Dragon in size.

Gergorio had been feeling better and insisted I stay for lunch, leading us well into the afternoon. And that left me working on very little sleep and still dressed in my sweaty Cadet Training Uniform. At least two lunches with Kitty meant two good and tasty meals; rather than protein bars or my attempts at cooking by throwing together whatever random components I could get my hands on for unenjoyable sustenance.

"PT tells me you don't know Magic Basics." Sorenson assaulted me with the statement before I'd even finished opening the door.

"What?"

"You were in a magic defence class yesterday, yes?"

"Yes."

"PT tells me you didn't display any knowledge of Magic Basics, like Shielding. We came to the conclusion that it's because you don't know them. Am I wrong?"

"You talk to PT?"

"We keep each other appraised, and he came to warn me you wouldn't make it to your lesson. How is your friend, by the way?"

"Better today."

She nodded. "That's good. I wish him well. Now, about you, and your Magic Basics."

I shrugged. "PT suggested we focus mainly on hand to hand combat."

"Merry, do you know Magic Basics like Shielding?"

A direct question. I winced. "No."

She pressed her lips together. "Alright... I can allocate one of your weekly sessions to Magic Basics. Dependant on your progress, I may schedule you in some extra classes."

Great. More to add into my already confusing

timetable. Between Cadet Training, extra training with Valencia, Sorenson's lessons, two hours of practice a day, helping Kalik with amulet research, and now patrols, I wasn't sure how extra Magic Basics lessons would fit into my timetable. It wasn't like Professor Sorenson could work around my timetable at the expense of her own. "Yes, Professor."

"Good. Now, today we're going to work on a different Holding Song."

I grimaced.

"We're going to keep looking until we find the one that works for you. This will be invaluable to you as your Guardian training progresses."

When the lesson was over, I trudged back down the stairs. Lior waited at the base of the tower, sitting under a tree on the edge of the park area in the centre of the Five Towers, bundled up in a bright red scarf. I loomed over xem until xe looked up from the book in xyr hand.

"We cannot do this outside again," Lior insisted, teeth chattering together in the rapidly freezing air.

"I might know a place..."

"Let's go!" Lior creaked to xyr feet.

I grabbed xyr hand and led xem across campus.

"How did you find this place?" Lior asked, cuddling the dark brown beverage xe had ordered while I had been finding a table. I was half convinced Lior had only sent me away to stop me from spending my own money. The Guardian stipend paid my rent and a little wage but nothing compared to working full time at Jhoto's.

"Kalik brought me here — and before you start

with your eyebrows," I pointed at said eyebrows, "we just had lunch."

"Sounds like a date."

"It was a work break."

Lior threw xyr head back and let out a single barked laugh. "You know what a break is?"

"Why does everyone think I don't understand what a break is?"

Lior tilted xyr head to one side. "I'm just teasing you."

"You and Kalik both," I grumbled.

Lior and I talked over Holding spell-songs – although I didn't know why Lior was learning Holding Songs when xyr focus was supposed to be commercial spell-singing.

Eventually our food arrived at the table, the server apologising for the delay. Lior and I both waved off her apology and told her we weren't in any hurry.

"Oh! I nearly forgot! This woman came by the club yesterday asking to see you," Lior announced.

"What woman?"

"I told her you didn't work there anymore."

"That's it?"

"Well, yeah. I don't know this woman and I figured with what I know of your long and torturous history." Xe touched the back of xyr hand to xyr head.

"Don't be so dramatic." I tapped xyr hand to pull it back down.

"Okay, fine. With everything that's happened in the past few weeks, I figured giving out info about your location to any old stranger who happens to know your name and that you might have once worked at Jhoto's Bar and Club, wasn't a great idea."

"Fair point. Thanks Lior." But who on Terya had that woman been? And why was she looking for me?

"And then I found out why Jen the bartender has been taking so much time off sick."

"Gossip," I accused.

"I thought the person who covered for Jen so often might care," Lior sniffed. "Excuse me if I got it wrong."

I sighed, giving in to my curiosity. "Tell me?"

Huiday mornings were completely outside my experience — beyond the pre-dawn amble back to my flat after a closing shift at Jhoto's where I'd occasionally pass the bakers heading in to their shops to light their ovens. Still, the way the cold air clung low over the streets was pretty, even if the chill had me stuffing my hands deep into my pockets.

"Not a morning person?" Kalik asked as he jogged over, black Guardian Uniform coat buttoned high up his neck.

"Never have been," I couldn't keep the grumble out of my voice. The sun hadn't even risen yet, street lights casting eerie blue and orange glows over the street depending on their magical or fire-based means of operation.

"Here." He held out a paper bag and a silver-coloured travel mug.

"This better not be tea," I warned.

Kalik smiled; exhale misting the air in front of him. "It's not, but good to know." He sipped at his own travel mug. "I stopped by the café on campus before I got here. Revvi asked if I was ordering for you." He shook his head as if exasperated but amused by Revvi's antics. "She said you've been coming in fairly regularly and suggested that." He gestured at the items in my hands.

"Thanks."

"Least I could do, making you work on a Huiday when you have training six days a week."

I canted my head as Kalik surged into motion.

"Patrols are a little outside my regular schedule so I've had to add in some extra work time and between my own duties and your lessons and such, Huiday was the only one that could work this week." His shoulders lifted, like he was trying to hide. "These patrol times might end up being incredibly variable, I hope that's okay."

"Yeah..." I wanted to ask why Kalik was the one who I had been patrol partnered with but the possible reasons and their repercussions kept the words lodged in my throat. Instead I shuffled the pastry out of the top of the bag and bit into it, revelling in the rich chocolatey taste.

Once we finished the drinks Kalik took the mug back and put it into one of the deep pockets of his Guardian Uniform coat. The sun crested the horizon, golden rays casting long shadows down the streets.

"Guardians!" A woman called, waving her arm at us.

Kalik stepped up to interact with her as I hung back, watching the way he smiled softly, the way he leaned just right to make her comfortable but show he was invested in her issue. Finally he nodded and gestured for me to follow him as he clambered onto the roof of the storage shed.

The scent of baking bread wafted up through the gaping hole in the roof.

Kalik climbed back down to pass me up some planks of wood to cover the hole. "Apparently," he said as he handed one over. "Jonathan is having a whole fiasco about what you should wear to the Guardian Cadet Graduation Ball."

"I have to go to a ball?"

"Every half-year there's a ball for people to graduate out of the Cadet Training Programme. Everyone involved with the Guardians has to attend."

"Oh... What do Cadets normally wear?"

"Everyone wears Formal Uniform — it gets confusing because pretty much every Formal Uniform is the same no matter your rank. The only difference is the accolade buttons — which every Graduate gets and then you earn them for various successes after that. But every ball is just a sea of white shirts and black trousers."

"Okay, so I wear Formal Uniform, what's difficult about that? Are we actually fixing this roof or...?"

"We'll send a repair crew; just cover the hole for now." Once we were both back on the ground Kalik continued. "Apparently, there's some debate from the University Board about your gender whether that means you should be wearing a dress of some kind."

"No." My voice was harsh.

"I think it's silly too," Kalik said. "You're a Cadet, you should wear a Uniform. Not to mention, if you wear a Uniform we don't have to start thinking up a whole new outfit, and employing a tailor, and whether it would be a dress or a shirt and skirt..."

My brain filled with images without my consent. The white dress, the barred windows, Larrings.

"Merry?" Kalik's voice battled the sound of my heartbeat in my head, the harsh rush of my breath tearing up my throat.

I knew I was breathing, I could feel it ripping my throat apart, pulling all the moisture from my mouth. But my lungs disagreed. My vision started fuzzing around the edges, like I'd been hit on the head.

When I came back to myself, I was staring into Kalik's deep brown eyes.

"You okay?" He asked.

"Sorry."

"Are the panic attacks new? An amulet thing?"

I grimaced. I didn't want to have this conversation. "Not the amulet," I said, "but still new."

"Do you want to tell me about it?"

"About what?"

"Whatever it is that stole your breath."

"No."

"Have you told anyone about it?"

"Lior, a bit."

"Liorellion Folcs?"

"What other Lior do you know?"

"It's good that you have someone you trust like that." Kalik examined me before nodding. "If there's anything I can do, just let me know. We have Guardian counsellors for these kinds of things, if it gets any worse protocol states you must meet with them for at least three months."

"It's a thing?" PT had mentioned it but I had thought that was just him.

"People can get hurt in all kinds of ways. Sometimes they see the counsellors for things like this, sometimes they get hurt and fall into depression, sometimes they lose someone important or fear losing someone important, sometimes people just have this kind of thing built in. The counsellors are there for any

Guardian that needs or wants to see them. If you go of your own accord, it's completely confidential. If you go because it's mandated, your attendance is recorded."

With that Kalik stood tall again and turned toward the main street once more. When we had ducked into a side street I couldn't have said, but I trailed after Kalik as we continued our patrol route. The sheer volume of tailors in the district seemed ridiculous, each one setting my heart battering tiredly against my ribcage.

Sorenson's spell bashed into my shoulder. "You're not focusing, Merry," she barked.

"Sorry," I panted, trying to ignore the way my body ached. Even holding back Sorenson's spells had battered me like a smashed block of ice for cocktails.

I could have mentioned how Kalik had requested my presence pre-Cadet Training to fit in enough hours of patrols this week, which meant our patrol had ended before the sun had even poked at the edges of the horizon. I could have mentioned that I had passed the six hour mark for working time without a break. But it didn't matter. Learning and practising Battle spell-songs when nearing exhaustion was useful experience for real battle — or at least that was what I had heard.

"Don't be sorry, be better."

I tried to pull my focus back to the Shielding spell Sorenson had taught me. Something about it wouldn't stick in my head, and I couldn't hold on to it for more than a few seconds.

Another blast to my shoulder had me stumbling.

"Focus," Sorenson demanded, pushing against

me with the power behind the word. Sweat dripped down her face, sticking her hair to her skin as she pulled magic.

I gritted my teeth against the pain and the pressure. I tried to pull up the Shield, like a cloak lifted from the floor but it wouldn't come. The cloak was imaginary and I didn't have the visual imaging to access it.

A roar of frustration escaped me and power pushed through the room.

Sorenson was on the floor. The windows were shattered. The cool outside air filled the room, gentle rain spattering the tops of Sorenson's shelves and the floor near me.

The breeze dispelled the metallic scent of magic, though the crystal ward didn't settle back into place.

Sorenson picked herself up off the floor before I could even think about moving. She organised her skirts around herself and took a deep, calming breath. Before I could apologise she held up a hand. "I think we'll leave it there for today," she said softly.

I nodded meekly and dashed down the stairs.

CHAPTER EIGHTEEN

I wanted to destroy whoever had painted the dawn sky in delicate pinks and iridescent blues. Magical exhaustion tugged at my limbs as I trudged toward the Guardian Gym.

I had put my shoes on the wrong feet twice that morning. Despite having crawled into bed almost immediately after breaking Sorenson's windows the previous day and sleeping all the way through to the morning, I still couldn't seem to get past the tiredness.

Valencia had been giving me odd looks the whole walk to the Guardian Gym

My shoulder ached as I stood in line with the other Cadets. PT paced back and forth in front of us, stressing the importance of drawing knowledge from many sources and the importance of knowing how to restrain without injury. "We can hardly be considered protectors if we are aggressive."

A murmur rippled down the line but I couldn't quite catch what was said.

"In order to help widen your knowledge base, I have requested the assistance of a Senior Guardian. Until you all get a handle on immobilising holds we will be utilising the knowledge and assistance of Colonel Kalik."

My head jerked around to spot Kalik slowing from a jog to a confident walk as he entered the gym. He didn't seem like the type to be late; I wondered what had kept him. The smile on his face seemed insincere but I couldn't decide why.

Once more he reminded me of the Kalik who had been sat in my living room the first time we'd met rather than the Kalik I had sat and researched magical artefacts with. Or the Kalik who had taken me to lunch. Or the Kalik who accompanied me on patrols. Or even the Kalik I had watched interact with the Guardian Private.

The fact that Kalik was the resident expert on immobilising holds put our previous sparring matches into a different perspective.

Kalik ran through a few examples of immobilising holds with PT, explaining that most of his holds utilised the opponent's momentum and strength against them. He stressed the importance of only using them on aggressors and, even then, using them with care and consideration.

"Any questions before we begin practising what Colonel Kalik has shared?" PT asked. "Yes, Cadet Jenkins?"

"You two seem fairly evenly matched. Will this still work if our opponent is much bigger and stronger than us?" He gestured to his own short stature and slim frame. "I don't exactly have that kind of power."

"It absolutely will," Kalik answered. "As I mentioned, the brilliance of this style is that it uses your opponent's power against them." His eyes roamed the line of us. "If one of the smaller Cadets might volunteer..." His attention landed on me, holding there. He wanted me to volunteer. When nobody else stepped forward Kalik said, "Cadet Arlan, perhaps you wouldn't mind?"

I scowled at him briefly before stepping up to him. He talked me through some of the movements before stepping back.

"Okay," he said. "I'm going to come at you now."

As I held the struggling Kalik, pain burned through my shoulder. He double tapped my hand, telling me the demonstration was over. This time his smile was easy, more honest than before.

"Does that help mitigate your concerns?" He asked.

Al nodded and PT and Kalik started partnering people up. Valencia edged toward me and I tried to fight the laughter bubbling in my chest at his lack of subtlety.

Valencia and I shifted through the steps, blocking out the movements.

When Kalik called for our attention to teach another movement he picked me out to help demonstrate once again. A flip over the shoulder this time, before pinning your opponent against the ground.

I managed to keep my discomfort and pain to myself until the last attempt where a hissed breath escaped between my teeth.

"Return to your earlier practice pairs," Kalik

said as he got to his feet. He turned to face me and quietly asked, "What happened?"

"I'm fine." I realised my mistake as soon as the words were out. That wasn't what he had asked. I closed my eyes.

"What is wrong?" His words were painfully clear.

I put a hand over my shoulder protectively, trying not to think about how much Nathaniel Larrings would have exploited a weakness like this. "I'm really fine," I said, opening my eyes to both Kalik and Valencia looking at me with concern written all over their faces.

"Let me see," Kalik demanded.

I huffed at him but wriggled out of my Guardian Cadet hooded overtop to reveal my sleeveless undershirt. It was one of the ones I'd picked up from the linen cupboard in the newly refurbished barracks, cut a little lower under the arms than I might have liked, exposing some of my sports bra, but it matched the other Cadets better than the ones Kalik had brought in the box.

I had to admit, my shoulder looked worse than I had thought, purple bruising spreading from my collarbone to halfway down my upper arm. "It's not a big deal," I said. "Just practise gone wrong."

"What practice?" Kalik asked.

"My lesson with Sorenson — it's really not a big deal. It's my own fault for not Shielding properly." I shrugged and vaguely regretted the motion.

"Wasn't that after Cadet Training yesterday?"

"Bruises always look worse the next day." I had plenty of experience with that.

"Yesterday morning?" Kalik asked. "When

Sorenson's windows were smashed?"

"Maybe," I replied. The amulet in my hand tingled.

"Why haven't you been to a Healer?"

"It's a bruise, Kalik. Give it a couple of days and it'll be gone. Anyway, you guys need to stop treating Cadets like babies, we need to be able to take a hit and keep going. What happens when we get bruises from training? Are we meant to trot off to the Healers every time? Bruised knuckles and scraped knees?"

"No, but—"

"I don't see why you're so bothered by this."

"Merry, this is hardly a scraped knee. The power required to shatter Sorenson's windows through her wards left magical residue for the rest of the day. She had to relocate. If she turned that power on you it could be more than a simple bruise."

"It's nothing," I insisted, not wanting to correct Kalik's assumption that Sorenson had been the one to shatter the windows. "When someone touches it wrong or I overuse it, it hurts for a bit, but it's not like it's impeding my movement. It's a bruise, I've had worse."

Kalik's face was severe. "It sure seemed like it was impeding your movement. And you are known for not going to a Healers when you need to."

"I wasn't referring to the whole Embassy fiasco when I said worse," I scoffed and turned to Valencia. "Shall I attack you or...?"

"I really think, if Sorenson turned all that power on you, you should go to the Healers," Kalik reiterated.

"She didn't turn that power on me," I snapped, losing the battle not to correct him. "My Shield kept failing and I got frustrated and I lost control, okay? I exploded her windows, are you satisfied now?" I hadn't realised I'd been advancing on Kalik with each statement until suddenly there I was, squared up and in his face.

I cleared my throat and stepped back, turning to face Valencia once again.

At the end of the session, Kalik left. I rolled my shoulders; the ache in them reminded me of Kalik's protective statements.

"You heading back to the flat?" Valencia asked.

I nodded, focusing my attention on lacing up my boots.

"I'm sure he'd be like that with anyone," Valencia said as we exited the Five Towers through the huge gates I had never seen closed.

"Huh?"

"Colonel Kalik. He's known to be protective of Guardians, Cadets especially so. He's not singling you out."

"Sure felt like he was. He didn't exactly call on anyone else to demonstrate with him." I shuffled my hooded overtop in my hands, unwilling to drag it on over my shoulders with the ache in them, especially since I fully intended on showering one I got back to the flat.

"I wonder if all sponsors are that invested," Valencia mused. "I never had one, I just petitioned Commander Whitclé."

I tied the hooded overtop around my waist, glad to have my hands free again.

"I don't think I'd have had the resilience to repeatedly petition like you did."

"You know about that?"

"Yeah. Kitty mentioned it. How did you

manage it? I'd have just taken the no and looked for something else to do. I don't know what, though. People skilled in Kinesis Magic aren't exactly in high demand outside of construction and I do not have the spatial awareness for construction work. I'd have gone back home and never even met Kitty."

Why had I been so resilient? What was it that had kept me going back to Whitclé's office over and over again? "Spell-singers have three options for employment using their magic: military and Guardianship, entertainment, or child care."

"Fair point. I know you don't like attention and I cannot picture you with a kid."

I snorted at the very idea. "You couldn't convince me near one."

Valencia grinned. "I guess that gives you good reason not to take no for an answer." He stared into the middle distance and heaved a sigh. "I can't imagine it though. How you kept going in the face of such adversity."

I tuned him out, not wanting to hear him reminding me of my stubbornness and how I shouldn't be where I am. He didn't stop talking all the way back to the flat, through the living room, and right up until I closed the bathroom door gently in his face.

The sting of hot water spraying on my shoulder made the little voice in the back of my mind whisper about going to a Healer. It sounded like Kalik. I pulled some healing ointment out of the cupboard under the sink instead. It didn't exactly smell pleasant, but if I slathered enough on I'd probably be all fixed up by tomorrow morning.

Once again, Kalik disappeared quickly when Cadet Training ended, dashing out of the Gym with barely enough time to put his shoes back on. The other Cadets started off to their own late morning activities and Valencia and I took up our semi-regular position toward the edge of the sparring floor furthest from the door.

Valencia's normally wavy hair was plastered to his forehead with sweat. We took the time to stretch, the pull pleasant on the residual ache in my shoulder.

Valencia's guard had improved to the point I was willing to introduce him to the de-escalation stance. It had quickly become a favourite for him, with him proudly declaring "we're protectors, not aggressors," almost every time he stepped into it.

We started to block out one of Kalik's immobilising holds, testing the movement required without the time pressure of the Cadet Training Session.

The clearing of a throat stopped us. We turned to face Cadet Al Jenkins, who was pulling on the ends of his overtop sleeves. "Are you two practising immobilising holds?"

"Yeah," Valencia answered.

"Would you mind if I joined you?"

"Of course not."

Al glanced at me as if to check whether I agreed. I shrugged. Al seemed nice enough, it wouldn't matter if he joined us this once.

After we'd blocked out the movement in all pairing variants we could think of, we started trying to incorporate it into short sparring sessions. Having an extra person allowed us to take short rests and let us each watch for both mistakes and clarity of movement.

When we were done, Al thanked us. "I ended up partnered with Cadet Manth when we were learning and... well I wouldn't say anything negative about a fellow Guardian Cadet but I didn't learn much that day."

"You can come join our sessions whenever," Valencia invited.

"You do this regularly?"

"At least twice a week," I supplied. "Every Deuday and Septday."

Jenkins smiled for the first time since I'd met him. "Thanks. I just might take you up on that."

I waited on the street corner for Kalik, shifting from foot to foot as the cold of pre-dawn seeped into my bones. The bell in the clock tower chimed the hour.

Kalik was late.

Had something happened to him? Had he just overslept? Was it because I hadn't gone to the Healers? Was it because I'd confronted him?

The distinctive silhouette of a Guardian jacket pulled my attention. My lips twitched into a cautious smile until I noticed that the figure was too short to be Kalik.

A Goblin Guardian Lieutenant stepped into the blue glow of the streetlight I stood under, his skin tinted almost green. He smiled blandly.

"Colonel Kalik sends his apologies, he's indisposed right now." His voice was deep and rich and not at all what I wanted to hear.

He had no reason to lie, though, right? There was no purpose to fabricating a reason Kalik couldn't make it. But then, why not just cancel? Why send somebody else to take his place?

"My patrol route is through the residential neighbourhoods on the East side of town," the

Lieutenant said, starting off in that direction.

East. Tension prickled in my shoulders. The likelihood that his route would pass the Elven Embassy was slim but paranoia clung to me as I trailed after the Lieutenant.

Three hours later, he waved his goodbyes as we separated at the gates to the Five Towers and I headed back to my flat.

Would he report back to Kalik? Did it matter? Was the cool disconnect I had with the Goblin what everyone else had with their patrol partners, rather than the casual banter Kalik and I shared?

"Hi," Kitty greeted from the kitchen as I untied my boots.

I waved vaguely in his direction.

"Everything okay?"

"Yeah." My hand stung with pain. I rubbed at it. Had I caught it on something or was it just stinging from the temperature change? The amulet under my skin drew my attention and I frowned down at it.

"You sure?" Kitty asked when I didn't move from the chair, halfway out of my shoes.

CHAPTER NINETEEN

Valencia chased after me as I hurried out of the Guardian Gym, face still burning hot with the anger and shame. Wasn't this just the perfect way to start a week!

"Hey, Arlan, wait up!"

Sweat stuck his hair to his forehead in the same way it stuck my shirt to my back.

I didn't want to wait. I didn't want to spend time talking over what had happened. Valencia liked to debate the different options available to people at any given moment. He liked to think about what he would have done differently or what he would have liked to do. Normally I could enjoy it, even if it sometimes made me want to snap at him about just taking the initiative and doing something.

But today PT had chewed me out for not partnering up well. "Guardians work in pairs at a minimum. Being a good fighter is no use to you if you can't work with your fellow Guardians."

I had stood there, biting my cheek to keep from reacting, fingernails cutting into my fisted hands, eyes burning with the need to cry. I had no voice. I was powerless in the face of PT's red-cheeked rage.

When we had been dismissed, one long hour after that, I had scurried for the exit, desperate to avoid the whispered gossip of the other Cadets. Their eyes burned into me as I yanked my shoes and overtop out of the cubby, not bothering to put either on before I headed outside.

Valencia caught up to me easily as I yanked my boots on to my ice-cold feet. It really was too far into winter to wander around barefoot, even if it felt like a reasonable reaction. I tucked the laces into the boots without bothering to tie them.

"That was quite the talk from PT." Valencia's voice was cheerful and it just made the burning in my eyes worse. "You holding up okay?"

"I'm an adult," I said, hoping Valencia wouldn't see it as the evasion it was.

"Don't feel like one when PT chews you out thought, right? Most of us Cadets have been there."

"Sure."

"No, really. I mean, I've seen everyone who joined after me on the receiving end of one—"

"Valencia, you really don't need to give me some speech about it. I'm an adult. It's not like I've never been criticised before. I'll take what he said on board. Can we stop talking about it now?"

"Okay, sure." He fell behind me as I stomped back to the flat.

I was a colossal jerk.

Kalik picked me up at the end of my street for our next patrol on Troiday evening as the sun was setting, casting a harsh orange glow over the buildings that didn't mingle well with the street lights.

He led me through the entertainment district, checking in with people loitering around street corners and chatting with the bouncers stationed outdoors, their breaths frosting in the frigid night air. Music floated out of Jhoto's as we passed by. I hesitated by the window but it wasn't Lior's magic.

By the time we got back to the Five Towers and finished writing up the paperwork — which mostly consisted of me watching Kalik scrawl illegible nonsense on forms — the records office was empty and dark.

We exited the wall-building between Tower Two and Three, facing the dark green in the centre of the campus. The trees shifted in the night-time breeze, silver moonlight glinting off the branches.

"You're all antsy," Kalik said as I turned toward the exit of the Five Towers campus.

"Sorry."

"This isn't an apology talk, Merry, I'm just concerned. What's up?"

I chewed on my lip. Did I tell him everything? Tell him that PT had chewed me out on Unday and in return I'd snapped at Valencia without reason. Tell him Gergorio and Kitty had been avoiding me since, scurrying out of the communal areas of the flat as I stomped about. Tell him that my stupid wounded pride and hurt feelings had got me kicked in the leg when the Holding Song I was working on with Sorenson had broken and her meant-to-be-thwarted foot had collided with my shin. Tell him that his absence last Huiday had worried me so much I hadn't been able to get it out of my head. "Rough couple of days," I said finally.

"Anything I can do?"

"Do you think I can work as a team?"

"Depends on who you're partnered with, why?"

"Something PT said."

"Want to talk about it?"

"I'd rather hit something."

"I'd have thought you'd get enough hitting things practice with your Cadet training but," he smiled, "sure, let's go."

The Guardian Gym was closed when we tried the door. It shouldn't have been surprising, it was fast approaching midnight. A sigh escaped me. Maybe it would be better to go home and get some sleep. I had Cadet Training in the morning and, as proven by almost getting my nose broken in my first week, being tired for those was a bad idea. But Kalik pulled a key from his pocked and brandished it at me. "Perks of being a Colonel."

I had never seen the Gym empty before. It was larger than I expected, which made sense seeing as it regularly fit a whole host of Guardian Cadets in it. With no lights on, the equipment created odd and monstrous shapes in the inky darkness. The dim light through the high windows cast enough glow that the sparring floor in the centre of the room was clearly visible.

Kalik and I fell into the swing of sparring easily, even though we hadn't done it since before starting the search for the amulet.

"What did PT say exactly?" Kalik asked as we

started another round, having taken a brief break to stretch our warmed muscles in the cold space.

"That I don't play well with others."

Kalik caught my arm, forcing it behind my back. "I'll let you go if you say it in a PT voice."

I tested Kalik's hold on me. Solid. Could be breakable but not without considerable pain for both of us.

"Being a good fighter is no use if you can't work with your fellow Guardians," I imitated. The words had been swimming around in my head since they had been spoken.

Kalik let me go. "Ah," he said. "PT's famous Talking To."

"What?"

"Anyone who might make it big in the Guardians gets one."

I stared at him as I stretched out the shoulder I had compressed.

"I got one too." He folded his arms, rolled his shoulders back and started imitating PT, "Cadet Kalik, you will never get anywhere in life if you don't start taking some pride in your appearance. How do you expect people to take you seriously with week old stubble pretending to be a beard?"

The attempt fell short but I couldn't help but laugh. "In his own domain, Kalik. You're making fun of the man in his own Gym."

Kalik launched himself at me as if to take me out at the waist.

I dodged.

"Not much he can do to me. I'm a Colonel. I'd watch out for yourself if I were you."

"And here I was trying to work with you as a team," I joked, flipping Kalik onto the mat.

"Considering what little I know of your history it's no wonder that you're inexperienced as a team player."

"I don't think PT is looking for reasons, just results." I looked down at him. "Are you planning on getting back up?"

"You should join me down here." He held up a hand.

"You want me to lie down on the sparring mats with you?"

"It's comfy."

"You're so weird," I laughed sitting next to him.

"No no no. You need to lie down."

"Why?"

"Because your teammate is asking."

I took a deep breath, playing with the cuffs of my trousers. "Lying down is too vulnerable."

"You don't have to if you're not comfortable with it."

"That's okay?"

"The most important thing about working on a team is that it's supposed to be give and take. Your team should be working with you as much as you're working with them. I asked you to join me; you went as far as you were comfortable and informed me of your discomfort. As your teammate, I take that, accept it, and accommodate."

I hummed.

"Giving is hard though," Kalik sighed. "It's why I hate working with other people."

"You hate working with other people?" I leaned back on my elbows.

With the Guardian Gym being at the base of Tower One, I had thought the ceiling would be the floor of the upstairs rooms, instead the tower reached up uninterrupted to its glass ceiling. If the quiet hum resonating from it was anything to go by, that glass was enchanted. Usually the Gym was too loud to hear the melody of it.

"Other people are the worst," Kalik said. As he espoused the issues of working with other people, I let myself lean further and further back until I was finally lying flat on the sparring floor. Kalik was right, it was comfortable.

The clouds shifted away from the moon, revealing its full silver face to me. The huge Midwinter moon, or, according to Goblin legends, the Moon Prince's Anniversary.

"Sometimes," Kalik said, voice quiet in the relative silence of the Gym, only the humming enchantment to work around — not that Kalik could hear that, I reminded myself. "At night, I like to look up like this. The moon seems so much smaller. It makes everything else seem smaller too, more manageable." He sighed again. "Not that I get much of a chance to stare up at the moon these days."

"I never really thought about it," I admitted. Moon stories belonged to Goblins and, while my great-aunt had told them to me and while I'd apparently held on to the knowledge, Tellyn Smeeten didn't appreciate my attempts to celebrate. After a while, I'd stopped trying.

"I expected nothing less from someone as focused as you."

"I think part of it is from spending so much of my childhood and adolescence with nothing to occupy my time. All the opportunities I have now, all the options, I just want to grab at them, do them as fast as possible, and grab at the next thing." I reached up toward the moon; from here it fit in my hand. "Even Lior has done more than me, and xe doesn't even have a goal in life."

"Done more than you?"

"School summer camp, holidays across the Goblin peninsula. Xe learnt skills just to discard them. Xe spell-sings because it's something to do and it's something xe's good at." I let my hand fall back on to the mat. "I have achieved a lot in the last few months, in the last few years but..."

"You feel like you started so far behind everyone else that you'll forever be playing catch up?"

"Exactly." I turned my head to look at Kalik. His dark skin shone with silver in the light, shadows casting his features into obscurity.

"I felt like that for a while," he murmured. "I think it's a pretty common experience actually... I was only a teenager when we joined the Guardians. Jonathan — Commander Whitclé, he was the one who implemented the age limit but I wasn't eighteen when I joined. I missed out on a lot of teenage experiences because of it."

"Do you regret it?"

"Not at all. Sometimes I wonder how it might have gone if things had been different, but my experiences led me to who and where I am today. How could I regret that?"

I thought on that, turning my face to the moon once again. Maybe he was right. If I hadn't run from Smeeten I wouldn't have ended up on Shima, which would mean no Lior, no spell-singing, no Arlan Tiernan. "What do you do about the things you do regret?" I whispered.

"I suppose that depends on what it is. If I can do something to fix it, I do that. Apologise, correct my behaviour, give an explanation and hope the other parties accept that sometimes there's a reason you did something and you can't always change it or promise to behave differently in the future. I'm a Guardian first and everything else comes after, which means sometimes I behave in a way that emotionally hurts the people I care about, but I made the choice to be a Guardian first and if they can't accept that, there's nothing I can do about it. And, if I can't do anything to fix my regret, I try to let it go. It's not always about finding positives; sometimes it's about accepting that things happened one way and trying to move on."

We lay in silence for a long time.

"Do you know the Goblin tale of the Moon Prince?" I asked.

"I don't think so."

"Once upon a time, a young Goblin boy was captured by Elves — this was during one of the wars, I guess. Anyway, the Goblin boy is captured and locked in an Elven cell with one barred grate between him and the outside. And every night he called upon the moon to save him."

"He called upon the moon?"

"Oh, context, Goblin mythology states that there are people living on the moon or that the moon is the source of all magic. I'm not sure, honestly. The point is, there are moon people."

Kalik chuckled.

"One day, when the moon was closest to Terya, a glowing man with skin as dark as the night and robes of sparkling starlight appeared on the other side of the grate. He held his hand out to the young Goblin but the Goblin couldn't take his hand through the grate. — I forget the next bit but basically the Moon Prince rescues the Goblin and takes him back to the moon where they get married."

"You're a terrible storyteller," Kalik laughed. "But that's nice. I wish I had a Moon Prince."

"Surely you would be somebody else's Moon Prince?"

"Maybe... but the thought of someone coming to rescue me is very appealing for a man who always has to have the solution to every problem."

"Being a Colonel is stressful, huh?"

"So stressful. And there's always the niggling concern that something will happen to the Commander, then the rest of the Council of Colonels and I will be in charge until a new one can be appointed or that one gets back to full health."

"You are aware that isn't currently a problem, yes?"

"It's always in the back of my mind."

"You don't want to be Commander, then?"

"Not even a little bit." He blew out a breath. "The amount of work, the amount of stress. At least Jonathan has Rakael to support him when things get tough."

I didn't say "for now" but it echoed inside my head. I lifted my hand to look at the amulet. From our cumulative research we had discovered most of the literature regarding the Amulet Of The Dragon Lord was about how it had gone missing and theories about retrieving it rather than how it actually worked.

"I think it reacts to dishonesty," I said.

"What?"

"The amulet. It... it vibrates when somebody near me lies."

"What about when you lie?"

"How often do you think I lie?"

"Pretty much every time you say 'fine'"

I turned to catch sight of his grin. "You're teasing me?"

"Mostly."

"I was never a good liar, and being a bad liar gets you in trouble, so I try to avoid it."

"Let's test this. Say something ridiculous."

"Like what?"

"That you want to kiss me."

I pushed up on to my elbows. "That's the first ridiculous thing that came to your mind?"

He turned to look at me. "Do you want to kiss me, Merry?"

Humming birds invaded my stomach. "You're absurd." My voice was breathier than I expected. I yanked my gaze away from Kalik's dark eyes. "After all," I continued when I had a little more control over my voice. "I go around kissing everyone so it wouldn't make you special."

"What?"

"Ow," I squeaked, gripping my hand tightly as if that would ease the pain.

CHAPTER TWENTY

"Partner up," PT bellowed his voice harsher than usual. "Now!"

We scrambled into pairs, shooting each other bewildered looks.

"Line up here," he gestured to the edge of the sparring floor.

We stood, solid floor surprisingly hard compared to the sparring mats.

"Final tests," Valencia breathed in wonder. "That's why PT's been on edge this week."

On edge? He'd been yelling at a different Cadet every day, I had just been the start of a weeklong reaming out marathon leading up to today.

"Cadet Jenkins, Cadet Edthorn, you're up. Step onto the sparring floor. No holds barred, use everything at your disposal. No maiming, no killing. Fight," PT ordered.

"We do this every half-year," Valencia hissed to me and the other newer Cadets who tended to hover around him. "Pair by pair, no hold barred sparring matches. It takes forever but PT uses it to assess each pair to see who is worthy of Graduating. It's usually just before or just after the Patrols Partnering though, not in the middle of them. But then, patrols were late this year."

Al and Edthorn sparred with one another. Al, scrappy and moving like he didn't want to be caught. Edthorn, built like a bruiser. Too many hits from Edthorn would flatten Al. But Al was too cautious, unless his aim was to tire Edthorn out he needed to make a move.

Their match ended with their exhaustion, each panting like they had been punched in the stomach too many times.

Another pair was called forward, their match beginning without preamble.

"I'm glad you're not upset with me," I whispered to Valencia.

"Huh?"

"You haven't been at the flat much this last week. I just... I wanted..." I took a deep breath. "I'm sorry I snapped at you on Unday, it was unfair and I regret it."

"Don't worry about it." But even as he said it some of the tension eased from his shoulders.

"I don't know how to stop it from happening again, which is why I haven't said anything until now."

"What are you talking about?"

"Kalik said the best thing to do about regrets was apologise and correct your behaviour."

"You didn't know that one on your own?"

"Well, no." Irritation prickled down my spine. "Sorry if we haven't all had a plethora of experience with social interaction."

"I didn't mean..."

"Valencia, Arlan, you're up," PT interrupted before either of us could say anything more.

We stepped onto the sparring floor, mats squishing under my bare feet. The buzz of the magic used in other matches mixed with Valencia's own, held close to the surface, ready to use. It prickled my skin like the beginning of a storm. The tang of salt and sweat stung my nose.

"Fight." PT's voice was sudden thunder, the boom of a book hitting the floor in a silent library.

Valencia moved. He was fast but I was prepared for that, having spent the last several weeks sparring with him.

He didn't go in for a hit immediately, instead moving around the floor, keeping his magic close to the surface.

The prospect of taking down or even just hurting a potential friend was difficult to contend with. I didn't want to beat Valencia with him being so close to Graduation, but I couldn't pull my punches just so he might graduate, anyone he had to fight post-Graduation wouldn't. Not to mention, if he did graduate I would be without my regular sparring partner.

My legs were made of stone. My feet became almost impossible to lift. I trudged around the floor, more focused on lifting each foot that I was on Valencia. The weight of his eyes glued to me heightened my anxiety, but I almost didn't notice when he bounced, coming in to grab me.

"You rat," I hissed when I realised what he was doing.

I pushed against the Kinesis Valencia was pressing on my legs. Shoving against the locking, wall-like sensation.

I stumbled out of it and straight into Valencia. He twisted me, pulling me toward an immobilising hold. I grabbed onto his shoulders and kicked him in the shin.

"Using your Kinesis is crafty," I said when I finally pinned him with one arm twisted behind his back, the other hand pressing into his shoulder.

"Can't believe you kicked me in the shin," he grunted.

"No holds barred."

"Still a dirty trick."

"Like using Kinesis isn't? Are you doing it again?" His magic raised the hairs on my arms and the back of my neck.

He broke my hold and we returned to circling each other. I tried to pull up the kind of Shield Sorenson had been teaching me. It didn't come easily.

The wash of relief from blocking Valencia's Kinesis Magic was short lived as my Shield flickered and died.

Valencia grabbed the opportunity with both hands. He moved fast as if to sweep my leg. I jumped. Straight into his oncoming attack.

"To the front, to the back, what could be your next attack?" I teased, weaving magic into my words. If Valencia was casting Kinesis on my legs, there was no reason not to use a little Disengaging Song on him.

We traded blows for what felt like hours. Valencia's fists flashed like lightning. We jerked, dodged, weaved. Moving from boxing likes hares to trying to trip one another to utilising our magics and back around.

Blood trailed down Valencia's chin from where

I had split his lip. A bruise was developing on his forehead.

My knuckles, feet, shins, and knees burned and ached from the multitude of attacks and blocks we'd traded and from fighting Valencia's Kinesis. If the stickiness on my face was anything to go by, I sported my own cuts and bruises there too.

Valencia seized my wrist. He yanked me forward and, in one quick twist, had me pinned.

I wriggled but only seemed to fold myself further into his grip. "Yield," I conceded.

CHAPTER TWENTY-ONE

I twisted my hair between my hands. How was I supposed to wear it to a formal event? Somehow my regular pair of plaits didn't seem suitable. If only I knew a Guardian with long hair who I could ask. Maybe Guardians didn't think it was important. I left it down. At least it wasn't too wild and untamed today.

"Merry," Kitty asked from the other side of my bedroom door, "are you coming with us? Or are you going to show up later? I know you don't have to be early like Gergorio."

I pulled open the door. Kitty was the smartest I had ever seen him. Being a medical and apothecary student it was rare for him to wear an unstained item of clothing. Now, however, he wore a delicate green tunic that offset the green in his hazel eyes, like whole forests full of hidden life set into his pale face. I'd never noticed Kitty's innate power before, never noticed how striking those eyes were in comparison to his hair, which had been pulled from ubiquitous scruffy ponytail into a neat half-up style clasped with decorated clips.

I turned to the living room, finding Gergorio standing in the centre. He was dressed in the same manner as me. A white button up shirt with the Guardian crest over the heart, paired with black trousers. It was still easy to move in but much more fitted than the day-to-day Uniform. It suited Gergorio, emphasising his defined musculature, making him seem tall and imposing and contrasting well with his golden brown skin.

It wasn't quite so neat on me, hugging my hips in ways it wasn't meant to and hanging off my shoulders in order to fit my chest.

All the way to the ballroom, Valencia couldn't keep the grin from his face. Every now and again he would try to sober his expression but the beam would break out like the moon on a cloudy night.

Kitty wasn't much better, playing with the base of his tunic, smoothing it out, looking at Valencia with such love and indulgence that I had to look away.

The ballroom was toasty compared to the chilled evening air outside. It was the first time I had been through the doors at the base of Tower Five — access to the library was through the straight wall-building next to it and up the stairs. Tapestries coated the ballroom walls depicting kingdoms, legends, historical events, and things I couldn't name. Elaborate light fixtures with a mix of candles and magical lights coated the ceiling. Even the floor was decorated.

A small stage had been erected to the south of the room, opposite the huge oak doors we entered through. Whitclé was directing a group of Guardians in some kind of task.

Valencia gave Kitty a quick, chaste kiss and headed over to the Commander. I made my way over to an elegantly gowned Rakael Valencia where she lingered in an alcove. She stood from leaning as I approached. Being near her made my hand ache. Was her appearance more golden than it had been before or was it the light shining off her shimmering ball gown?

"I remember when Gergorio was born," she said. "I was fourteen and very unimpressed by him. It didn't take me long to change my mind. That boy has a way of charming even the most stubborn — then again you would know that, wouldn't you, Cadet Arlan?"

"Merry is fine."

"I think this is a night to be called a Guardian, Cadet Arlan."

I smiled, watching the Graduating Cadets milling about near the stage as Whitclé talked to them, pointing this way and that. Valencia caught my gaze and rolled his eyes.

"Most Guardians put their hair in a bun for the Graduation Balls," Rakael said.

"You've been to them before?"

"I come with Jonathan every time." The soft smile she wore when talking about Commander Whitclé suited her.

"I don't know how to do that," I admitted.

"Let me."

I turned to let her at my hair, not even having to bend thanks to her height. "It needs to cover my ears."

"How come?" she asked, calloused hands already in my hair. She paused when she exposed the forward pointed tip of one ear. "Oh. I see."

The ceremony was short. I had expected more pomp and circumstance and exceedingly long speeches about what it meant to be a Guardian. Instead Commander Whitclé spoke for no more than ten minutes about the values these new Graduates presented, impressing the importance of keeping them strong throughout their Guardian careers.

PT and Commander Whitclé completed a kind of trading off ceremony with the Graduates, handing them their Graduate accolade buttons. The head of the University spoke a little about the value of continuing education, extending the offer of repeated free education to all Guardians, where non-Guardians had to pay for a second degree.

I had assumed that the ceremony's completion would end the event but instead music began and people started to dance. I slunk to the edge of the room when Gergorio asked Kitty to dance.

"Couldn't tempt you onto the dance floor for anything less than fully-fledged Guardianship, I bet," Kalik whispered from behind me.

I laughed and turned to face him. The Formal Uniform suited him, the crisp white shirt contrasting beautifully with his dark skin, silver accolade buttons glistening in the light.

My eyes landed on the hand on his arm. "You brought someone," I stated, looking between his face and hers. She looked gentle, ladylike; everything my uncle wanted me to be.

"All the higher officers are expected to bring a

date to these things."

"A date?" I sputtered.

"Merry, what's wrong?" Kalik detached from his lady to brush gentle fingers against my shoulders.

The noises of the ballroom were fading, like my head was submerged in water. All I could see was the ice blue of Kalik's date's dress. The ice blue of Tellyn Smeeten's eyes.

Soft fingers on my face made me flinch for the slap that was coming. Pay attention, Meredith! You can't space out all the time. You're useless. It's really no wonder nobody wants you.

By the time I came back to myself, we weren't in the ballroom anymore. Kalik smiled at me crookedly. "There you are," his voice was soft. "I got a little worried."

"What...?" I started, trailing off when I realised I didn't know what to ask.

"You got all distant so I brought you out here."

"Why?"

"I was hardly about to abandon you in the ballroom when you weren't okay."

"What about your date?" My voice cracked a little on the last word. I leaned my head back on the wall; it was cool against the ache taking root there.

"She won't mind."

"You seem fairly certain of that."

"I know her fairly well."

I rubbed my face. "Of course you do. Come on, Merry, you know how dating works."

"Oh yeah?" Kalik asked, leaning against the wall with me

"Abstractly."

"You've never been on a date?"

"You've met my uncle, how do you think he would have taken the idea of me dating?"

"You're an adult now. You still haven't tried it?"

I shrugged. "I guess I'd have to trust a person first and I've never been good at trusting people."

"I had noticed that," Kalik admitted.

I finally turned to look at him. He was staring at the opposite wall. The torchlight played with the brown of his eyes, turning them red and gold.

"You and Lior never?"

"Never. Lior flirts, sure, but xe doesn't date. Aromantic, you know?"

Kalik nodded.

"If you're trying to think of someone else I spend time with, that's it. There's you now, but you already have a date." After I said it I knew it was the wrong thing to say. What had I even meant by that? I didn't want to date Kalik, did I?

Kalik blinked at me, licked his lips and finally said, "I doubt Jonathan would have taken it well if I had brought a Cadet as my date. I can see his face now. 'A Cadet! Do you know what this looks like!'" He laughed.

In the following silence, music drifted to us from the ballroom. Cheerful and bright. Nothing like the kinds of music performed at Jhoto's. Nothing like what Sorenson taught me.

"I should go home," I said finally.

"I'll walk you."

"I can take care of myself."

"Anybody who has met you knows you can take care of yourself, Merry. But you're still feeling the after effects of... of what happened in there."

I pushed myself off the wall, too tired to argue,

and realising I had no idea where we actually were. The idea of following the music back through the ballroom was less than appealing.

"I know the back way out," Kalik offered.

"Won't your date miss you?"

"She can manage a little while longer."

The night air was cool on my skin and soothing to my headache. "Do you really believe I can be a Guardian?" I asked quietly, almost hoping Kalik couldn't hear me.

"Do you think I shouldn't?" he asked. An evasion.

"I don't know. I want to protect people. I don't want anyone to end up where I was before... But... with everything that's happened, the whole thing with the Elven Embassy and the artefact in my hand and I can't even look at a certain kind of blue or contemplate wearing dresses without—" my breath hitched and I stopped walking to gather my composure.

"Ultimately, it's your own self-belief that will pull you through the Cadet Programme. That or stubbornness."

I laughed weakly.

"I'm serious. You've been through some shit, Merry, but who got you out of it?"

Smeeten had been away for business, as he so often was. He'd taken most of his estate guards, leaving me, Nathaniel, and maybe a dozen other employees.

As I had expected, and dreaded, Nathaniel came for me in my rooms. There had been nowhere to run, but still I had tried, shoving myself behind the vanity table. The mirror fell. Smashed. The noise of it drew both of our attentions.

I'd grabbed a shard. Even now, the thin lines of

scars decorated my palms.

I'd lashed out with it. And I had run. It was easy enough to get past the few border guards lingering on the edge of the estate.

"Me, I guess," I answered.

"And who got you into the Guardians?"

"You."

"No, I didn't. You petitioned and petitioned. I just sped up the process."

We had made it to my door.

Kalik reached out to touch my face, his fingers soft and warm. "You can do anything you set your mind to, you just have to believe in yourself."

"That's easy for you to say." I couldn't tear my eyes from Kalik's.

He smiled softly. "Maybe so. I think you can make it as a Guardian. I think you can get through the Cadet Programme, no matter what it throws at you. And I think you're going to make a better Guardian than half the current lot. You bring a new perspective, and Shima knows how much the Guardians need to be shaken up. You said it yourself, it's a thousand years old, it needs an update."

His fingers twitched toward the back of my neck. The moon had waned only slightly from earlier in the week, too close to Terya to shift as quickly as it normally did. It shone through the window in the hallway, lighting Kalik's face, glinting off the accolade buttons on his shirt. His eyes were dark.

I couldn't say when we had moved closer together but now his breath ghosted my face, as warm and gentle as the rest of him.

The air in my lungs was suddenly too light. I could float away at any second. Only the touch of Kalik's warm hand where it had woven its way into my hair kept me from ending up in the Moon Prince's Realm.

Finally his hand fell away. "I should let you get some sleep."

CHAPTER TWENTY-TWO

Jen opened the supply door at the back of Jhoto's club. It was early morning, the sun only recently having crested the horizon and Jen should have been home hours ago. "Is Lior here?" I asked.

"Haven't seen xem." Jen shrugged. "Try upstairs?"

I headed up the back stairs.

Lior's bedroom was empty. The door left ajar, the bed covers messy, and the blinds clicking against the glass of the open window. There was no way Lior would leave it like this. Xe was meticulously neat.

Jhoto emerged from her personal office. "Merry," she froze, glancing between me and the empty room.

"Have you seen Lior?" I asked.

A pause. "No."

I frowned. "Any idea where I can find xem?"

Again the pause. "No."

"Jhoto, what's going on?"

"Liorellion is missing."

"How long?"

"Three days."

"Why haven't you gone to the Guardians?"

"Even if they would help me — which I doubt, between my previous relationship with Rakael and my status within Goblin society — I can't be seen to choose their aid over the aid of the Goblin Peacekeepers."

"You're putting politics above the safety of your child?"

"It's not as simple as all that, Merry."

"How is it not that simple?" I snapped. "Lior has gone missing on Shima! How is that not a Guardian matter?"

"In all likelihood the person who took Lior is a Goblin purist."

I flinched away from the word. Purists came from all walks of life, the people who thought their race was better than all others. If they had taken Lior, it would be because xe was a Half-Elf. "So what if that's true?"

"In order to pull something like this off, they have to be skilled or connected, meaning it's someone with high status. Even if the Guardians could find out who it was, they wouldn't be able to touch them."

"They can hand evidence to the Goblin Embassy, or whatever relevant Embassy."

"Just leave it alone, Merry. It's none of your business."

"I can't. Jhoto, I can't just leave it. Lior is my best friend."

"Why would you care? You abandoned our

family for the Guardians."

"What?"

"Oh, come on, Merry! You go off to help Raka and then don't turn up to work for weeks, and, as if all that weren't bad enough, then you quit. Next thing I know Lior's devastated because you've abandoned xem. This is none of your business."

"You told me to go with Rakael!"

"Your mind was obviously made up before that."

"Is this all some twisted jealousy that Rakael left you for Commander Whitclé?"

Her expression turned to stone. "You go to *him* and you could be putting Lior in more danger."

"It's better than doing nothing!"

On my way up the stairs to Commander Whitclé's office I shoved bodily into Kalik. My heart tried to leap up my throat and out of my mouth at the sight of him.

"Whoa, Merry, what's wrong?" he asked, holding me by my shoulders.

"Do you come to everyone's rescue or am I just special?" I asked in a rush, my eyes fixed on his knees rather than his face. What was wrong with me? Why couldn't I look at Kalik? I so desperately wanted to talk this whole thing over with Lior, for xem to make a ridiculous comment that sent us both into fits of laughter. "Don't answer that. Listen. Lior has gone missing. Xe has been gone for three days but I only just found out. Jhoto's worried a Guardian investigation will cause more trouble than it's worth but..."

"Okay," Kalik took a moment to process. "First

things first, we file a missing person's report. Come on."

"Well done to those of you who showed up even though today is the first day of Winter Holiday for the University," PT said to the sparse numbers of us who gathered on the sparring mats.

The midwinter cold had seeped into the Guardian Gym; making most of us shift from foot to foot. I saw no sign of Al and a wave of loneliness washed through me at the realisation that Valencia wouldn't be attending Cadet Training anymore. I'd known it, but experiencing his absence hit a little harder.

"For the next two weeks," PT continued, "you all get the pleasure of working with weapons. It's almost unheard of for Guardians to use weapons these days, but with low numbers, between the recent Graduation and the Winter Holiday, weapons training is a non-essential training that makes good use of your time."

He pulled a wooden sword from a barrel set in the centre of the sparring floor. We watched as he demonstrated a proper stance as well as how to advance and retreat. That done, he called us up to each grab our own sword and try out the stances.

As I reached for the barrel somebody shoved me away with a hiss of "Colonel's bitch."

I stumbled to one side, searching for who had pushed.

Manth shot me a wide smile. His fangs weren't extended this time.

I shook my head and waited for him to move away before I grabbed my own sword.

The lack of lessons with Sorenson made fitting in patrols a lot easier. The sun stared down at me, glinting off the icy ground and blinding me to the clock face at the top of Tower Five.

It felt like I had been waiting in the freezing cold air forever. I half hoped Kalik wouldn't show. The phantom feeling of his hand in my hair kept springing to mind. I rubbed at the back of my neck to dispel it.

What was I supposed to do with these stupid new feelings? Kalik had already told me it was inappropriate for a Colonel and a Cadet to... And even if it wasn't inappropriate there was no guarantee he felt anything for me. And why would he? I wasn't exactly Ms Dateable-Attractive-Woman.

"Merry," Kalik called.

I jogged over to him and we walked out of the Five Towers campus together.

"Is something up?" he asked. "I mean beyond the 'my best friend is missing and I feel a little helpless about it because I just have to trust other people to look' thing."

"Why would you ask?"

"You won't look me in the eye."

"I..." I trailed off. I couldn't lie, and I didn't want to risk saying something adjacent to a lie. But I couldn't tell Kalik that I didn't have the social training to figure out what I felt about him after the night of the Guardian Graduation Ball. And that without Lior, I was completely unable to function as an adult being from an emotional standpoint.

"It's a lot of change," I said finally. "Valencia is a Graduate now, and it's already Midwinter, and I'm kinda worried about Rakael Valencia too because I'd never really considered her as a person before but then you said about how Commander Whitclé leans on her, so without her the Guardian leader is less stable."

"I said that?"

"You said that he leans on her, I filled in the rest."

"You want some distractions?"

I shrugged. "Sure, I guess."

"When I was a Cadet and set to patrols, I ended up with a really angry Lieutenant. He didn't like my attitude."

"Why?"

"I was a very lazy Cadet. I know it's hard to believe now, but I think I've told you before, I only joined the Guardians because my brother wanted to and I had nowhere else to go."

"I don't know if it's fair to call you lazy for that?"

"Apathetic then. Or struggling maybe. I don't know. The Lieutenant wanted me to be in clean pressed Uniform every day, he wanted me to always be on time, and he wanted me to be attentive to the needs of the Guardians who he saw as a military organisation. I failed on all counts. My Uniform was always creased, I stopped for every stray cat and crying child whether I was on patrols or not."

"That definitely doesn't sound like laziness, apathy, or you struggling. That sounds like someone who cares too much."

He hummed. "You're not like that."

"Excuse me?" My gaze jerked to his face, hoping he would have his cheeky grin to show he was attempting to tease me. Instead I found him thoughtful, staring into the middle distance.

"Nobody could call you apathetic. You started out with the mentality that people need to be protected. It's how all Guardians should think." He turned to me. "It's a heavy burden to bear, the knowledge that everybody should be protected and saved. One day you'll find yourself facing down someone you don't want to save. That will be your make or break moment."

I focused my attention on my boots where they crunched through the ice on the ground. Someone I didn't wish to save?

Before I could give it much thought we were set upon by a young woman who had lost her engagement ring.

After locating and returning the ring, and then finishing our patrol route Kalik turned to walk me home. "I fully intend to procrastinate the paperwork until tomorrow, if that's okay with you."

"I guess."

He hesitated at the end of my street. I half thought about leaving him there, pretending I hadn't noticed him stop and heading upstairs. I didn't know if I could take another charged moment with him without combusting.

"At some point you will need to learn how to dance."

My nose scrunched. "Why?"

"You'll be attending Guardian Graduation Balls twice a year for the rest of your career. Eventually somebody is going to ask you to dance. I think all Cadets should be taught, but PT doing the teaching is... less than appealing."

"Why would people ask me to dance?"

"People like to dance with the Cadets. And dates usually want to dance."

"Let's be honest, Kalik, if I bring a date it's going to be Lior and xe won't make me dance, so that's fine, right." The realisation that Lior was missing and might not be found hit me like a bat to the gut, leaving me breathless.

"You are far too captivating to expect to be left alone at the Guardian Graduation Balls."

I blinked at Kalik. Captivating? Me?

"I'm offering to teach you to dance, Merry."

"You really think it's that important?"

"Either that, or I wanted to dance with you at the Guardian Graduation Ball and I'm disappointed that I didn't get the chance."

"There's no music." Again my voice came out breathless.

Kalik stepped up close to me, taking one hand in his and guiding my other to his shoulder. His hand on my back was warm and gentle. The hold was soft, easy to break, but solid and reassuring at the same time. He looked deep into my eyes. His shoulders moved with his breathing – he obviously had never been taught to sing or to breathe effectively.

My own breath synchronised with his. The world around me got distant. The cool air was warm in Kalik's hold. The humming birds invaded my stomach again.

"Ow!" I cried, hopping my newly bruised shin up and dropping Kalik.

He laughed. "You have to move with me."

I shot him a glare.

His beam didn't deplete as he held up his hands again.

I stepped back into his embrace, my ears heating at the close proximity.

This time I moved with Kalik. It was stilted and a little awkward but his body pressed close to mine, warm and soft and reassuring. I laid my head on his shoulder, his cheek pressed against the top of my head. My heart pounded in my ears in a way I wasn't used to, no feeling of panic followed. My heartbeat was loud, slow, and even.

We moved to the metronome of my heart. I wondered if Kalik could hear it.

He squeezed my hand gently.

"Fuck, Merry!" Kalik gasped, jerking out of my hold. "I know I kicked you first but you don't have to take vengeance."

I laughed, still standing close. "It was an accident."

"I know." He smiled crookedly.

"Maybe I should just refuse to dance with anyone."

"Maybe," he breathed. "For someone who can move so well in a fight you really don't have any innate dancing talent."

"If High-Borns do it, I probably can't," I joked.

"Why is that?"

I froze at the unexpected question. "I... uh, I've always been like this. It caused my uncle no end of shame and despair."

"Maybe I should teach you to lead," he offered.

PT split us into two lines with our wooden practice swords. The aim of the session was for us to step up and attack while our partner stepped back to block, then swap until PT called for us to find new s'partners. It had been going well. With my experience working on a pirate ship, it was easy enough to get into the swing of repetitive motion.

Step up, attack, step back, block. Step up, attack, step back, block. The clack of wood on wood bounced around the room, undercut by the whisper of feet moving on the sparring mats.

PT called for us to swap s'partners. I waited for the line to finish moving. Looking at my new partner, I gulped. Manth grinned at me, his fangs extending slowly as I watched.

I tightened my hold on the wooden sword. Step up, attack. Manth blocked perfectly but instead of waiting for me to step back he countered. His wooden sword thwacked into my arm.

My hand spasmed, sword clattering to the mats at my feet.

Manth stepped forward and swung his sword in an arc toward my head. I jerked back. Manth kept coming for me, his sword flashing left and right, up and down.

I dodged as best I could, desperate to avoid Manth's sword. One heartbeat of distraction as I tripped over the edge of the sparring floor and onto the stone edge of the room, and Manth's sword rammed into my stomach.

My breath shot out of me as I doubled over. Another crack as it hit across my back.

"What is going on here?" PT bellowed.

"She challenged me!" Manth protested as I scrambled back to my feet. "Like with Valencia."

The lie stung up my arm to where Manth's wooden sword had bruised me. I cradled my hand to my chest.

"Arlan?" PT asked.

I shook my head.

"Swap partners," PT demanded.

Two more partners down and the session was over. Exiting the oak doors of the Gym, I headed straight for the edge of campus, ready for a hot shower in the comfort of my flat. A hand on the back of my shirt dragged me inside the wall-building and down a corridor.

As I was shoved heavily into the stone wall, I yanked my shirt collar away from my neck.

Manth stood close to me. Too close. His fangs seemed longer in the shadows of the disused corridor. "No Valencia to hide behind now," he snarled. "Are you going to be a good girl and quit or are you going to force my hand?"

I shuddered, trying to blink away the image of Nathaniel Larrings that wanted to overlay Manth's too-close face. When he reached out to brush aside a hair that had escaped my plaits, hand trailing along my neck, my vision fizzled at the edges. My breath hitched.

"Aww," Manth's breath on my face was wet. "Does the little girl have a little crush?"

"Let me go," I hissed. My gums itched as my fangs begged to extend.

Manth leaned into my neck, his wet breath pushing me back into the wall.

I shoved at his shoulders, tripping over my feet as I dashed out into the sunlight.

CHAPTER TWENTY-THREE

I slammed the book closed and shoved away from the desk.

My room could never have been considered tidy but right now it was too tidy, too stifling, too close to what Smeeten would have wanted.

I tossed my duvet and pillows onto the floor but it didn't help.

Lior was missing. I had a stupid amulet in my hand that I was no closer to figuring out. Manth had decided I was a target for some reason. And I couldn't even begin to figure out my stupid feelings about Kalik which would not go away.

Kitty and Valencia had been murmuring to each other all morning. Loving little murmurs that made their way through the wall to me. Loving little murmurs that made me jealous of the connection they shared.

I jogged down to the Guardian Gym, not even

bothering to tie my boots since I'd have to take them off again anyway.

I found a free punching bag and attacked it with all I had. Form didn't enter my mind as I pounded into the bag until my knuckles and shins began to sting.

"Arlan," a deep clear voice called across the Gym.

I turned, breathing heavily. Commander Whitclé stood at the edge of the room, just inside the huge oak doors. He gestured for me to follow him, leading me all the way up to his office.

When he sat behind his desk, I perched in the chair opposite, shoving away potential answers to the question of what he wanted to talk to me about. I didn't want to listen to my own answers.

"I have received a request for your official statement regarding being named heir to Lord Smeeten." He cocked an eyebrow, waiting for me to say something.

My throat was painfully dry but I pushed the words out anyway. "I filled out a form with Kalik..."

Commander Whitclé sighed and rubbed his eyes. "Can you fill out another form please?"

I nodded.

He threw an envelope across the mess of a desk at me. "Bring it back tomorrow."

I waited for Kalik at the end of my street. The paperwork Commander Whitclé had given me was complex, written in human script, with paragraphs regarding the legal aspects of being claimed as an heir and being in the Guardians in whatever way, shape, or form.

Having already reached my limit for trying to understand complex language and wording with amulet research earlier in the day, I put the document aside for now. Commander Whitclé may have demanded its return by the next day, but I knew better than to sign a form without having read and understood it.

My knuckles stung as I fisted and unfisted my hands, stretching where the skin I had split on the punching bag was healing. At least the pain distracted me from my thoughts.

Finally Kalik appeared. I trailed after him, wading through the swamp of thoughts bogging me down, where Kalik skipped along like a bee flitting from flower to flower.

"What has got in to you?" I demanded.

"We've had a break in the case."

"Lior?"

"No."

My shoulders drooped.

"An expert in magical artefacts. She's agreed to come to Shima to help us."

I couldn't muster up any enthusiasm, even in the face of Kalik's palpable relief. There was no guarantee this artefact expert would be able to help us anyway.

If his stunt in the corridor earlier that week was anything to go by, Manth's insistence on partnering with me wasn't out of camaraderie. Unfortunately, his twisted investment seemed to be creating a chasm between me and the other Cadets who had remained in training over the Winter Holiday.

I tried to push away the easy comparison between Manth and Larrings. Larrings had pushed a wedge between me and the other Laymen Smeeten employed — not that it had been much of a relationship before.

Isolation, my long term companion.

"Arlan," PT called when he had dismissed us. "A moment."

Manth grinned, tapping Edthorn on the arm and gesturing back at me. My shoulders slumped in defeat. Please don't let PT be planning to chew me out for my inability to manage partnering up well again.

"Help me put away the practice swords."

I hefted the other side of the barrel to PT.

"I've noticed the way you look at Colonel Kalik."

I frowned at him as we carried the barrel over to the cupboard.

"At the ball last week."

"What do you mean?" He hadn't noticed the panic, had he? But what would that have to do with Kalik?

"You were jealous," he stated plainly, pulling open the cupboard door.

"Jealous?"

"I'll tell you now, Arlan. Inter-Guardian relationships don't work. I've been there."

"You have?"

"Garrett," he sighed. With the barrel safely stored in the cupboard he shut it, twisting the keyless lock. "He was..."

PT's whole face changed when he smiled, opening up, angles and lines softening. "He was a hero, and an idiot, and my partner and paramour for three years. Then he got himself into some trouble with human royals — this was before the revolution, of course. There was a huge fight. He lost his Guardianship and I almost died."

My head snapped up.

"It's a big part of the reason I'm not in the field

anymore. Almost got my leg torn off. Lot of physio and counselling to get me back in fighting form. Garrett..." he huffed out a sigh. "He ended up marrying some girl and having a kid. Named it after himself, because heroes get things named after them but nobody saw him as a hero anymore. Etta or something."

"Etta Amaranth?"

PT's bushy eyebrows drew together. "You know her?"

"She's the first person who taught me to fight."

PT laughed. "I wouldn't want to get into it with you and a dagger, Arlan, not if Garrett's kid taught you to fight."

I jogged over to my boots and pulled the dagger Etta had given me from the holster built into the left one. I held it out to PT.

He examined it, that soft smile stealing over his face again. "That would be Garrett's dagger. And you should not be casually carrying that around to Guardian Cadet Training." His face hardened again. "Take my advice, Arlan, don't start a relationship with a fellow Guardian."

"I wasn't planning to."

He nodded once, sharply. "Dismissed."

I sheathed the dagger in my boot once again before pulling them on and heading out into the crisp wintery air. On my way off campus, someone charged into my shoulder.

"I am going to murder that woman if she even — sorry. Merry?" Sorenson smiled at me.

"Professor Sorenson," I greeted. "I thought you wouldn't be here, it's the holidays."

"I was in the middle of a research paper that's due in spring so I thought I'd spend my lesson-free time building on the project." A scowl overtook her features. "Until that meddlesome bitch showed up."

"What meddlesome bitch?"

"Professor Simonde. I don't know why she's here but I left the Peninsula to get away from her so I very much don't appreciate her presence."

"Oh, that sucks."

"It does." Sorenson sighed. "Anyway, what about you? Not heading home for the holidays?"

I scrunched my nose. "I am home."

Sorenson put her hand over her face. "And I've just made an ass of myself. Sorry, Merry."

"It's fine." I rubbed away the pins and needles in my hand.

"Since you're here, we could touch up on your Magic Basics if you wanted."

I hesitated. It would be good to know more Magic Basics, but would I really be able to learn anything with Lior still missing? "Didn't you want a break from teaching?"

"It'll be nice to one-up Simonde; she doesn't have any students here."

I laughed. "Okay."

"Come see me in my office tomorrow after Cadet Training."

CHAPTER TWENTY-FOUR

"Charm," Sorenson said. "What is it?"

"Making people like you?"

"Encouraging people to do as you ask through making yourself more appealing to them."

"So it's just Persuasion Magic?"

"It's like small scale Persuasion, yes. Do you have any experience with Persuasion Magic?"

"Only from the receiving end." Although there was that Illusion dispelling I had managed in Smeeten's clutches, but that might have been a one off.

The format of the lesson followed the same formula as Sorenson's spell-singing lessons. She talked me through the basics of Charm: how it worked, the kind of magic you should draw on, the level of power that would make it work without making it noticeable.

"I'll demonstrate and then you try."

Sorenson's face gained a luminous soft quality, her hair turned from plain to glossy, even her eyes seemed brighter. "Merry," she began.

The rest of her words dissolved into the pain attacking my left arm. I clutched it to my chest, my eyes screwing shut.

"Merry? Merry!"

"I'm—" I hissed a breath in and out. "I'm okay. I'll be okay."

"What's going on?"

I squinted at her. When had I knelt down? "I have a magical artefact connected to me. Apparently it doesn't like Charm."

"What artefact? Is that why Simonde is here?"

"Maybe."

Sorenson settled cross-legged on the floor next to me. "You're not working with her yet, then?"

"Not yet."

"She's probably not so bad to everyone else, try not to let my own issues colour your opinion of her."

"Sure," I scoffed.

"What is that supposed to mean?"

"I've been working with you for a year and a half. You think we're not on the same wavelength?"

Sorenson smiled. It was her normal one, no softened edges, no weird glow. A rare sight. "I suppose you could easily have transferred to another teacher if you wanted to. I think it's safe to say, Charm might be out of your reach for now."

I sighed heavily.

"It's okay, not everybody gets all the Magic Basics. Charm is usually easier for spell-singers since both are about influencing other people, but just because something usually works doesn't mean it always does."

I nodded mutely.

"I'm going to let you go for the day."

I traipsed down the steps of Tower Four and back to my flat, rubbing at my hand distractedly.

Was Simonde on Shima to help me? Was she the artefact expert Kalik had mentioned? Or was she here for some other reason?

Why did Charm set the amulet on fire? Was it dishonest? Or was there some other issue? How would I manage being a Guardian if Charm Magic sent me to my knees?

Kitty greeted me with a wide smile when I sat to take off my boots.

I sent him a vague wave only for him to launch over the kitchen table and grab at my hand. His warm fingers gently examined the amulet then pulled a pot out of one of his pockets.

Kitty slathered some thick cream over my hand. It was soothing but I let out an exasperated sigh anyway.

When Kitty finally let me go, the scent of mint emanated from my hand instead of the disgusting chemical smell healing ointments normally had. "That's good stuff, where did you get it?"

"I've been experimenting with different concentrations of ingredients."

"You made it?"

"Yup. Here," he put the tub in my hands. "I get the feeling you'll need it easily accessible for a while."

"You're not asking questions?"

Kitty shrugged. "I figure we have a solid friendship, you'll come to me when you need me." He wandered back into the kitchen. "Oh, while I remember, Kalik came by earlier, asked me to send you to him."

A tired sigh escaped me but I pulled my boots back on and headed back to the Five Towers campus. He couldn't have come to get me during Cadet Training?

Kalik's office door was ajar when I arrived. I didn't need to knock before he looked up. "Merry, come with me."

I trailed after Kalik to the wall-building between Tower Four and Tower Five. He led me into one of the empty artefact lab classrooms where a Goblin woman in a white coat stood, examining some old-looking texts laid out on a lab bench.

A group of Guardians loitered in one corner, chatting amongst themselves.

"Professor Simonde," Kalik called. The woman looked up. "Let me introduce Cadet Arlan. Merry, this is Professor Simonde."

"A pleasure," Simonde greeted without looking up.

"Right. I'll leave you all to it."

"Kalik?" I called after his retreating back but he either didn't hear me or didn't want to stop.

I chewed on my lip as Simonde called me forward and held out her hand expectantly. I placed my own amulet-bearing hand into hers. She twisted it this way and that in a much more forceful manner than Kalik or Kitty had.

"It looks like this has permanently bonded to you," she mused, scribbling something down in a blank notebook next to the ancient tomes. I wondered if she ever got it wrong and accidentally wrote on priceless ancient manuscripts. "But that doesn't mean it's impossible to use. Have you been experiencing anything? The Colonel mentioned you had experienced some adverse effects when people were dishonest with you."

"Yeah," I spoke hesitantly. "Lies make it buzz, I guess? And, um, Charm Magic is... not great."

She raised one eyebrow. "Can you be more specific?"

"Pain."

She hummed and shifted to flick through the books spread over the lab bench. Goblin script filled it; both printed text and scribbled notes. I couldn't make out much of either so I turned my attention to the Guardians. Valencia shot me a little wave, I returned the greeting. He extracted himself from the group and strolled over to me. "How's things?"

I shrugged, not wanting to unpack that question. "How is Graduateship treating you?"

Valencia's smile went on for days. "It's amazing. I mean, it has its difficult bits. Some of the older Guardians especially, we disagree on some important stuff but it's everything I expected."

"Because you expected that," I finished. It was what Kitty always said when he started something new. Valencia and I laughed.

"Right," Simonde interrupted. "Miss Arlan—"

"Cadet," I corrected.

"Cadet Arlan, if you could stand here."

I moved to where she indicated.

"This may cause the amulet to react; I need to know what it does."

I nodded, clenching my jaw against the nerves bubbling in my stomach.

One of the Guardians stepped up to face me. "I'm taking my spouse out this weekend."

The amulet vibrated in my hand. "It's

buzzing," I told Simonde.

The Guardian stepped back and another took his place. "I always hated PT's sessions."

The sensation spread up my arm. "Worse," I said.

Three of the Guardians traded off telling lies and truths as Simonde wrote down my experiences. My head began to swim and ache.

"Professor," Valencia's voice cut through the haze I'd slipped into. When had that happened? "Maybe we should stop for now?"

"But I'm just beginning to get a clear picture of how the amulet reacts." Enthusiasm filled her voice.

Valencia didn't argue but the expression on his face was the one he pulled when Kitty started making potions in the kitchen instead of the student labs.

"We'll only continue for a few more," Simonde said.

My vision blurred.

Another Guardian stepped up.

My mouth was numb and fuzzy.

"Professor?" Valencia's voice again but I couldn't quite seem to make him out.

More voices. The ache in my head exploded.

"Merry!"

CHAPTER TWENTY-FIVE

Waking up outside my own bed and my own bedroom had my heart thundering in my chest, a thousand horse stampede.

Darkness surrounded me. What time was it? My head ached dully. Where was I? What had happened? The last thing I remembered was Kalik showing me into the lab and introducing me to Simonde.

I rubbed my face, stopping when I noticed the bandage on my hand. Logically the bandage had a purpose but I pulled it off anyway. A red burn-like quality surrounded the amulet, travelling a little up my wrist and up to the knuckle on my thumb.

Burns were complex to heal, magical ones even more so. A medic-mage could heal a broken bone or a stab wound in a few minutes, or hours depending on severity. Burns though, they took several sessions, and healing ointment, and time. Most medic-mages ended up focusing on containing the burn so it wouldn't spread rather than actually Healing it.

I checked my pockets for Kitty's ointment but I must have left it in the flat.

I clambered out of the bed and tried the door. A relieved breath escaped me when it opened easily. I emerged into the corridor.

The dim lights revealed that I was in the Healers tower. That made sense.

A very tired looking Kalik leaned against the opposite wall. "Running away?" he asked.

"Going home."

"You're really not supposed to leave until you have been cleared by a Healer."

"I'm fine."

"You were unconscious more than a day."

"PT's going to be mad I missed a session."

"He'll know you're here. Valencia is incredibly organised."

"What?"

"Valencia. He brought you to the Healers. According to Filicious he was very insistent that nobody else touch you but him. He sent Filicious to get me, Diamos to Jonathan, and Worthing to PT. Apparently Valencia had complete control of the situation before you even properly hit the floor — at least according to Filicious."

"I'll have to tell him you're impressed," I muttered. "Are you here to keep me from leaving?"

"No."

"Are you going to stop me?"

"No."

"Why?" I started toward one end of the corridor — I'd find an exit eventually.

Kalik followed me. "I'm here because I found out my friend was hurt, and because as a Guardian Colonel they couldn't kick me out when visiting hours were over. I'm here because I knew you would want to leave as soon as you woke up and I didn't want you falling unconscious on your way home with nobody around to catch you."

"I'm fine," I insisted.

Kalik didn't respond and, to his credit, he also didn't comment when we reached a dead end and had to turn around, passing the door to the room I'd woken up in.

"We're friends?" I asked as we started down the stairs.

"At the very least."

"But I've been avoiding you." The truth slipped out. I blamed the amulet. I blamed the tiredness. It didn't matter. "Not that I've been doing a good job."

"I thought you might have been," Kalik sighed.

"You knew?"

Kalik shrugged. "You haven't come to research the amulet with me. You haven't been pestering me every minute for updates on Lior's case — which, by the way, since you didn't ask but I know you want to, yes I am leading. And every time you're near me right now you won't look me in the face." He rubbed the back of his neck. "For what it's worth, I'm sorry for whatever I did wrong. Was it the dancing thing? Because you're really not unteachable or anything — wait that sounded bad."

"It's not the dancing. You haven't done anything wrong. It's just me..."

"I should have stayed with you. In the lab, I mean, with Professor Simonde. If I had, you probably wouldn't be hurt."

"It's not your fault."

"I got you into this whole mess. I'm the one who convinced you to help Rakael, I'm the one who convinced you to break into the Elven Embassy, I—"

"Nobody forced my hand here, Kalik." I interrupted. "I didn't have to take the bet, I didn't have to break into the Elven Embassy, I didn't have to do any of this. If you're only here to assuage your guilt, I don't think you should be here at all. If you're only calling us friends because you want to feel better about your actions, that's not really friends. I don't want to spend my time with people who have ulterior motives."

I pushed myself to walk faster, blasting through the doors and into the frigid night air. Light-headedness washed through me, making me stumble.

Kalik's hand under my arm steadied me. "I'm not here because I feel guilty. — Okay, maybe here right now helping you home is a little guilt-motivated. But I do like you, Merry, a lot actually. You're clever, and funny, and fierce. And you care, so much, about other people."

I hoped the dim moonlight wouldn't illuminate the way my cheeks and ears heated. I hid behind the curtain of my loosened hair — sleeping in my plaits, whether on purpose or apparently even in unconsciousness always pulled most of the hair out of said plaits.

I untied the ends as Kalik and I made our way out of the Five Towers campus and through the dark streets of Shima back to my flat.

Kalik accompanied me into the building and up the stairs, where we lingered outside the door.

"For what it's worth," I said softly, looking up into Kalik's face. "I don't think your presence in the research session would have changed anything. Try not to beat yourself up about it."

Kalik brushed a piece of hair behind my ear, trailing from my forehead down. He smiled when he caught sight of the forward curved point of my ear, usually carefully covered.

"Get some sleep," he breathed.

"I just don't understand why I can't do this!" I snapped, covering my face with my hands. I itched to pace Sorenson's classroom space. The buzzing of used magic pulsed on my oversensitive skin.

"Everyone has a latent magical ability," Sorenson explained, grabbing a crystal wand from her desk and waving it around the room. Each time she walked through her new pink quartz wards they infused the air with the taste of spun sugar. "In theory anyone could learn any form of magic, but each person is drawn to a particular type more than others — or not drawn to magic at all. You're drawn to spell-singing, which is a presentation of magic. Technically any magic type can be expressed through spell-singing from Elemental to Healing to – well anything really. Vocal is the natural expression of your magic. Which means every other presentation will be more difficult, at best. On top of that you have magic types: Persuasion is usually what spell-singers have an affinity with. You sing a song to Persuade someone to feel a certain way or do a certain thing."

She perched on the edge of her desk. "When you blew out my windows, you did it with a blast of Vocal Magic. No words, no delicate power balance, no specific intent. You reacted instinctively; you used your magic in the most natural way to you. Having such a strong affinity for one presentation of magic is great; it means you've learnt more spell-songs in this year and a half of lessons than most students get in the full three or four year course. On the other hand, it makes accessing other presentations of magic extremely difficult."

"That... makes a lot of sense."

"This is the kind of thing taught in every school, Merry. There's not paying attention or not accessing the memory well, but you seem like you've never heard this before."

My face went cold. How was I supposed to respond to that? I couldn't tell Sorenson that I had never gone to school. That would lead to more questions. But, with the amulet still in my hand, and still feeling the lingering burn and exhaustion from Healing I wasn't eager to play with what the amulet decided was or was not a lie. "Wait, I didn't magically *Persuade* the windows to smash."

"No, you didn't. What's fascinating about that is that I'm still not entirely sure what magic type you accessed. There are a lot of potentials: Kinesis, Wards, Elemental — just to name a few. What's your family background?"

The clock rang out. "I have to go," I blurted. "I'm supposed to be meeting Kalik."

I didn't wait for Sorenson to react before I dashed out of her classroom and back down the stairs.

"Oh Meredith," my uncle sighed. His face was filled with disappointment. "I would have thought you would find someone better than a human. At least an Elf."

"What do you mean?" my voice floated through the space but I couldn't think when I had opened my mouth.

"Your little human. The Guardian with whom you spend inordinate amounts of time." His fingers traced the same route Kalik's had when he'd tucked my hair behind my ear, except Smeeten's followed the edge of my face to my chin. "The one you keep having such lewd thoughts about."

"Guardian partners are supposed to be varied." Again my voice sounded but my chin didn't press against Smeeten's fingers with movement.

"He is not who I want for you."

"Who you want for me?"

"As a marriage prospect, Meredith. Even the Folcs child would have been a better choice."

"Marriage prospect? Who is getting married?"

"Please, Meredith, tell me you are not coupling with the man without marital intent."

"Coupling?" This time my chin did press against Smeeten's fingers but they disappeared like mist. "Wait!" I called after his fading form. "Wait, have you seen Lior?"

I jerked awake, chest heaving. A tidy desk sat in front of me, two neat piles of books stacked atop it. A comfortable-looking chair perched opposite me, empty of inhabitants.

Kalik, watching me, sat in the chair to my side.

"Are you real?" I asked, my voice a whisper.

"As far as I know," he replied, tilting his head to one side.

I took a deep breath.

"Shall we call it there for the day?" Kalik asked, flipping the book in his lap closed with a small clunk. He stood, stretching his arms above his head, shirt rising to reveal a stripe of the flesh of his stomach.

Ears heating, I looked away from him.

The words from my dream echoed, "He is not who I want for you."

I cleared my throat. "Have there been any updates in Lior's case?"

Kalik huffed out a frustrated breath. "I keep finding leads that go absolutely nowhere. I tried to hire Rakael Valencia to use her Finding Magic, but her curse is really starting to take a toll, so Jonathan said if it's not urgent we shouldn't bother her."

I nodded slowly, closing my own research book with gentle fingers.

"I'm not giving up, Merry. Try to have a little faith in me."

"It's not that," I whispered. "It's just... the longer Lior is missing the worse it's likely to be when we find xem." I was resolutely avoiding the word if.

CHAPTER TWENTY-SIX

I dragged myself up the stairs to my flat. The sword training session had been painstaking. Manth had decided, once again, that the best way to try and make me quit was to partner up with me for sparring and try to physically batter me out. I didn't know what his problem was but I sure wished he would stop making it mine.

PT had asked me to put the swords away with him again, this time before the Cadets had put them back in the barrel, meaning I'd spent countless minutes walking all over the Guardian Gym gathering and counting up discarded swords.

Kitty was pacing the living room when I opened the door. He turned at the end of the room, spotted me, and froze. His hands twisted together in front of him.

"Everything okay?" I asked cautiously as I

dropped my keys into the bowl by the door.

"I think Gergorio is missing."

"What?"

"He hasn't been to see me in days, not since Sixday last week when he came to tell me what happened to you. I know he moved into the Guardian barracks and that he wanted to spend some time there, getting to know the other Guardians and stuff, but this is excessive. So I went to check on him and none of them have seen him either." He had a smudge of something green on his forehead, presumably something he'd been mixing today. "So I went to ask Rakael and she hasn't seen him, so we filed a missing person's report but the official Guardian processes say that since we're not officially living together and we're not married, they can't tell me anything."

His chin length hair hung bedraggled around his face. He ran his hands through it, fingers catching in more of the green stuff that marred his pale face.

"Okay," I said, not sure if I was stalling for time or agreeing to help Kitty before he even asked. I closed the door behind me and moved toward the kitchen. Valencia would make tea in this situation, which would probably comfort Kitty, so I would make tea.

Lior going missing was one thing. Jhoto hadn't been wrong; there could have been a multitude of reasons for xyr disappearance. But Gergorio going missing less than two weeks later implied a pattern. Gergorio wasn't even a Lackey; he had no familial affiliations with any Elven Lords. I wasn't even sure if he'd grown up on the Elven Isles. Purity couldn't factor into that equation. Unless it was Gergorio's relationship with Kitty?

But why take Lior for xyr parents and Gergorio for his current relationship? It was a poor pattern. Goblin purist wouldn't want Elven Gergorio, but an Elven purist wouldn't want Lior who had been raised by a Goblin parent.

"Merry?" Kitty asked.

I rubbed my face. This was too much. I hadn't thought friends would ever be a part of my life and now that I had some, somebody was taking them away. My breath hitched with the threat of tears. I kept making tea.

"Merry?"

"Lior went missing on the Sixday before last."

The dining chair creaked against the floor as Kitty all but fell into it.

I placed the steaming mug of tea in front of him. "Drink your tea. I'll look into this tomorrow, okay? Find out who's running the case, tell them what I know about Gergorio, let them know there might be a link."

The door to Simonde's lab stared at me, mocking my cowardice. I'd got nowhere trying to investigate Gergorio's case; nobody could even tell me who was heading it up. I'd been working nonstop since sword training had ended, leaping from office to office in a desperate attempt to find any information.

With hands only mildly trembling, I pushed open the door.

Two lab techs stood with the animatedly talking professor. In one corner, Kalik sat, scribbling furiously, a pile of folders tucked close to his feet. With all the extra work that sponsorship, amulet investigation, Rakael's case, and Lior's case would be putting on him, it was no wonder he was using any time he had to keep up with paperwork. His hair flopped in front of his face, tight coils that must be obscuring his vision. I wanted to move it for him, but his dark hand darted up to pull it away, noticing me as he did so. He shot me a quick smile but didn't stop what he was doing.

"I would like to investigate the effects further," Simonde announced to me.

"That seems a little counter-productive."

"Excuse me?"

"Look, I get it. To you this thing—" I waved my hand with the amulet embedded in it at her "—is a fascinating artefact that wants to be studied to an absurd degree so you can write a paper about it. But this thing has an actual effect on my life and we have two main jobs here. Fix me and fix Rakael."

"Cadet Arlan, I have been seconded by order of the Goblin Monarch to research this amulet for use in aiding Miss Rakael Valencia in being freed from her cursed oath. To do that, I need your full cooperation."

"Maybe if you bothered to listen, you would find that I am giving you my full cooperation."

"I am listening to you, Cadet Arlan."

"Professor Simonde," Kalik said from his chair. "Is there any way we can go about this differently? Cadet Arlan was fairly seriously injured after the last attempt, as I'm sure you remember."

"If we had more time I would agree with you. As it is, Colonel, my options stand that I complete the task in question with haste or I do not complete it at all."

She didn't have to say that the curse would have taken its effect before we figured out how the amulet worked. We all knew it. But I would have respected her more if she had come out and said it.

Simonde gestured to one lab tech, who spoke.

The words didn't matter. From the first one, the intent was clear. Now I knew why it felt like I was being burned. My knees didn't have the energy to keep me up for even a second longer. The tang of blood in my mouth from where my newly extended fangs split my lip, it melded with the sweetness of the venom. Then both were lost to me as the world melted.

This time it didn't last so long.

My senses filled back in, on my knees in Simonde's lab. I surged, unsteadily to my feet. Flashes of light, like fireflies filled my vision as I shoved the door open and stumbled down the corridor.

When I reached the stairs I hesitated but some intrinsic part of me demanded I keep moving. Danger lay back there and I needed to be as far from it as possible.

CHAPTER TWENTY-SEVEN

I didn't expect to find a Guardian on my doorstep on a Quaday morning, but there he was. "Commander Whitclé needs to see you," he demanded.

I took enough time to pull on my Guardian hooded overtop before I followed the Guardian all the way to Whitclé's office. Whitclé called me in as soon as I knocked on his door.

He wasn't wearing his Uniform. Instead he wore a pastel blue button down shirt with tiny stars printed on it. He gestured for me to sit in one of the chairs opposite him, forearms bared where he had rolled up his sleeves.

"You walked out on a meeting with Professor Simonde."

It wasn't a question but I answered it anyway. "Yes, kinda."

His eyebrows rose. "Kinda?"

"Well, it wasn't a conscious choice. She—" I took a deep breath, trying to battle down the rising panic at the memory of the pain, and the urgent need to flee.

"Professor Simonde is an expert in magical artefacts. She knows what she's doing."

"She knows more than me about what the amulet it doing to me? She knows how it feels better than the person it's acting upon? I'll be sure to look at her burned hand next time I see her, shall I? I'll go visit her in the Healers tower when she loses consciousness because she won't stop!"

Commander Whitclé sighed. "I understand that she's putting you under a lot of pressure."

I wanted to argue but the words stuck in my throat. Pressure wasn't what I would have called it.

"I also understand that you have been taking it upon yourself to bother other Guardians in an attempt to shadow more cases. Perhaps if you weren't exhausting yourself with additional activities beyond your duties as Guardian Cadet, you wouldn't be struggling so much with these research sessions."

"I don't think you understand." The words came out barely above a whisper.

"I understand that the Guardian Cadet Programme can be challenging and I understand you are in a unique position, as the first female Cadet. But we have honed the GCP over years of careful consideration. I'm sorry you have had to take on the amulet responsibilities beyond the base curriculum, however, it does you no credit to attempt to build your knowledge outside the Programme."

"No—"

He held up a hand. "We are working on a time limit with regard to Rakael — Miss Valencia. Your primary focus needs to be that, especially during this holiday period when Cadet Training is optional."

"My primary focus?" The words were bitter.

"Perhaps if you were more invested this would be going a little easier for all parties."

"I am invested!" I snapped, surging to my feet. "I am doing everything in my power to complete the task assigned to me. I don't half-ass things, that's not who I am. I was already putting nine hours a week into independent research. I get that you think I'm not super-into saving your paramour or whatever, but please remember that this isn't just about her. I have a magical artefact in my hand burning me when people lie! Unless you're counting injuries to me, Simonde has made no more progress than Kalik and I did before she got here. I know this is close to your heart because it pertains to your paramour but–"

"Cadet Arlan!" Commander Whitclé was on his feet, hands fisted on the desk, muscles in his arms standing out. "That is quite enough. You are to follow orders to aid Professor Simonde in her research. Desist harassing the other Guardians regarding the missing persons cases. Stop pestering Colonel Kalik to work outside his duties; he has quite enough to do without babysitting you through Professor Simonde's work, let alone taking on random cases when his case load is already full. If you cannot follow my orders in these matters I will consider it your resignation from the Brotherhood of Guardians Cadet Training Programme."

CHAPTER TWENTY-EIGHT

It took exactly two days for me to lose my dedication to Whitclé's demands. If I was quiet he probably wouldn't notice. If I snuck down to Kalik's office after sword training, who would even tell him about it?

Kalik's office was empty when I pushed open the door. Weird. Didn't he usually lock his door when he wasn't in the office? But the desk was in order so the prickling sensation at the back of my neck was probably just paranoia.

I couldn't go to anyone who might report back to Whitclé. Who was the most outside his realm of focus? Who was most likely to be able to help me without feeling the need to alert the Commander?

PT's office door was closed but I could hear him moving around inside. I knocked hesitantly.

"Cadet Arlan," he greeted after swinging the

door open. "What can I do for you?"

"I was looking for Kalik. He... um... we don't have particularly regular patrols so I like to check in pretty regularly..." It wasn't strictly a lie but the amulet buzzed in my hand anyway. It could shut up.

PT frowned. "Commander Whitclé is the most likely to know where any on-duty Guardian is."

I sighed. "I knew you would say that."

"But if you don't want to bother the Commander, you could check his rooms."

"His rooms?"

"Colonels don't live in the barracks. They get assigned family suites or a living allowance to live outside the Five Towers."

Following PT's directions to Kalik's rooms proved easy enough. The door was locked and nobody responded when I knocked. The prickling sensation at the back of my neck intensified even as I tried to tell myself that nothing bad had happened to Kalik. He was a Guardian Colonel; he could take care of himself.

With Commander Whitclé's orders to leave well enough alone, I couldn't report Kalik missing even if I was convinced of it.

I headed back to the flat.

Kitty was clattering around in the kitchen when I sat to take off my boots. "Potions or food?" I asked.

"You've been gone ages," he greeted, wiping his hands on a towel and leaving orange stains on it. The same stains decorated his face and the thing on the cooker smelled like it might be pumpkins. Soup?

"Couldn't find Kalik for an update," I sighed. I

pulled two cups out of the cupboard and started making tea. I still didn't like it but it gave me something to do.

"Thanks for trying," Kitty said as we waited for the water to boil. The kettle blobbed with bubbles. "You don't think...?"

"I'm trying not to, but it's not adding up to a good picture." I poured the water into the cups. The fact that Kitty also thought my inability to find Kalik sounded like he needed to be added to the list of missing people was not reassuring.

"Oh. You have a letter."

"A letter? You're kidding me."

"It's in human script." Kitty danced across to the table by the door and picked up a cream coloured envelope. "Meredith Smeeten — I figured that was you."

The sound of Kitty reading my uncle's surname made me jerk, spilling tea all over my hands. I hissed in a breath and put the mugs down, shoving my hands under the cold tap. "Ah! Could you read it?"

"You're not worried about personal content?"

"Because I get all the letters," sarcasm made my voice dry. "It's probably spam. Somebody trying to convince me to spend money I don't have on things I don't want."

Kitty shrugged. "Dear Miss Arlan, if that is what you call yourself. You may have noticed the people important to you have begun to disappear."

Kitty grabbed a chair and sat before his legs gave out.

I stopped feeling the water running over my hands as my whole body turned numb.

"I am holding them," Kitty breathed. "What do I want? I presume you're asking that question if you have any sense in that pretty little head of yours. I want the amulet you stole. You will return it to me. I take it you're clever enough to figure out my leverage here. A Lackey of mine will meet you at Jhoto Folcs's club at opening hours and escort you to the transfer location."

Kitty looked up at me, green eyes filled with fear and hope.

I turned off the tap and dried my hands. How was I supposed to return an amulet that was embedded in my hand? Was the use of the word Lackey because this was an Elven Lord or just to throw me off? Why did they want to meet at Jhoto's? Was Jhoto involved?

"Merry?" Kitty asked. I realised I had been staring at nothing. "What are you going to do?"

"I don't know."

"You have to give this to the Guardians." Kitty launched into action, soup forgotten. "Maybe they can do something with it, like get someone with Finding Magic to search for the writer."

"They'd would only be able to Find you and me; we've imprinted our feelings onto it now."

"Okay, but maybe they can find a handwriting match. Or at least they'd know Gergorio was taken and hasn't run away!"

"It doesn't say who was taken," I countered. I grabbed the letter from his hands, growling at the human script, still fairly incomprehensible unless I was really focused. "And it isn't signed!" I flung the paper down on the table. "If all these people were taken because they're friends with me then..." then it was my fault Lior had gone missing. It was my fault the Guardians thought Valencia had left Kitty.

Who could want the amulet that much?

"You can't be thinking of going to that

meeting," Kitty said.

"What?"

"It's obviously a trap. You need to tell the Guardians about this so they can try and fix this without you going in clueless, or if you have to go they can back you up. Promise me you'll talk to the Guardians about this letter."

"I promise," I lied, clenching my hand around the stinging amulet. At least with the rigours of Simonde's research I was a little more resilient to its effects. "Just let me go change."

Maybe I would have gone to Whitclé, provided I wasn't climbing out of my bedroom window and heading to Jhoto's club instead.

Maybe if Kalik hadn't been missing, maybe if Whitclé and I hadn't argued, maybe if things had gone to plan for a change, I might have asked for Guardian backup. As it stood, they wouldn't provide it anyway.

Not to mention, even if they did, if Whitclé wanted me to sit back under Guardian protection while other people stepped in to deal with the problem I wouldn't be able to handle the guilt. That was if Whitclé even believed the letter was real and not some concoction I'd made up for attention.

I queued up with the other visitors of Jhoto's club, cold air turning our noses and ear tips flushed.

The bouncer was new and requested proof of age but eventually let me in when I railed at him about being old enough to have worked there thank you very much. The mass of people inside swayed me from side to side like a boat caught on heavy tides.

I tried to stay near the entrance but when the

crowd got too much I found myself a relatively quiet corner to hunker down in, hoping the letter-writer's Lackey would notice me.

My heart pounded in my ears over the sounds of the club, drowning out the band on the stage and the conversations of the people on the floor.

How long had that letter been sat in my flat without me noticing? Nobody I knew would ever write to me so it wasn't like I checked the little pile of post on the table by the door. What if I was too late?

I exited Jhoto's, dejected. I'd failed and I would have to climb back into my flat through my bedroom window.

I would take the letter to Whitclé and let him decide what to do with it. Hopefully he wouldn't hold it against me, or consider it me inserting myself into the missing person's cases. It wasn't like I had chosen to receive the letter, but that might not matter to Whitclé.

The shortcut home was pleasantly sheltered from the elements, which often made it a haunt for people between homes, or ruffians between jobs. The lack of people should have tipped me off but I was too busy wondering what I would do with my life after Whitclé kicked me out of the Guardian Cadet Programme. He'd never wanted me to join in the first place.

Something covered my eyes. A gruff voice whispered in my ear, "no trouble now. Unless you want your little friends hurt, you'll come quietly."

CHAPTER TWENTY-NINE

"You," I breathed when the blindfold was removed.

Greasy pale hair, pallid complexion, clothes that should have been neat but never seemed to fit.

I glanced around, unwilling to take my eyes off him for too long. A windowless stone room surrounded us, dimly lit by the blue toned light globes hovering over Larrings' shoulder. "Alone?"

Larrings was never alone – where Smeeten went, Larrings followed. He never did anything without Smeeten's say so. He didn't have an original thought in his head.

Larrings didn't answer my question. Stepping closer, he reached for my hand. "Has that idiotic Goblin Professor told you how this works yet?" he asked.

I pulled my hand away before he could grab it. I stepped back, colliding with the warm solid form of Larrings' hired goons. Their hands didn't reach up to grab me. Not yet.

"Of course she hasn't." A sneer coated his face. "She wouldn't be able to figure it out." He laughed, setting my skin prickling with tension. "I've been researching the Amulet Of The Dragon Lord for years and when I found out you were on Shima with it—"

"What?"

"I didn't tell Smeeten, of course. If he knew I was looking to remove the oath he placed upon me when I became his Lackey he would have stopped me." He stroked a hand down the side of my face. I jerked away from his touch and his sneer grew. "Oh, my little mongrel, you have always been the solution to my problem, but now..." He laughed again.

"You knew I was here?" I managed in a whisper.

"I always knew where you were," he snapped. "You take me as much for a fool as your uncle does."

I shook my head minutely. Never had I considered him a fool the way Smeeten did. Just trodden down. Crafted expertly into what Smeeten wanted. But if Smeeten had failed to make me the perfect Elven Lord, why wouldn't he have failed to make Larrings the perfect Lackey?

"I thought Smeeten would provide my route to Lordship, especially with someone like you in the picture. Unfortunately he was a little more ambitious than I had bargained for. But there was every chance he would have let me marry you and become his heir."

I stepped back again. This time solid arms closed around me. My brain raced to come up with an escape plan but there was no way out. I was trapped by the goon. I was trapped by Larrings. And this was never going to end well for me.

"The loving husband taking on the Lordship for Smeeten's reclusive niece. And then you had to go and ruin that plan!" His face darkened, scar twisting in a way that must have hurt once upon a time. "You never did take direction well."

He started to pace. Five steps one way then five the other. Metronome-like. "So, then I thought Smeeten might name me his heir, with you missing and presumed dead. But no. I was never good enough for him."

"He's a purist," I whispered.

"And I'm just supposed to let that be?" Larrings roared. "I'm just supposed to take indentured servitude to a Lord because I was born into it?"

"You could have left." But even as I said it I realised the absurdity of the statement. Without the funds to get off the Elven Isles, Larrings would never have been able to escape being treated as a Lackey. And if he'd taken the time to build up the money through Lackey work he would still have ended up stuck — skill set too specialised for other jobs, work experience list showing one Elven Lord's name. And, if that had been his plan with Smeeten, then what? Smeeten wasn't exactly known for letting things go.

"That's the aim." Larrings' hand shot out.

My arms jerked up to block his strike in a way they wouldn't have if not for weeks of Cadet training two hours a day six days a week.

He grabbed my left hand, putting pressure on it until it opened. He pressed my palm, and the amulet, against his own hand. The words he spoke were incomprehensible.

Nothing happened.

Larrings' nostrils flared. "Why isn't it working?" He snapped at the goon holding me. "What's barring it?" He turned blazing blue eyes on me. "What do you have?"

From behind me, a hand appeared, holding an amber crystal. Larrings snatched it and scanned it over me. It shone bright over my heart where the charm Arlan Tiernan had given me lay. The Ring of Concealment.

Larrings ripped my shirt down the front until he found it. He twisted his hand in the chain. His attention on the charm rather than me let me move again.

I fought against the hold of the goon as Larrings tore the chain from my neck. I kicked their shin, head-butted, stomped on their foot. My hands were free so I put them to use, grabbing and scratching and desperately trying to break their hold.

The goon's hold shifted and somebody grabbed my legs. More trapped than I had been before.

Larrings grabbed my left hand again. He pressed his palm against the Amulet Of The Dragon Lord, speaking those incomprehensible words once more.

Pain rushed up my arm, spreading across my chest, shoulder, and back. Speeding up my neck and into my head. The world sounded like I was underwater. The taste of it bitter and harsh, lemon and chili and salt.

Larrings morphed in front of me, disappearing into licking blue flames of power.

CHAPTER THIRTY

I snatched at the hand on my shoulder. Agony radiated up my arm, freezing me mid-motion. The amulet.

"Merry?"

"Kalik?" I blinked to see him in the darkness. Bruises marred his dark skin, over his eye, down his jaw, onto his neck. But the soft wash of relief that flew over his face at my response reassured me he would heal. "Where are we?"

"Underground somewhere," someone else grumbled.

I pushed myself into a sitting position to look past Kalik. Gergorio Valencia slumped against the opposite wall. "If my Elven senses are anything to go by."

He looked healthy enough. Healing bruises dotted his face and arms, his eyes were shadowed with lack of sleep, and he looked hungry. But he was alive and whole. Everything else was fixable.

Bare stone walls surrounded us; cylindrical iron bars separating our cell from the corridor beyond — not an Elven space then, Elven cells used flat bars for ease of putting wards on them. If I peered just right, a tiny glow of orange light extended from the end of the corridor; it might have been a turning but it was too dark and too far to tell.

I shivered in the cold, damp air, pulling my ripped shirt closer around me with my uninjured right hand. I ached all over, like too much training followed by a restock at Jhoto's, hefting huge barrels of alcohol.

No sign of Lior.

"Kitty's worried about you," I said eventually.

"He's okay?" Valencia shifted as if to sit up straighter but winced and sank back down into his slump.

"Last I saw him. How long have I been here?" I went to rub my face but stopped when I noticed my hand. The soft red glow coming off the amulet lit the space eerily, showing a harsh burn on the rest of my hand and travelling up my wrist in tree-root like patterns. I closed my hand into a fist and set it in my lap.

"Only a little while. They dumped you in here unconscious," Kalik said, his voice soft, his eyes glued to me.

It had been early evening when I'd given up to go home from Jhoto's. We had walked for a while, which meant it would be late evening or early night by now. "Kitty might be in bed," I mused.

Some of the tension in Valencia's shoulders dissipated.

"When they dropped you off," Kalik said, "they took your friend Lior away with them."

"Why? What for?"

"They're not exactly forthcoming," Valencia grumbled. He shifted again, hissing at the pain it caused.

"What happened to you?"

"I didn't come quietly."

"He's got a couple of cracked ribs, at least as far as I can tell," Kalik offered. "Provided he doesn't get hit again he should be fine even without a Healer."

Provided he doesn't get hit again. That would make escape somewhat more challenging. That, and the fact that the only person who had any semblance of an idea that we were here was Kitty, and that relied on Kitty realising I was gone. "Larrings does love to go for the ribs," I muttered.

"Larrings?" Valencia asked.

"The guy in charge of all of this."

Kalik's eyebrows drew together. "Isn't he—"

"Lord Smeeten's Lackey?" I interrupted. "Yup. But apparently he's gone rogue."

"You know this guy?" Valencia asked.

I chewed on my lower lip as I nodded.

"Great! How do we get out of his clutches?"

Valencia and I tried very quickly to move on from Kalik's suggestion of "escape the cell, find Lior, and go for Guardian backup." I informed him that wasn't an actual plan, and asked if he had learnt anything from the Elven Embassy escapade.

Valencia suggested we try to grab a key off the guards when they next made an appearance.

When a pair of goons did appear, with no Lior clutched between them, one crouched by the edge of the cell near where I leaned against the wall. "Hello," he greeted.

The other one pulled keys from his pocket and approached the cell door. Kalik shifted in his crouch.

"Mr Larrings asked me to tell you something," the one near me continued. "He told me to tell you that the sky was green, the clouds purple, and the—"

But the rest of his words were lost to the agony racing up my arm. I might have screamed, I wasn't sure, I couldn't hear anything. My eyes were screwed shut in pain as I clutched the amulet to my chest and writhed.

When the pain faded I found Valencia breathing shallowly, hand clutched around his ribs and face having taken on an ashen sheen visible even in the near darkness.

Kalik was gone.

CHAPTER THIRTY-ONE

"Meredith?" He stopped in his tracks.

Something was different about my uncle. He was somehow less perfect than the last time I had seen him but I couldn't quite figure out how. His hair was, as ever, perfectly clean and styled. His ice blue and silver robes were sleek and smooth, silk shoes peeking out from under them. Yet something looked unputtogether as he stared down at where I sat holding Valencia on the floor of the cell.

I pushed down the urge to scramble to my feet. Valencia needed me.

"Uncle," I said, at the same time Valencia asked, "Who's this?"

"Good answer," Valencia muttered. His voice rasped with every breath. Something was very wrong. He needed a Healer.

"What in Terya are you doing here?" Smeeten

asked.

"You really didn't have anything to do with this, did you?"

"Of course not! I could never throw you in a cell, Meredith."

"You literally did throw me in a cell only weeks ago."

"Meredith," he snapped, covering whatever it was that Valencia wheezed. "What is going on here?"

"Larrings," I started, hesitating when Smeeten's face paled. "What?"

"I've lost my magical link with him." Thoughts flickered across his face before his Courtier mask fell over him once more. He shifted over to the chain locking the cell door to the cell bars, laid over the original lock. He pressed a long fingered hand against it.

Cold filled the room, teeth-chattering cold, as if it were ready to snow at any given moment. With a blunt snap the chain clattered to the floor.

Cautiously I helped Gergorio to his feet.

Smeeten stepped up to him. "I expect you to get my niece out of here safely," he demanded.

"That's absurd," I countered. "Gergorio can barely breathe for a start."

"Excuse me?" Smeeten turned raised eyebrows on me.

"And," I continued, "Larrings has Lior and Kalik. I'm not leaving them here."

"What about your friend? As you said he can barely breathe."

"You don't get to turn it around like that. You can't demand he take care of me and then use the fact that he currently can't as a tool in your arsenal too."

Valencia tapped on my arm. "I can make it to

the surface. I'm a Gold Elf, I can sense it."

"You sure you'll be okay?"

"If I run into anyone, I'll hide."

I wanted to give him the Ring of Concealment, at least for now, but it lay somewhere discarded on the floor of the first room Larrings had brought me to.

"You need to go with him, Meredith," Smeeten demanded.

"I am not some fragile flower and I will not be treated as such. I am a Guardian Cadet; I have a duty to help these people. If you really want to keep me safe then back me up for once in my life."

The dark corridor opened into a blue-lit room filled with surprising items of comfort. A plush sofa sat against one wall, a great oak desk opposite it. Directly in front of us lay a delicate cerulean carpet coated in patterns that looked like snowflakes. It filled my head with thoughts of long winter nights spent staring out of the window.

At the end of the carpet sat an overstuffed and somewhat ratty chair upon which Nathaniel Larrings waited, cleaning his fingernails with a metal file.

Something was different about him. His eyes were brighter than I had ever seen them, his smile cleaner. He'd changed clothes. Instead of Smeeten's ice blue, he wore a crisp white shirt and a deep blue jacket. It looked soft, expensive, and shockingly flattering. For the first time since I had met him, Larrings' hair was soft, pulled into the same half up half down style that Kitty had worn to the Graduation Ball — though Larrings' hair was much longer and paler than

Kitty's.

He sat tall, in a semblance of relaxation, but the tension in his jaw hinted at hidden anxieties. Confidence exuded from him.

"I have to thank you Meredith." Even his voice seemed less slimy. "You have finally done something right. You made the Amulet Of The Dragon Lord work and now I am free from that ridiculous Smeeten Oath. How pathetic," his voice dripped disdain, "enchanting your Lackeys to do whatever you wanted, to be whatever you wanted. Now I am my own master."

"You believe I would let you go that easily?" Smeeten snapped, stepping into the room with me. "You believe yourself intelligent enough to outsmart me?"

"Intelligent enough, perhaps, to keep your own niece's location from you for four long years?"

Four years. That meant it had taken time for him to find me. I had managed to hide, at least for a little while.

Larrings threw his arms wide. "I am freed from my oath, old man. Your heir provided me that service with an amulet stolen from you, no less."

"You and I both know that Meredith could never steal anything from me. Anything she asked would be freely given."

"Everything but her freedom; that which she most craves." His hands flopped over the arms of the chair. My eyes tracked the movement to a head of pale brown hair.

"Lior!" Without thinking I darted toward xem. Smeeten's hand on my arm was little deterrent. Larrings' spell-trap woven into the carpet was a different matter.

"What did you do to xem?" I demanded,

frozen as I was in his spell. The volume of magic in the air coated my tongue.

Lior remained still, passive. Xe knelt at Larrings' side, a war prize. Blue light from the light globes set around the room glittered off the ice xe had been set in.

"The little half-breed was just my tester. Lord Smeeten is no longer syphoning my powers, I needed something to practise on."

"Lior isn't a thing! Xe is my friend!"

"Had you been a more willing ally, perhaps I would have taken that into consideration. Then again, I thought you'd be more distressed with the state of your Guardian." He gestured to the other side of his throne. Kalik knelt in a stand of ice just like Lior; only his face wasn't blank and unresponsive. Silently he watched us.

"You surely do not desire allies, or you wouldn't have worked so hard to break your oath to me," Smeeten snarled.

Larrings rose from his chair to circle each of us in turn. "Allies, old man." He hesitated in front of Smeeten. "I'm done with being your guard dog, taking your orders with wagging tail in the desperate foolish hope that you might one day feed me a treat or pat me on the head."

He shifted to circle me, rounding me over and over. "I might have allied with Meredith here since she knows what it's like to be at your beck and call." He touched his index finger gently to my face, trailing it around my jawline. "We are the same you and I."

Were we? I'd drawn the same comparison myself a time or two. Both broken down by Smeeten, arranged into what he wanted us to be, at least on the surface. But, just like me, Larrings had clawed his way out from under that control.

My hand fisted around the amulet, pain stinging up my arm, as Lior caught my attention once again. I had failed xem. Worse, I had put xem in this position. No matter what, I needed to get Lior out of this alive.

Everything else was fixable.

My ears popped and sudden lightness filled my limbs. I was free?

Kalik's eyes, fixed on me, widened. He shot a look at Lior then back at me. Telling me to go? To remain where I was pretending to be frozen? Did he have some kind of plan? Did it matter? I couldn't tell what his obscure glances meant. I was on my own. The decision rested solely in my hands.

With no finesse I yelled, "Hold!" at Larrings.

None of the Holding spell-songs Sorenson had taught me had worked, but the theory was somewhere in the back of my mind. I threw power into the word. It wouldn't last long, if it worked at all.

I ran to Lior. Xyr eyes were glassy and far off. I tilted xyr chin up. Xyr head moved easily, as if made of air.

"Lior," I whispered. "Come on, everybody else is mad at me. I need my best friend back."

Lior didn't respond. Xyr eyes remained blank.

I yanked the metal file off the arm of Larrings' chair and shoved it into the ice trapping Lior's legs.

"You Fuck!" Larrings' voice rang out in the small chamber.

I kept chipping at the ice. It was agony on my burned hand. The shards attacked my skin, tiny cuts peppering my hands and arms.

I kept chipping. Even as the solid, heavy footsteps approached. Larrings was coming and I had failed.

His hand ripped me away from Lior, throwing me against the nearest wall. Blood filled my mouth, the sting of a bitten tongue followed. I touched a hand to the back of my head and when it came away clean I pulled myself, achingly, to my feet.

Larrings could do what he wanted to me as long as I got Lior home safe.

The crackle of magic being pulled from the air sparked around me, the light globes in the room dimming. The ice in Larrings' eyes froze me in place even before he loosed his magic.

Something hit his shoulder. He stumbled forward. Another blast and he turned away, unleashing his magic at his assailant. I didn't care who it was. I didn't care why. I turned back to continue chipping at Lior's bonds, searching the floor for the dropped file and scrabbling with my fingers when I couldn't find it.

The teeth-chattering cold of Tellyn Smeeten's magic surfaced in the miasma. The distinctive white sparks of it fluttered behind my eyelids every time I blinked. It didn't make sense but I didn't have time to think about it now.

"Come on, Lior," I whispered desperately. "What am I supposed to tell your mama? 'Oh, sorry Jhoto, I'm the reason your child was kidnapped, tortured, and killed, but since I basically told the Commander of the Guardians to go fuck himself can I have my old job back anyway?' How well do you think she is going to take that? Because I think she's going to take it about as well as you would take me saying that I'd made a new best friend — which I'm telling you now, is never going to happen!"

Finally, a crack appeared in the ice block. I

pulled at it, stumbling back when it broke free. Dragging Lior from the ice, I turned to look for the best route to the exit and stopped when I registered what had been happening behind me.

Smeeten stood protectively in front of me, facing Larrings. He pulled as much magic to him as he could. The wall of ice shielded us against Larrings' constant barrage of attacks.

Smeeten's hands trembled with the effort. Staring up at him from the ground as his magic swirled around him, a flash of my childhood came to me. Smeeten standing above me, summoning snowflakes from thin air and making them dance as I laughed and clapped and cheered.

"Meredith, take your friend and go," he hissed.

I hefted Lior, half dragging, half carrying xem toward the doorway. As soon as we emerged from the ice shield, Larrings focused his attention on us.

"Do not count me out yet, Lackey," Smeeten snapped. His shield shifted into a barrage of ice chips.

As I dragged Lior to the doorway, Kalik once again caught my eye. Frozen in place he watched the battle between Larrings and Smeeten.

I shifted direction and pulled Lior behind the blue sofa, out of the line of fire but not abandoned in the corridor. I wouldn't have been able to make it all the way to the surface with xem even if I had been willing to leave Kalik behind.

I lifted xyr face, staring into blank brown eyes that dragged at my heart. "I will be back for you. I promise. I said I wouldn't abandon you and I won't. 'Til the rays of the sun turn blue from the strain."

Overturning the sofa for better protection, I peeked around it into the room again. Larrings and Smeeten seemed to be at an impasse. Larrings had the clear advantage, he'd just come back into his power, he practically radiated it. Smeeten, on the other hand, had just lost a portion of his and, if the energy emanating from Larrings was anything to go by, it was no small portion.

Larrings knew the room better than Smeeten and, if the spell-trap in the carpet was anything to go by, he had set it up for the fight.

There was no way I would be able to drag-carry Kalik out like I had Lior, but I was hoping he was only trapped by the ice and, once I'd chipped him out, he'd be able to help me get Lior out of here.

I scooted around the sofa, clinging to the wall in the hope I would fade into the background.

A wave of powerful Persuasion Magic washed through the room. It forced me to my knees. In front of me, Smeeten crumpled. The compulsion was strong, the weight of hands pressing on shoulders, of burdens too heavy to bear.

Larrings turned from Smeeten toward me. "You didn't really think you could sneak around without me noticing, did you?"

I desperately fought to get to my feet but I couldn't push past the Persuasion.

"I'd offer you the honours of taking his life, but I'm not sure I could trust you to follow-through. And I certainly can't risk him taking this back to the Elven Court. Not if I want my Lordship." He threw a quick glance over his shoulder at Kalik whose face was twisted in pain under the Persuasion. "Same goes for your pet

Guardian, I suppose. You can choose! Who first? No, I know your thoughts. I've seen the way you look at the Guardian, we all have, even Smeeten sees it. You'd do anything to protect that Guardian, to get him to look at you with as much sickening puppy-affection as you look at him with. You think we didn't see you at the Guardian Graduation Ball? Oh yes, we were invited, everyone who is anyone is invited. And, since you were there, we went too."

Smeeten's eyes flicked to look at me. I couldn't compose my face; it fell into a stunned expression. They had been there? How had I not noticed them? How could they have been so close to me without my realising?

"You want to be free of forever looking over your shoulder for Smeeten, don't you?" Larrings asked, tone shockingly conversational as he hefted Smeeten by the back of his collar and tossed him down like a piece of litter at Kalik's ice stand. "But, since you do so long to be your own person, prove your independence and choose anyway. Maybe I'll even let the other live, contained of course. Like I said I'm not risking my Lordship. So, who do you choose to kill first? Your secret sweetheart or the man who kept you beaten down most of your life?"

"Too afraid to make your own choice?" I pushed out between gritted teeth.

"What?"

"You've never made a decision in your life and now, when you finally have the chance, you're still looking for someone else to do it for you."

Larrings' face twisted into a sneer, then he broke into a laugh and clapped his hands together slowly. "You have grown strong in your time away, haven't you? Who on Terya taught you these tricks? It can't be your pet Guardian; he couldn't even break the initial Hold trap that let me encase him in ice. Yet here you stand, having broken out of my trap and now attempting to force your way out of my concentrated Hold."

He leaned forward, face shifting to serious and eyes like pools of almost frozen water. Treacherous. "Unfortunately, all that strength means nothing to the Guardians if you can't follow an order. Isn't that what Commander Whitclé always said? You didn't really think he was giving you a fair chance did you?"

The pity in his eyes filled my chest with emptiness. He was right. I couldn't follow a simple order, couldn't make an easy choice like this. This was why I struggled to make friends, an inbuilt problem with my very self.

Lior was wrong: people didn't like me. Valencia tolerated me because I lived with his boyfriend. Kalik worked with me because we had made a bargain. Kitty put up with me because I paid my rent.

Still, Kalik had wanted to dance with me, and Kitty had given me the ointment when I needed it, and even if I couldn't make new friends I had Lior. Sure, I was bad at following orders without reason, but that would be beneficial if I ever made it up to Lieutenant. And Kalik wasn't the only reason I had managed to make it into the Guardian Cadet Programme. I had petitioned Whitclé incessantly. Kalik had even said Whitclé would bend eventually

The cloud of Persuasion disappeared; fading like the morning fog over the ocean.

"So," Larrings continued. "Will you choose? Take the step toward what you want."

My hands had fisted, fingernails digging into my palms. Warm, sticky blood coated my fingertips.

"Or will you allow yourself to be controlled by a petty little man for the rest of your life?"

When I said nothing Larrings snarled and thrust his hand toward Kalik.

Kalik's face contorted with pain.

With a yell, I dove at him, the last of the Persuasion Magic catching my ankles. I dragged his hand away from Kalik. Every piece of me that connected with Larrings burned with cold. Pain escaped me in a hiss of a breath, frosted air forming in front of my face.

Larrings met my eye, weaving Persuasion Magic into my mind. My knees turned to jelly but I clung to him. I let the Persuasion Magic tell me what it would, focusing all my energy on keeping my fingers latched to his arm. If I let go, Larrings would hurt people.

The slap across my ear and cheek was disorientating. As the world swam around me, my grip slipped.

Larrings pressed his advantage, looming over me. He pressed a foot to my chest. I had never noticed his preference for sturdy boots before, just like my own. I had always assumed he would wear silk shoes like Smeeten. Yet here he was, pressing a sturdy boot into my chest. I could barely take a breath and with each passing second the pressure increased.

I scrabbled at Larrings' sensible boot as he crushed the air from my lungs. My vision started to cloud. My focus was gone.

I couldn't breathe.

I couldn't think.

"NO!" somebody roared, the sound of it

pushed past the buzzing in my ears.

The pressure disappeared.

I sucked in a breath. Ribs aching, I scrambled to my feet, desperately searching for the next attack.

I found it just in time to watch Larrings plunge an ice spear into Smeeten's chest.

I stumbled, piecing together what had happened. Larrings had been going to kill me. He was mere seconds away. Smeeten had broken the Persuasion and tackled him. Bodily tackled Larrings.

I stared as blood pooled around my uncle's body.

Larrings pulled the spear from him. He approached me, blood dripping from the spear still in hand. Smeeten's blood. My uncle's blood.

Emotion stole my voice as I stared at Larrings. As I stared at the bloody floor. The blue blood melded so nicely with the decor.

Larrings raised the spear.

CHAPTER THIRTY-TWO

I tore the spear from Larrings' hands, tossing it to the side. The tinkling pretty sound it made as it shattered made no sense.

For one blink, surprise stole over Larrings' face: eyes wide, face slack. One step backward.

I rammed into him. We fell. He slammed a fist into my stomach, flipped us so he pinned me. I scrabbled for escape. He seized one wrist. I shoved my knee into his ribs.

Reaching down to my boot, I grabbed Etta's knife from its holster. I slashed it across Larrings' bicep.

He dropped my wrist to clamp a hand over the wound, reaching for me with his injured arm.

I swung the knife back, catching whatever part of him I could. The air buzzed with the sharp and sudden disappearance of Larrings' magic. Darkness coated the room for one, two, three slashes of my knife.

A small silvery light shone, bounced on the edges of my vision. Larrings scrambled back, hands jerking up to protect his face and throat. I couldn't stop slashing at him, desperate, feral.

"Merry!" Kalik's voice rocketed through the heartbeat pounding in my ears, in my head, in my whole body.

My head jerked to find him. When had he escaped the ice stand? How?

A silver light globe hovered over his shoulder where he knelt in a pool of blood. Blue. Not his. Humans bled red, dark red. I didn't look at the body lying next to him.

My uncle.

I turned to Larrings. He cowered against the wall. This was all his fault. He represented everything wrong in the world, in my life.

And yet.

Fear shone in his ice blue eyes, so similar to my own, to my uncle's. Larrings didn't have family or friends who would miss him. The cycle of revenge would end here.

And yet.

"I could kill you." The force in my voice surprised me.

Larrings lowered his hands from his face. Arranging his features, that infuriating smirk slipped into place with practised ease. "Go on then, get it over with."

"I could kill you," I repeated. "It would be easy. I won't. Not because I'm weak. Because I made the *choice*."

Rage bubbled in his face as Kalik swooped in to clasp cuffs around his wrists, light still bobbing over his shoulder.

The thunk of feet echoing down the corridor

had me dashing to stand protectively over Lior, still propped against the wall where I had left xem, still guarded by the sofa. Still glazed over.

I couldn't take on Larrings' hired goons. I couldn't. But as I stood over Lior, I knew I wouldn't stop until I got xem out of this or died trying.

My knees trembled.

Flickering lamplight cast an ominous orange glow across the floor as the footsteps approached.

Gergorio cradled his ribs as he led Commander Whitclé and a swarm of Guardians in battle armour into the room.

"Jon," Kalik sighed, relief washing through him. Stumbling, he handed Larrings off to a pair of Guardians I vaguely recognised, before his legs gave out from under him.

Whitclé moved to the body.

"It's too late." Kalik's voice was hushed.

Whitclé shifted to approach Kalik but he shook his head and gestured at me and Lior.

"Can you break a Persuasion Spiral?"

Cautiously, Whitclé approached me, eyes on my hand. I looked to see what captured his attention. The knife. I still clutched Etta's knife in my hand. The only apparent weapon in the room. The weapon and my hands both coated in blue blood. The same blue blood pooling on the floor and coating Larrings' arms. No, not the same blood as on the floor.

My hands trembled.

"Arlan," Whitclé spoke quietly. "I'm a Healer; can I try and help your friend?"

I hesitated. Did I trust Whitclé to keep Lior safe?

My knees buckled and I collapsed to the floor,

knife clattering against the stone tiles as my numb hands let it go.

The residual magic in the air mixed with Whitclé's Healing. Flames over snow, a piece of frozen clothing melting in the heat of a hearth.

CHAPTER THIRTY-THREE

Dragging my eyes open revealed a dim room; the only light a thin strip forcing its way under the closed door. A room in the Healers tower. With the pain coursing through me it made sense. My chest ached, my left arm was entirely numb, and I had more pain than I could name, but I wasn't in a cell and that was what counted. For the first time in my life the plain white walls comforted me.

I tested my limbs, looking at my bandages. Magic burns were one of Kitty's areas of expertise, maybe the Healers would ask him for some of his special salve. If they didn't I would.

Logic told me the best course of action was staying in the bed. The Healers needed me to stick around. And the pain building behind my eyes, travelling from the back of my head to the front the longer I stayed awake, didn't bode well for my ability to make it home. But my breathing turned ragged and everything hurt and I wanted the comfort of my home, my bed.

I pushed myself out of the bed. The prospect of waiting around for a Healer, of leaving myself vulnerable after everything that had happened, of being easy to find... it was beyond my capabilities.

When the door opened on the first try and there were no Guardians stationed outside the room to keep me in it, my shoulders dropped with a sigh of relief. Definitely not a prisoner.

The Healer's desk at the end of the hall was empty of a Healer but full of files. I cast my eye over them. The entire ward had been dedicated to people injured in the Larrings escapade. Several files titled with ranks and names of Guardians. Larrings' goons must have fought Whitclé's troop on their way to find us.

Graduate G. Valencia. Mx L. Folcs. Colonel E. Kalik. Cadet M. Arlan — me.

Spending time deciphering the Human Script would be too much for my tired and aching brain to process, even if it wasn't a complete violation of my friends' privacies. I wanted to know they were all okay, but this wasn't the way to do it. Larrings would have looked. Smeeten would have looked too. He would have been disappointed in me leaving my friends medical files private. But his opinion didn't matter anymore, did it?

I wanted to reject Larrings' statements about me, but he was right, for the first time in my life I was my own person, no longer searching for the ever present shadow of Smeeten.

I shook my head and turned toward the other end of the corridor. What was it with me and this place? I could never go the right way the first time. But home was calling, my flat with its messy bedspread and all my things.

"I don't have my keys," I muttered. And, if the low level light globes stationed around the desk were anything to go by, it was the middle of the night. Kitty would not take well to my knocking to be let in and I could hardly climb back through my window. Actually, Kitty would be grumpy and would just cart me back to the Healers anyway.

I leaned on the Healer's desk with a sigh.

"Should have known I'd find you out of bed," Kalik's teasing voice called.

"Says you," I accused, pushing back to standing.

He stood in the middle of the corridor with a soft, tired smile on his face. Gait stiff, he approached me. "I was just going to the bathroom."

"How are you?" I asked before he could ask me.

"Been better."

"Ever been worse?"

"Nothing comes to mind," he admitted, sitting heavily in the Healer's chair. "But being encased in ice was never going to be good for me, especially when put there by magic. The Healers assure me I'll be back to normal in no time, though. How about you?"

"I haven't heard from a Healer yet."

"How are you feeling?"

"Fine." The word slipped out before I could think about it. My breath hissed between my teeth at the sudden stabbing from the amulet.

"Not so fine," Kalik murmured when the stinging died down a little.

"Coping," I corrected.

He nodded in the direction of the amulet. "That seems worse than when I last saw it."

"Larrings did something," I said, pressing my hand into the amulet itself even through the bandages. I ignored the pain from the healing burn as the buzzing faded. "He used it to free himself from an oath."

"Is that why you're so badly burned?"

"Burns on top of burns," I sighed, perching on the edge of the desk.

Kalik winced in sympathy. "That can't be good."

"I've been better," I repeated Kalik's earlier words. "But it doesn't change anything."

"Excuse me?"

"If I can remember the words Larrings used, or we can get him to tell us, we can free Rakael Valencia from her curse."

"What?"

"If he freed himself, we can use the same—"

"Merry, no."

"What do you mean no? It solves the problem. We use the amulet, free her from her curse, and then we look into getting rid of it."

"Merry, no! It's causing you injury. Jon's not going to allow us to do that."

"What's your brother got to do with — oh! Commander Whitclé is your brother!" How did I not see it before? They even looked similar! And Kalik had talked about his brother entering under a different name. And was cagey about his brother's current whereabouts. Kalik's word had sway with the Commander.

"I didn't mean to tell you that," Kalik said. "It isn't common knowledge."

"I'll keep it to myself."

"I found this," Kalik held out the Ring of Concealment, "in the aftermath. I've been waiting to return it."

I took the ring from him. There was no sign of the broken chain so I slipped it onto my right ring finger, noticing the hum of magic for the first time. I frowned at it then shrugged off the feeling; I already knew it was magic. "Thank you."

"I know it's important to you."

"His name was Arlan Tiernan."

"That's where you got the surname?"

"His suggestion."

"Because you were hiding."

"Quite the detective, aren't you?" I teased.

"Well, I am a Guardian, don't you know," he grinned.

"I miss him," I sighed, looking down at the ring again. "He gave me my first real home."

Kalik placed his hand over mine.

I smiled at him. "I know how to make my own home because of him. But everything with Smeeten — my uncle — Tellyn — I don't even know what to call him anymore!"

"It can't be easy."

"And I can't even lie my way out of it." It was supposed to be a joke but instead of a laugh, a small sob bubbled up in my chest.

"I'm here," Kalik said. "If you need me. And before you try to blame yourself for this whole thing — don't try to argue, you'll get hurt if you lie — what happened to me and to all of us, what Larrings did, it's not your fault. I wouldn't have changed anything about our friendship even if it meant I wouldn't have had to face Larrings."

"Friendship," I murmured, looking at Kalik's hand on top of mine. I held in the sigh. I didn't

feel like I deserved even that, but a small part of me, the same part that got wrapped up in Kalik's dark eyes and Lior's Moon Prince talk, wanted something other than friendship, something more than friendship — or different. Somewhere, somehow I had started to think maybe Kalik felt something like that for me. He had wanted to dance with me.
I took a deep breath. No matter. Like all wounds, it would hurt for a while, but it would pass eventually.

CHAPTER THIRTY-FOUR

Clean white sheets and pale pink and blue curtains surrounding me. I pushed myself up in bed. This wasn't right.

I pushed open the curtains to see Smeeten stood behind a blue blood ward.

"If you'd come home on your own, I wouldn't have had to do this."

The bedposts grew hands, grabbing at me and holding me still no matter how hard I fought. I looked back over to Smeeten, ready to beg his aid.

A puddle of blood surrounded his collapsed body.

I jerked awake, wincing at the residual pain lingering in my body. I kicked out of my bedsheets even as I breathed a sigh of relief at them being my own messy green ones. No curtains to be found.

It was still dark outside but I got up anyway. The Healers had advised as much sleep as possible, but they'd also recommended avoiding stress.

Puttering about in the kitchen was too likely to wake Kitty, which would inevitably engage his protective instincts, which would result in sleepy tea and being sent back to bed.

I scribbled a note about visiting Lior — although it read more like my name, an arrow, and Lior's name — and headed, quietly from the flat.

Lior was still trapped in Larrings' mind prison. When I had cut Larrings' skin with Etta's dagger, he had dropped all his active magic, but residual effects could last forever.

Gergorio had told me Larrings wasn't being very forthcoming during interrogations but that didn't surprise me. Smeeten had taught us both how to keep our mouths shut.

Jhoto wasn't letting me anywhere near Lior during official visiting hours. She blamed me for putting xem in harm's way. I couldn't fault her logic; it was almost a weight off my shoulders to have someone else angry with me. My friends' empathy should have been comforting but it just made the pressure of guilt in my chest that much harder to bear.

The Healers had made Lior as comfortable as possible, Healing xem of all injuries, including the ice burns on xyr legs. Now xe lay in a deathlike trance until someone could figure out how to break the spiral.

I pulled up a chair by Lior's bedside and sighed. "I miss you," I said. "Apparently Gergorio and I are friends, and Kitty and I are friends. But I could have all the friends in the world and I'd still miss you. It's different with you. I don't know…"

Lior's chest rose and fell evenly.

I laid my head on xyr bed. "I keep having nightmares about what happened. I guess you probably do too but you can't wake up from yours." I sat back in the chair, restless and forever uncertain of what to say. "Lior I'm so sorry."

Still nothing from Lior. I watched xem breathe, trying to sync my own breathing with xyrs.

"Do you remember when we ended up on that boat to one of the little islands to the south and we were gone two whole days? Your mama was so mad; I thought she was going to explode." I laughed weakly. "But she just pulled you aside and talked really calmly with you. You never told me what she said but I always thought that must be what she was like when she was mad. Turns out I was wrong. That's what she's like when she's mad with you."

I reached forward to smooth Lior's hair off xyr face, using my right hand since my left hand was still bandaged beyond belief.

Lior gasped awake.

We stared at each other. "Merry?"

"Lior?"

"Are you real?"

"Far as I know."

"Did you just wake me up?"

"No? Maybe?" I looked at my right hand and the Ring of Concealment. Could it have? I looked up at Lior. "Does it matter? I'm just glad you're okay?"

I wrapped my arms around Lior in a smothering hug. Xe clung tightly to me.

When we were done hugging, Lior shuffled over in the bed, demanding I climb in next to xem. Xe told me what the mind prison had been like, all xyr insecurities and fears laid bare and used against xem. Completely convincing, no matter how unlikely or impossible it was.

We talked nonsense, and fairy tales, and fears, and reliefs until the sun came up, peeking through the flat medical curtains. A Healer came in to check on Lior.

The Healer was incensed upon realising that I was in the room, demanding to know how I'd got in and how long I'd been there before checking over every millimetre of Lior for unnoticed injuries.

After the Healer left I climbed back into the bed with Lior to keep talking.

"**I** might have guessed you'd be here," Kalik said from the doorway. He had a crutch tucked under one arm — temporary, he'd assured me when I'd last run across him. "Once I knew Mx Folcs was awake."

"Hi," I greeted.

"I really prefer Lior," Lior corrected. "Or Liorellion if you like formality, which I don't but that's your prerogative, Guardian-man."

"Well, just so you both know, Lior's mama has been notified that her child is awake and will inevitably be here any minute."

"I should go." I clambered out of the bed.

"What? Merry?" Lior touched weak fingers to my wrist.

"Your mama isn't exactly happy with me for getting you into this mess."

"But—"

"Thanks for the warning, Kalik, I'll be right out."

Kalik closed the door, leaving me alone with Lior. I started pulling on my boots. "I have to go; I can't deal with Jhoto right now. I'm not..."

"Okay, okay, but before you do."

I paused.

"You and your Moon Prince?"

"Kalik is still not my Moon Prince."

"Really?" Xe slumped. "Nothing happened between you two?"

"No—" the beginning of pain in my hand made me modify, "not really."

"Not really? Dish!"

"Lior I don't—"

"It'll make me feel better, make me feel normal. Please?"

I huffed out a sigh. "Fine. At the Guardian Graduation Ball he walked me home. At the end of a patrol he taught me to dance — I was terrible so it probably wasn't important to him and..."

"And?"

"Once, we talked about you saying he was a Moon Prince."

"Merry! That was private!"

"I'm sorry. It just slipped out. We were under the Midwinter moon and talking about the legend and I just... said it. Anyway, he said he doesn't want to be a Moon Prince, he wants a Moon Prince to come rescue him."

Before Lior could respond, Jhoto swept through the door and pulled xem to her chest. Regardless of the fact that one of my boots was unlaced, I snuck out before she noticed my presence.

I couldn't call myself happy to be entering Jhoto's club. But Lior had practically begged me to come. "It's my debut back to the stage. I need you there Merry, you give me confidence. You're the only thing that ground-feeder couldn't use against me."

So I had agreed to come, and I wasn't about to let Lior down. Likelihood was I could avoid Jhoto anyway. So the only problem would come from trying to go home at the end of the night.

I searched the floor for somewhere out of the way to sit. It was busy, but Jhoto's always was. One table at the front, just below the stage, had only one person at it. I manoeuvred my way through the crowd to ask if they were saving the seats for other people. "Excuse me, are you — Kalik?"

"Why yes, I am Kalik." He grinned.

"What are you doing here? It doesn't really seem like your sort of place."

"Lior asked me to come. Said something about a thank you for helping xem out."

I took a seat next to Kalik. We chatted about nothing until Lior emerged onto the stage. Xe caught my eye and a little tension eased out of xyr shoulders. Xe began a song. The Shields at the base of the stage glowed with the silvery light, allowing only a little of Lior's magic through.

Xe sang, under a spotlight, mostly still instead of xyr usual sensual dance routines. More of a ballad than xyr normal energetic pieces.

My face broke out into a dopey grin before realisation dawned. "That little rat!"

"What?" Kalik asked.

"Xe's making romance!"

"So what if xe is?"

I put my head in my hands. "Lior still wants you to be my Moon Prince. I tried to tell xem that you want your own Moon Prince not to be someone else's, but apparently it didn't go in."

"That's okay. I have a Moon Prince."

My head jerked up. "Who? Since when?"

"Someone in my life who changes everything, and she came to my rescue too. She's everything I didn't know I wanted, and most of the things I did."

"Is it that Healer?" I asked, mind racing. I knew my one sided feelings would cause me pain for a while. I had thought it wouldn't be so bad, but if Kalik started dating, and talking about it, and spending time with someone...

"What Healer?"

"The pretty one that always seems to treat me."

He had every right to date whoever he wanted, provided his date consented. It was none of my business. It was my own fault for bringing up the Moon Prince thing in the first place. Or maybe Lior's fault for trying to make romance — not that I could be mad at Lior right now.

"No."

"Revvi from the café?"

"No."

"Your date from the Graduation Ball?" My voice had got squeaky.

"That was also Revvi and no," Kalik laughed. "Merry. It's you."

"It is not!" I protested. "You're only saying that because Lior's song is making you all squishy and romantic."

"Is that what the amulet is telling you?"

"No..."

"I've got my personal Shields up — usually do

— can't you sense it?"

Now that he mentioned it, he did always smell a little like grass after it rained. "Why?"

"Why have I got my Shields up? Well, I'm an expert in most forms of Basic Magic, and Shielding is a particular forte of mine."

"You are the most irritating person I know," I snarled without venom.

"I used to think I wanted the same kind of partner as Jon. I thought we had similar taste in romantic partners — except that Jon is straight and I am decidedly not."

"I'm nothing like Rakael Valencia."

"A few years ago I realised that, not only was that thought process coming from a place of idolising my brother, but also self-sabotage. I was so focused on bettering the Brotherhood of Guardians that I didn't have time to make friends or romantic partners so I didn't let myself do that by subconsciously looking for the wrong kind of people."

"You make friends with everyone."

"What?"

"The Healer, Revvi from the café. You have friends everywhere."

He sighed and circled a finger around one of the watermarks left by one of the multitudes of glasses that had sat on this table. "I'm not good at making time for people."

"You always have time for me."

"Yes, Merry, that's my point."

"What did I do?"

"You bested me in a sparring match."

"You've felt like this since then?"

"No." He smiled but he wouldn't look at me. "That was just the first step. That was the thing that caught my attention. And once you caught my attention, I couldn't stop seeing you. You were committed to the job in the same way I am, even though it was a job you didn't really want. You're the most persistent person I've ever met. You make me want to be better."

"Better than what?"

He laughed, eyes crinkling at the corners. "I realised we could be friends, real friends. After that, you kept taking more and more on and I realised you needed a tempering influence. You needed someone to tell you it's okay to take a break."

"Is that why you made me lie under the moon with you?"

"Part of the reason." His fingers played over the water rings, following a random pattern where the rings overlapped. "It was the Guardian Graduation Ball that really put it into perspective for me. I wanted to protect you and put you first, but I didn't think you'd want that, didn't think you'd want me. It wasn't appropriate. So I tried to put it aside — and if you want me to put it aside I absolutely will." He sighed wistfully. "Then you came to my rescue. You came back for me, twice. You faced the scariest thing in the world to you, and you did it because I needed help. Nobody has ever come to my rescue before."

He looked up at me, cheeks flushed. "So, like I said, if you want me to, I'll put these feelings aside and I'll get over them. But, on the off chance that you feel the way I do...?"

My head reeled. The moment after the Guardian Graduation Ball with his hand on my neck. Teaching me to dance, his warm fingers on my waist. Talking with me about Goblin legends, trying to take my mind off my troubles. It wasn't all in my head.

"What do you say to a confession like that?" I managed.

"You either say you reciprocate the feeling, or you say 'thanks but I don't feel the same'"

"I've never done anything like this before."

"I know."

"It's scary."

"That's fair."

"But... I think with you... it's not so scary."

CHAPTER THIRTY-FIVE

The door to the counsellor's office loomed at me, bigger than it should have been. The Healers had mandated I go to at least ten sessions. "Due to traumatic experience," they had said. "For the grief," they had said.

I wanted nothing more than for things to go back to normal. No counselling, no update from Gergorio about Larrings, no worry that my place in the Guardian Cadet Programme was over and done with.

Right now, normal seemed a million kilometres away. Normal wasn't an option for me. Had it ever been?

Since the Winter Holiday hadn't ended yet, I was still signed off sessions both with Sorenson and with PT — regardless of whether I still had a place; the Healers had demanded no training or physical exertion, and no fighting until the counsellors okayed it.

I flinched as the door swung toward me. Expecting a counsellor, I was surprised to find Kalik emerging from the room.

"You're in counselling?" I blurted.

He laughed. "Nobody greets me as nicely as you do, Merry."

I winced.

"Mandated by the Healers — I presume that's what brings you here too. Not that I'm asking if you don't want to disclose."

I nodded, shifting on my feet and pulling on the sleeves of my overtop.

"It's not so bad," Kalik reassured. "A little awkward at first but not the worst thing I've ever done."

"This coming from the man who said he wasn't in the worst pain after being trapped in an ice prison for who knows how long," I snarked. "It doesn't exactly fill me with confidence."

Kalik ran a hand through his hair.

Guilt washed through me. Attacking Kalik like that because of my own fear was mean. "I'm sorry," I whispered. "I just... I can't lie and..."

"You're not supposed to lie in counselling."

I rolled my eyes.

"What are your plans after?"

"I was thinking of investigating the amulet a little more."

"Yeah?"

"Yeah. There's this... uh... poetry book I've been trying to decipher."

"Bring it by my office; I'll add it to the stacks of work I have to catch up on."

"That bad?"

"Apparently the work doesn't stop just because you got kidnapped."

"I'm sorry. I'm sure I can manage the poetry–"

"No. Bring it over. It might be nice to look at poetry instead of endless reports. Anything else you're thinking of looking into?"

"I thought about, maybe, possibly, going to see Larrings."

Kalik's eyebrows shot up, hiding in his flop of hair.

"He knows how to use the thing. He's apparently been researching it for years. I thought... even if we just find out his sources, it could be good..."

"Let me know how it goes when you bring me the poetry book?" Kalik's voice was soft, his hand twitched toward me but he didn't touch.

I twisted my hands together, wincing at the residual pain the Healers couldn't get rid of. "You're okay with this?"

"I'm here for you if you need me. Be it as colleague, friend, or..." he glanced at the open door behind him.

I ducked my head.

"I trust you." He finally reached out and squeezed my shoulder lightly. "I should get going, and you have a meeting."

Kalik dodged around me.

I couldn't see the counsellor, even with the door open. I hesitated. Did they know I was here? Could I leave and try again another day?

I pushed the door wide and stepped inside.

Larrings' smile was still weaselly, but he looked surprisingly well groomed for a man in a cell. He'd been stripped down to a plain shirt and trousers — no shoes I was glad to note. The clothes framed him well, not like the ill-fitting garb Smeeten had had him wear. The sleeves of his shirt were rolled up, exposing pale forearms marred with criss-crossed pink slashes of half-healed wounds.

I tried not to rub my sternum where his boot had pressed. The damage had been Healed but the memory persisted.

He stepped up to the bars. "Well this is a surprise."

For one brief instant I couldn't speak. "I understand you haven't been very talkative."

He didn't respond, shifting on his feet as if bored.

"I want to know about the amulet."

Larrings stepped closer, pushing his face close to the bars. The wards crackled at his proximity, shooting green sparks up and down the bars and across the spaces between them. His face held a severity I'd never before witnessed from him. "What do I get in return?"

I examined him as the green light danced over his face, drawn closer by his intensity. What did he want? What could I offer? "Name your price?"

"Shall I presume my freedom is off limits?"

"I don't know what kind of sway you think I have with the Guardians..."

"Your little pet is a Colonel, is he not?"

"He's not a pet."

Larrings shook his head. He looked so much like Smeeten when he did that except that his hair, now hanging loose around his face, shifted with the movement. Had his hair tie been confiscated? "Tell me, are you going to accept the Lordship?"

"What?"

"He named you heir, if you recall. Which means, now he's dead; you're the next Lord Smeeten."

"I already refused that." Provided I had remembered to return the papers to Whitclé.

"Not according to my sources. And, since it didn't go through the Embassy, or the Court, it doesn't count." A dangerous smile swept over his face. "Which means you're the heir, and you have to find someone else to take on the role if you don't want it. Will you give up all your hard won freedom and return to the role you ran from? Will you become the new Lord Smeeten and have to deal with the Elven Court? Have people working for you? Navigate high society where one wrong move can destroy your entire power base? — Not that you have a power base to speak of. Will you let down your uncle like that? Or will you search out a viable heir? But wait—" he put his hand up to his mouth in a mockery of a shocked expression "—how will you manage that around your studies and the Cadet nonsense or whatever it is you do here?"

I waited. Larrings would have a point to this. We both knew I wasn't going to take up the title of Lord Smeeten.

His voice dropped. "Name me Smeeten heir and I will tell you everything you want to know."

I stared at him, open mouthed.

He stepped away from the bars and shifted to sit on the cot under the barred, warded window. A wooden frame with a canvas top, it looked much more comfortable than the wooden pallet bed from the Elven Embassy. "I'll be here when you decide."

I walked up the stairs in a daze. What was Larrings' aim here? What good would it do him to be named the next Lord Smeeten? Was he just that obsessed with the idea of a title? That didn't track for Larrings, even in his most submissive and subservient state. A state he had very purposefully murdered.

I was too busy thinking through all the possibilities that I almost walked straight into PT on the stairs.

"Cadet Arlan?"

"Sir," I greeted. The fact that he was still calling me Cadet was promising.

"How are you healing up?"

"Well enough."

"Will you be back at training on Unday?"

"I— I'm not sure."

"Did the Healers give you a time frame?"

"Not exactly."

PT nodded sharply. "Not a physical healing." He frowned down the stairs toward Larrings' cell. "Get anything out of him?"

"He only respects the Elven Justice System. I doubt he'll talk to anyone within the Five Towers system."

PT hummed, turning on his heel and leading me back up the stairs. "That is inconvenient. Do you think we could fool him with an Elven Guardian?"

"Probably not. He was Lord Tellyn Smeeten's Lackey, one of his favoured Lackeys at that."

PT invited me into his office and sat in one of the stiff wooden chairs on the door side of his desk, gesturing for me to sit in the other.

"He's been to a lot of Court meetings," I continued. "He's met the vast majority of Elven Lords and their respective Lackeys, he'll know if an Elf is outside that system. And if they're outside the system, they hold no power over him."

PT's eyebrows drew together and he opened his mouth.

"I mean in the way that Larrings cares about. Obviously he's imprisoned by the Guardians, but he reasons he must be remanded to the Elven Justice System, so anyone with no sway over that is of no consequence, which means an Elven Layman with links to the Guardians is no threat, and without the threat he won't talk." Did I sound like Smeeten when I phrased it like that?

"But he talked to you."

"We have a... history."

"Then what do you suggest?"

"Maybe we could reach out to the Elven Embassy for aid — although that brings the issue of their potentially wanting to claim Larrings for their own justice system. Or just them not agreeing to help." I twisted Arlan's ring around my finger as I thought.

"You could talk to him for us," PT suggested. "In an official capacity."

I swallowed, hand still on the ring. "In theory."

"However?"

"As a Cadet my position is somewhat more precarious than a fully trained Guardian. I wouldn't know what I was doing. Plus there's my history with Larrings..."

"What exactly is your history?"

"He was my uncle's Lackey."

PT leaned back in his chair, examining me.

"He may talk to me but I don't think he's going to answer my questions. He's really good at making bargains... I'm not so skilled."

"Who in the Guardians knows about your history with the prisoner?"

"Kalik knows a little."

PT raised an eyebrow.

"I didn't think it was relevant."

"With regard to this recent turn of events, it

might be best to report this to Commander Whitclé. Have you made your official report yet?"

"No."

"Why not?"

I didn't know how to tell PT that I had been worried if I handed a report to Commander Whitclé he would tell me I no longer had a place in the GCP. "It wasn't exactly a planned expedition."

"It all has to go in the report, Arlan, even if you'd rather it didn't." PT sighed heavily, taking on a far off look like he had when he'd talked about Garrett. He shook his head and rifled through the drawers under his desk. He handed me a file with a sharp nod.

Kalik's office door was, as always, ajar. I took in the neatly stacked piles of files and paper surrounding Kalik. They had even spread on to one of the chairs. He sat, hunched over the desk, pouring over one file and muttering to himself.

I hesitated. Should I come back? He had said to give him the book, but this was an awful lot of work that I definitely didn't want to add to.

I knocked.

His head shot up, smile emerging like the moon on a cloudy night. "Merry."

"I brought that poetry book. I've written down some attempts at translation but they're pretty word-for-word so they might not make sense."

He held his hand out for the book and I passed it to him. His fingers traced the cover as he examined it, just as mine had when I found it.

"I'll let you get back to..." I gestured at the piles of paper.

"Merry, wait."

I stopped.

Kalik cleared his throat, tidying the stack of papers in front of him. "I, uh..." he wouldn't look at me. "About being — our being in — our relationshi—" he cleared his throat again.

I waited.

Finally he looked at me, smiling that crooked smile. "Never mind," he sighed. "Are you free on Deuday? Evening?"

"Sure."

"I'll pick you up."

CHAPTER THIRTY-SIX

Two days and two attempts at writing a report later found me taking up a spot in one of the chairs stationed outside Commander Whitclé's office. I'd tucked the letter from Larrings inside the folder PT had given me.

"Arlan?" Commander Whitclé asked from his doorway.

I shuffled to put my feet on the floor from where I had curled up in the chair to write. "Commander Whitclé?"

"Did you want something?"

"I was just..." I pointed at the file in my lap, "writing a report."

"Outside my office?" When Whitclé frowned like that, a little amused quirk of his brow and a hint of a smile, I could see the family resemblance between him and Kalik.

"Yes."

"Is there a reason for this choice of location?"

"Kitty and Gergorio are in my flat very happy to have been reunited. The library is too quiet. The Cadet stipend doesn't pay enough to spend all day in the café. And it's cold outside."

Whitclé's face shifted into a real smile. He jerked his chin toward his office. "Come inside, Arlan."

I followed Commander Whitclé into his office. He took up his regular spot behind the desk with a sigh. "What brought on this desperate desire to write a report?"

"PT reminded me it wasn't done yet."

"I already have Colonel Kalik and Graduate Valencia's reports, is there something yours could add?" He held out a hand for the barely started report file.

I handed over the poorly filled out report and told Whitclé everything that had happened from getting the letter to going to see Larrings in the cell and my subsequent conversation with PT, though I kept my conversations with Kalik to myself. That last conversation, when I had given him the poetry book would have been impossible to recount anyway.

"So he wants to be an Elven Lord?" Whitclé mused when I was done.

"Yes, it's what he always wanted but I don't see what he could gain from it in his current position."

"Did Lord Smeeten hold a place in the Queen's Court?"

"Yes." Tellyn Smeeten had always been going away on 'Court business'. Sometimes he would take Larrings; sometimes he would leave Larrings in charge of the house. The poetry books had always been gifted after Larrings had been away, apologies for leaving me alone. Smeeten gave apology gifts too.

I swallowed past the lump in my throat. I didn't know what to do with the feeling that came whenever I thought about Tellyn Smeeten. It was almost like grief but that made no sense.

"Lords on the Queen's Court have to be tried under Elven law. We would have to relinquish him into Elven custody," Whitclé said.

"Wait, if I name him heir, he would be tried by the Elves?"

Whitclé nodded.

"Where he would be tried as an Elven Lord?"

Whitclé nodded again.

I pinched the bridge of my nose. "And since he would be heirless, they would choose to sweep the whole thing under the rug. Crafty." I shook my head. "I've been wracking my brain trying to come up with something else that will get him to talk but I can't think of anything."

"Talk? Talk about what?"

"He knows how to use the Amulet Of The Dragon Lord — that was going to be in my report. That's what created this whole issue. Smeeten had him under magic oath and Larrings had been trying to escape it. He used the Amulet Of The Dragon Lord to do it. If he tells us how he did it we can finally remove the curse from Rakael Valencia and maybe even detach it from me."

CHAPTER THIRTY-SEVEN

The Guardian Gym hadn't changed, even if everything else had. Still a well-worn room with its huge glass ceiling to let in the light. Still filled with the smells of sweat and the undercurrent of blood that made me think of split knuckles and broken noses.

Joining the Cadet line was easy enough. I was a little late so PT was already talking through the proper form of an open handed hit or grab and where it was appropriate as opposed to a punch.

Everything was fine until we tried to partner up. Edthorn tapped Manth on the arm, whispering to him and gesturing in my direction. I told myself they weren't talking about me but I didn't believe it.

Manth sidled up to me. "You're here."

"I am a Guardian Cadet and this is Guardian Cadet training."

"I thought Commander Whitclé had seen

sense and kicked you out."

"Maybe he's just an idiot then," I smiled.

Manth strode away, partnering up with Edthorn. I searched the room for a friendly face but Al was nowhere to be found and everybody else had paired up already.

"Looks like we're an odd number today." PT's voice was surprisingly quiet. His eyes flicked over the pairs who had already started sparring. "Well, Arlan, looks like you'll have to s'partner with me for now." He shifted into a fighting stance.

The aim of open-handed strikes was to subdue with minimal harm. Subduing a man as solid and sturdy, not to mention practised as PT with minimal harm was no small feat.

His foot shot out toward my knee. I yanked my leg back. Too late I noticed him swap his weight, lashing out again. I grunted at the new pain.

A fist flashed at my face. I shoved it away. Open hands. I twisted out of the hold PT tried to pull me into. We traded blows, boxing and dodging like hares.

Subdue with minimal harm, I reminded myself.

Huffing out a few even breaths to lower my creeping up panic. I should have worked on a punching bag, or someone safe like Kalik or Gergorio before I came back to Cadet Training. But I wasn't sure if either of them were allowed to spar again yet.

PT kicked out again, aiming for my ribs this time. I blocked. His leg connected with my hand, my hand connected with my ribs. I clamped my fingers closed around his calf, yanking him off balance.

I traded leg for wrist, pulling his hands behind his back and muttering, "clink clink," the noise cuffs made as they closed as I held him immobilised.

"Yield," PT called.

I let him go, bouncing off the residual pain in my arm and ribs as I brushed down my shirt.

The silence stopped me. I looked around, searching for who was hurt. Most of the Cadets were watching us.

"You've improved," PT commended.

"Thank you." My voice was meek.

"Back to the task at hand," PT's usual brash tone returned.

At the end of the session I aimed to sneak back out without too much notice but Manth blocked my exit. Edthorn trailed behind him like a child with a half dropped safety blanket.

PT hovered by the door to his office.

"You need to quit," Manth snapped. "Since Commander Whitclé and PT don't have one pebble of sense between them, you need to do the right thing and quit."

I sighed. "I really don't have time for—"

"Make time," Edthorn injected.

"Where else do you need to be, little girl?" Manth sneered.

I tried to step around Manth but Edthorn stepped up to block me.

"If you won't quit on your own, we'll just have to make you," Manth said from behind me.

The blow to the back of my head made me stumble.

Edthorn's fist in my gut threw the air from my lungs.

I fell to my knees on the mats. Manth and Edthorn snickered. Edthorn pulled back one leg for a kick. I yanked on his standing knee, sending his sprawling to the mats.

"What the—?" Manth muttered as I spun to my feet, bouncing away from the both of them.

Manth snarled, face screwing up, fangs peeking out of his mouth. He threw himself at me. His arms swung out wildly. I blocked, stepping to the side again to allow his own momentum to throw him to the ground.

I huffed out a few quick breaths. This new panic-adrenaline was not pleasant. Should I be bringing it up to my counsellor? Ugh. Counselling.

Edthorn jammed a fist toward my head. I ducked under it, stepping in to strike his stomach. While he relearned how to breathe, I caught Manth's next swing and pulled him into one of Kalik's immobilising holds.

"Are we done? Can I leave now?" I asked.

"Edthorn!" Manth snapped.

My head swam with the force of Edthorn's blow. As I stumbled, my heart rocketed from exercise-mode to panic-mode. I could practically feel the adrenaline blast out of it like a broken water balloon.

One of them grabbed me and my fangs clamped around the arm on the end of that hand.

"Enough!" PT bellowed.

The tang of blood mixed with the sweetness of my venom. I scrabbled away from whoever I'd bitten, hand flying to my mouth. Shame, revulsion, panic. It would probably be fine if I'd bitten Manth, Manth was a Goblin, he would be immune to the venom, right?

"Manth, Edthorn, the Guardian Cadet Programme will not accept bullying. Get him to a Healers and get a handle on yourselves. If I find you've continued this behaviour you will be expelled from the GCP."

"She bit me!" One of them cried.

"Hazard of a job like Guardianship. People bite. Go."

The scuffle of feet as Manth and Edthorn fled the Gym.

PT crouched by me. "You alright there, Arlan?"

I nodded slowly even as panicked tears prickled my eyes. I wanted to vomit. "I'm sorry."

"You're going to the mandated counselling, right?"

I nodded.

"Then I'll let them know this happened for you."

"I am willing to make you an offer in return for information regarding the Amulet Of The Dragon Lord," Whitclé said.

Larrings lounged on the canvas and wooden cot at the back of his cell, watching the way the sunlight played through the wards on the window bars.

"The Lordship is not an option," Whitclé continued. "But I am willing to transfer you to be tried under Elven Law."

Larrings snorted, turning his head just enough to look at me. "Hiding behind a big strong man? I thought you'd decided not to do that."

"I'm not in charge here," I countered quietly.

He stood and sauntered over to me. "What good would it do me to be tried under Elven Law? I'm a Lackey who killed his own Lord. Here or there, execution is my future."

I swallowed thickly. "Unless the Smeeten heir-apparent speaks in your favour."

"Colour me shocked. Meredith Smeeten willing to speak in my favour." He let out a short laugh.

I suppressed the urge to snap at him. The residual tang of blood in the back of my throat wouldn't go away even after brushing my teeth, eating, and brushing my teeth again.

"Tell me this, though. Why are you so interested in the Amulet Of The Dragon Lord?" He reached out as if to touch me. I flinched even as his hand stopped before the wards could crackle. "Just desperate to cause yourself more injury on behalf of this disgusting Human institution?"

"What?" Commander Whitclé interrupted.

Larrings sighed delicately. "Alright, I'll give you a tidbit, a trickle of information and then you can decide what my life is worth to you." He waited for Whitclé's nod before continuing. "I see your left hand, where the amulet is, is bandaged. Why is that?"

"Magical burns," I answered, staring at Larrings who in turn stared at Commander Whitclé.

"One of the aspects of the Amulet Of The Dragon Lord is magical interruption — that's why it can remove oaths and curses. Which you knew."

"I did," I whispered. Sort of.

"If it is to remove an oath or a curse, it must be fed. Since it is bonded to our beloved here," he gestured at me, eyes still locked with Whitclé. "She is the only fuel available."

"Every time she uses it the burns will get worse," Whitclé concluded.

Larrings spread his hands and bowed elegantly. "Let me know when you change your mind about my offer."

"No," Commander Jonathan Whitclé said flatly.

"What do you mean no?"

"That is not acceptable."

"Why not?"

He sighed, leaning his elbows on the desk and steepling his fingers. He'd led me away from Larrings' cell and up to his office, leaving me sat in a chair on the door-side of his desk and him in his regular seat. "Firstly, I would never put a Guardian in that position. Secondly, if I allowed you to do this, to harm yourself in aid of someone else — especially someone as important to me as Rakael — it would set a precedent."

"What precedent?"

"You use the Amulet Of The Dragon Lord to remove Rakael's cursed oath, at great expense to your own health. The next person who needs a cursed oath removed would come to us and expect you to do the same for them. It would be endless."

"But—"

"No, Arlan. If we refused the next person, it would add credulity to the idea that Rakael, as my paramour, is being prioritised over the other civilians asking for our help. I can't do that."

"But—"

"We will find another way to help her and we will find a way to separate the amulet from you."

"Time is running out for her."

"You think I'm not aware of that," he snapped.

"I'm volunteering my ability to help her!"

"And I am refusing your offer!"

CHAPTER THIRTY-EIGHT

Rakael Valencia was surprisingly easy to find. Between figuring out the logical locations she would hang around in, and following the discomfort the amulet provided. I found her in, what appeared to be, Commander Whitclé's personal rooms. She had a pair of Guardian Lieutenants acting as bodyguards.

The Lieutenants wanted to accompany us, but after a quick and persuasive word from Rakael about my being a Guardian Cadet and my own promise not to take her outside the Five Towers, they agreed to wait behind.

"What are we doing?" she hissed as I led her down the stairs near the Guardian Gym to the cells below.

"We are going to use the amulet to free you."

"But we don't know how."

"No, we don't. But he does." I stopped in front of Larrings' cell for the third time since Lior's return to the stage.

"No Guardian this time?" Larrings asked, rising from his cot and sauntering closer.

"No. Tell me how to break the curse."

"What's in it for me? What do I gain if I help you?"

"It is illegal under Elven Law to syphon off your Lackeys' magic to boost your own. Your word wouldn't count for enough in the system. Mine will, especially with this." I held up my bandaged hand.

Larrings took his time considering my words.

I glanced toward the stairs; half convinced Commander Whitclé would sense what I was doing and appear at any moment.

"Take the bandages off and put your palm against hers."

I did as Larrings ordered.

He rolled up his sleeves. A small satisfied smile touching his face, it softened his features.

A little burn for someone's life. It seemed a fair bargain.

As Larrings began speaking those incomprehensible words again the amulet started to buzz. It heated, scaldingly hot.

Burning.

Agonising.

I couldn't see. I couldn't stand. The pain tore up my arm, into my chest.

"Don't let her go!" Larrings snapped, his voice carrying through the pain as it always had. "If you stop now, you lose it all!"

The bed was hard. The blanket rough. I felt like I had been dragged along a dirt road by a horse for several kilometres.

I squinted my eyes open.

Healers tower. Again. And, if the dimness of early dawn light was anything to go by, I had missed my date with Kalik.

I groaned as I pushed myself up with my right arm, realising too late that not only had my shirt been removed, but I wasn't alone.

I yanked the rough blanket up to my chest. Sports bra or no, that was a lot more exposed than I was used to. I immediately regretted the action. Should have used my right hand. Stupid amulet in stupid dominant hand.

"That is a hell of a way to get out of a date," Kalik joked softly, head lifted out of his hands.

No bandages this time but the Runes drawn all the way up my arm were pretty in their own way.

"You know," Kalik continued, "if you didn't want to go you could have just said so. You didn't need to go to this kind of extreme."

"I do want to go," I said to my hands.

"But?"

I looked over at him. Kalik sat in one of the uncomfortable visitor's chairs, elbows resting on his knees, leaning toward me.

"I couldn't not do it," I said. "I couldn't. Our bet—"

"Said you would help us find the amulet," Kalik interrupted.

"Commander Whitclé—"

"Ordered you to help with research."

I opened my mouth but I had no excuses left.

Kalik shook his head, eyes closing.

Disappointment? He sighed and pushed to his feet. He pulled off his overtop and handed it to me. "I'll let the Healer know you're awake."

"Kalik, wait, I—" but he was out of the door before I finished my sentence.

The harsh yellow light that streamed in through the open door hurt my eyes. I probably deserved it. How many people had I hurt with this thing?

I awkwardly pulled Kalik's overtop on around the ache in my arm, trying not to disturb the Runes, but they were stained on in some way and didn't smudge. It smelled like him, a little musky and residual wet-grass Shielding smell.

I was half way out of the bed when Kalik returned with a Healer I didn't recognise. The Healer carried a flame lantern, casting yellow light all over the room. A light globe would probably interfere with the Rune Magic.

The Healer ordered me back into the bed, scanning over me with magic that pushed the air like a spring breeze. I sat on the edge of the bed while the magic worked. "The Runes should hold. You need to leave them be for another forty-eight hours and I'd really rather you stay here. And sleep." Then the Healer swept from the room.

Kalik lingered, loitering by the doorway.

"I'm sorry," I said finally, standing on trembling legs.

"The Healer just said you needed to rest. Do you ever do what you're told?"

I sank back on the edge of the bed. "No."

"No?"

"No. I never do as I'm told. Not really. Not anymore."

"Not anymore?" Kalik's quiet voice carried

through the room like a melody.

"It took me a long time to start trusting myself. Trusting my own instincts, my abilities, my own decisions. I still struggle with it." I sighed, playing with the too-long sleeves. "I know it's important for a Guardian to follow orders, but I can't mindlessly do as I'm told. If I don't agree I have to... at least consider which is the better option. Maybe Whitclé was right when he said I wouldn't be a good Guardian, maybe I do have a problem with authority."

Kalik perched on the bed next to me.

I hid my chin in the borrowed overtop, ducking down like a turtle into its shell.

"I'm sorry," Kalik said. "I was worried about you. I told you knowing that everyone deserves to be saved is a heavy burden, and here I am holding it against you when you made the only choice you, Merry Arlan, could have made." He reached for my hand, letting out a tiny laugh when he found it encased in his own sleeve. "Here's my question though, Colonel Arlan," he nodded at the green Colonel stripe on the overtop I was bundled into. "If a Guardian Cadet had done this, what would your next course of action be? What about if Lior had done it? Or if I had?"

I thought his question through before I tried to answer. This was serious and an off-the-cuff response wouldn't do. "I'd make sure they knew how foolish it was to take this risk, especially without asking for help."

"And you know that?"

I nodded. "It's just... I don't think I'm dealing all that well with everything. I wanted to feel like something was finished. I wanted to feel like I could do some good. Help someone." I snuggled deeper into the overtop. "I bit another Cadet. With my fangs."

Kalik threaded an arm around my shoulders. I leaned my head into the contact, chin popping out of the overtop. "Please don't take a risk like that again — or at least take someone with you next time. I'd rather not have to find my paramour unconscious in front of her enemy's cell after my brother's very light-headed partner stumbles into my office to inform me."

"I worried you would try and convince me not to do it."

"Why?"

"Because you're sensible. Because everyone else did. Whitclé practically forbade me from doing it."

Another soft laugh, one that reverberated over the shoulder leaning into his chest. "I'm glad you see me trying to persuade you not to do this as the sensible option. And you're not wrong; I probably would have tried to stop you. But, if you'd asked me to trust you, I would have. I wouldn't have been happy, I would have told you to at least let me read that poetry book first, or Simonde's reports, or something. But we're a team."

"Give and take. I should have trusted you." I smiled hesitantly at him.

His eyes were pools of ink in the darkness. A sense of wanting unfurled in my chest, unleashing the humming birds that so often emerged when I was around Kalik.

He leaned toward me, lips brushing softly against my own. "Can I kiss you?" he breathed against my skin.

"Yes."

For News About My Latest
Releases
Sign Up To My Mailing List At:
WillSoulsbyMcCreath.com

ABOUT THE AUTHOR

It's pronounced "Souls-Bee-Muh-Kreth"
As a cosplayer, Table-Top Gaming nerd, and videogamer; fantasy has been a staple of Will's life forever. They like to corrupt their friends into joining these pass-times, or at least reading their stories.
Obsessed with every way to tell a story and every possible use for one, Will had few choices other than becoming a writer. A little too nosy for their own good they like to invest their time fixing other people's problems, and when that doesn't work they hand out stories to make you feel better.

TURN THE PAGE FOR A
PREVIEW OF BOOK 2
MERRY ARLAN: FINDING THE HEIR

PREVIEW,
MERRY ARLAN: FINDING THE HEIR

CONTENTS SUBJECT TO CHANGE

"No," I said to Commander Whitclé.

His shoulders slumped. "What do you mean no?"

"I mean 'no, I'm not the Smeeten Heir.' What do you think I mean, no?"

This late in the day, stubble had started to present itself along the Commander's jaw. His Uniform shirt had wrinkled at the elbows, and he slouched in his chair behind the desk strewn with papers that separated us. For once the lamp that I always fixed my eyes on when I couldn't stare him down was actually lit, blue glow casting awkwardly over the room, fighting with the lingering pink and orange sunset shining through the window. "I have a letter here from the Elven Queen."

I waited.

"Regarding your new position following the death of Tellyn Smeeten."

That name hit me like a punch to the gut — which was something I'd already experienced in Cadet Training that morning.

Whitclé let out a huge sigh. "What happened to you filling out that form?"

"I did. I filled it out with Kalik the first week of Guardian Cadet Training, and then I filled out the same thing just after I got let out of the Healers."

"That is after the death of Tellyn Smeeten, which nullifies that paperwork."

"Well, I'm sorry that my best friend was kidnapped, I was wading through Guardian Cadet Training and patrols alongside doing research on the Amulet Of The Dragon Lord, and the fact that I couldn't do it by myself."

"You couldn't do what by yourself?"

I gulped. Weakness would be exploited, usually. "The form," I admitted.

Whitclé frowned. "Why not?"

"Because it's in formal human and I struggle with basic human."

"What do you read?"

"Elvish." Because I was raised by an Elf on the Elven Isles. Although my varied heritage left most people mistaking me for a Human, so I could hardly blame Whitclé for not thinking of it. Plus the official Language of The Guardians and the Five Towers University on Shima was human, which means I was supposed to be fluent.

Whitclé scribbled something down on what looked like a napkin for its stains and crumpled nature.

He put his pen down and leaned his elbows on the desk, one open folder crinkling under the pressure. Hopefully that wasn't an important pile of documents. Then again, did anything that entered Commander Whitclé's office come up uncrinkled? "Cadet Arlan, I'm not trying to be difficult, but you have been named Smeeten Heir and since the paperwork regarding your refusal of that title has gone missing you are now Lord Smeeten."

I flinched at the title. "Please," I whispered. "Don't call me that."

"Because of your current status as—" he stopped and rubbed his stubbley jaw. "Because of your current status in the eyes of Elven Law and the Elven Queen herself requesting your presence, we will have to pause your progression in the Guardian Cadet Programme."

"What?" I gasped, aghast. "I've only been a Cadet for one season!"

"This is not me kicking you out. I want to be very clear on that. Not only is there no current reason to, unless we cannot resolve this issue, but I don't want to give the impression that your assistance in the Rakael Valencia case is the only reason for your presence in the GCP. This is entirely fixable. And, you don't have to cease training with the Cadets for now — plenty of people send their young men to train with us purely for the title of being Guardian Trained."

He rifled through some of the papers strewn across his desk and pulled out a red paper folder with the stamp of the Elven Queen on it. Smeeten had received post with that stamp all the time, at least once a month, often resulting in his extended absence from home. It was that stamp that allowed me the chance to run.

Whitclé also grabbed a plain brown paper folder from the cabinets behind him, the Guardian crest sat on the front of that one. He flipped both folders open and turned them toward me as he started talking me through the Guardian Rules and their relevance compared to Elven Law and my current situation.

ACKNOWLEDGEMENTS

Let's start out with my mum. You made me love books and, well, what kind of an author would I be if that were not the case?

Then there's my In-Laws, always so astounded by my progress. Thanks for reminding me that this actually is a big deal when you're not super bogged down in the minutiae.

James & Stewart, thanks for your distraction, for appreciation, for the sheer volume of laughter, and for being friends when I struggle to make and keep those. And Megan, for being willing to be my walking billboard of advertising.

Everyone who put their publishing experiences out there on the internet for free for people to see and learn from, I'm so grateful for that information, I know I wouldn't even be halfway here without it.

And, saving the bexx-st for last, my wife: Bexx, you're my sounding board, my editor, my proof-reader, my logic-brain. Thank you. Without you this book wouldn't exist for more reasons I can name on one single sided page. Shout out to your endless patience with my rambling and my insistence that you read and re-read and "have you read those new edits yet?" – you must have read this 1,000 times over. How you still love me at this point even I'm not creative enough to figure out.

Thank You So Much For Picking Up A Copy
of
Merry Arlan: Breaking The Curse.

For News About My Latest Releases Sign Up
To My Mailing List At:
WillSoulsbyMcCreath.com

Or come find me on Social Media, when I'm
there I'm
@nopoodles

Enjoy my FREE Short Stories over on
nopoodles.wordpress.com